I0670324

In Darkness Peering:
Tales from the Bent Side

An Anthology Edited by
David D. Warner

doorQ Publishing ❘ Playa del Rey, California

In Darkness Peering: Tales from the Bent Side
Copyright © 2015 David D. Warner and the respective authors.
All Rights Reserved.

No part of this book may be reproduced in any form or by any means, electronic, mechanical, digital, photocopying or recording, except for the inclusion in a review, without
permission in writing from the the publisher.

Published in the USA by
doorQ Publishing
8675 Falmouth Ave #306
Playa del Rey, CA 90293
www.doorq.com

ISBN-10: 0692561137
ISBN-13: 978-0692561133

Front cover photograph by Creatismas

Printed in the United States of America

*For my husband, Marc Wittlif, and my dear friend,
Marilyn Blimes. You were the first to believe in me
as a writer. Just look at what you've unleashed!*

Table of Contents

Foreword

There's nothing like a good scare to get your blood pumping. Ironically, at least for me, it was at those times in my life when I have been most afraid that I have also felt the most alive.

Like many other kids who came of age before interactive video games such as *Resident Evil* or *Silent Hill*, and 24-hour streaming video services such as Netflix or Hulu, my sisters and I grew up reading books and going to the movies. More often than not we gravitated toward those books and movies most likely to scare the bejeezus out of us. We stayed up late on weekends and on hot summer nights camped out in front of the television in our sleeping bags watching back-to-back horror flicks on syndicated programs such as *Creature Feature*,

Cemetery Road and *The Midnight Horror Show*. We told each other, and our neighborhood friends, scary stories—the scarier the better—often times stories that we'd made up ourselves.

It is not at all surprising, then, that horror and dark fiction are still the genres that, more often than not, dominate my writing. For some of us—those not too afraid to take a trip down into darkest cellars of our minds—writing horror serves a useful purpose. It gives us a safe, expedient, and socially-acceptable way to cope with our most personal of demons and, ultimately, it's a hell of a lot cheaper than years of therapy.

One thing that has always disappointed me, however, is the lack of a positive LGBTQ presence in horror fiction. More times than not, when I have encountered a gay or lesbian character or any other sexual minority portrayed in mainstream horror, the characters are typically drawn as victims and rarely as protagonists. They are often depicted as weak, aberrant or damaged individuals, often deserving of the dire and sometimes gruesome fates that befell them. Things are, thankfully, somewhat better in this regard in the early part of the 21st century, but we still have a long way to go.

It was my intention when I started this project to compile a collection of original horror stories written by LGBTQ authors and featuring one or more LGBTQ protagonists. What you hold in your hands is the result of that dream. I present to you the fruits of my efforts and, most importantly, the labors of love of the authors who contributed their hard work to this anthology. I hope you enjoy reading this collection as much as I enjoyed bringing it to fruition.

David D. Warner
August 2015

Ellie

by David D. Warner

Stephen Matheson drummed his fingers, nervously, against his thigh as he paced back in forth in waiting area of the Valley Station for the Palm Springs Aerial Tramway. Despite the air-conditioning, it was hot inside this modernized structure, but not nearly as hot as it was outside. Earlier, when he'd parked his car in the adjacent lot, the exterior temperature gauge on his dashboard read 118-degrees, Fahrenheit—definitely a scorcher out there—but Stephen knew it would be at least 20-degrees cooler at the top of the mountain

If they ever got there.

He dialed Barry's number one more time and let it ring ... once ... twice ... three times ...

"C'mon, Barry," he grumbled aloud to himself, "pick up the goddamned phone."

The woman sitting on the bench to his left—the one with the little girl beside her—gave him the stink eye.

"Sorry," he mouthed silently to the frowning woman, glancing in the direction of the child.

He didn't think it was possible, but the corners of her mouth turned down even further at his apology and she turned her head away.

His call went to voicemail and he listened to the familiar recording.

You've reached the mobile phone of Barry Montgomery. I'm unable to take your call right now. Please leave your name, telephone number, and a brief message after the beep, and I'll return your call as soon as I can. If you're trying to sell me something I don't need, or hitting me up for money I don't have, go directly to Hell. Do not pass Go, do not collect $200. Have a nice day!

Stephen wondered how many times he'd heard that recording already today. He didn't bother to leave another message.

Ten minutes passed since his last attempt to reach Barry and Stephen was really starting to get worried that his husband would not make it in time. Even though the ride up to Mount San Jacinto State Park took only 10-12 minutes, the tramway ran on a strict, half-hour schedule. If they were not on the 2:30 p.m. departure, they'd miss Ellie's arrival.

As he ruminated about Barry's absence, Stephen's cellphone—still clutched in his hand from earlier—began to vibrate and he looked at the screen. It was Barry.

"Where the fuck are you, Barry?" He didn't care this time what the scowling woman thought about his choice of words. He was agitated. And she didn't matter anyway. He had much more important things on his mind … like where the hell Barry was and why he wasn't here.

"Calm down, Hon … I just turned off North Palm Canyon and I'm driving up to the parking lot now. I'll be there in a couple of minutes."

Stephen checked his watch again.

"Barry, you know that Ellie is supposed to be here at *exactly* 3:37 p.m., Pacific Daylight Time. You've got exactly 8 minutes before the tramcar pulls away. If we're not on it, we miss our chance. I've already got your ticket. Just ditch the car wherever you can find a spot, and run if you have to."

"I'll be there, Stephen."

"Barry, I really want to be up there when she gets here, and I want you with me when she does. You promised me we'd do it this way."

"I know Stephen. And I'm here now, aren't I? I know how important this is to you. And … for the record … it's important to me too."

"What took you so long?"

"I had to run an errand."

"What could be so important at a time like this?"

"You'll see."

To Stephen's great relief, Barry entered the Valley Station through the glass front door less than 5 minutes later. He was carrying a blanket and a picnic basket from Jensen's Market, and he was wearing that devilish grin that never failed to melt Stephen's insides.

Stephen looked at him, smiled broadly, and shook his head in amusement.

Barry shrugged. "No reason we should starve."

"No reason at all." Stephen chuckled. "What'd you get?"

"I picked up some fried chicken from the deli and a couple of those little mini-cheesecakes that you love so much. Plus …" he paused for dramatic effect, "… a bottle of Hendrick's gin because I know it's your favorite."

Stephen laughed and patted himself on the waist.

"Are you trying to fatten me up now? It's a little late for that."

"Oh, c'mon Stephen … live a little. You can let your guard down just a bit, can't you? Today of all days?"

Stephen chucked again.

"I can. I can indeed. And I'm sure it'll all be delicious. Let's go."

The 12-minute ride should have been routine to Stephen after all the years that he'd lived in Palm Springs, but he still got a thrill every time he made this journey up the sheer face of the mountain. The precocious boy in him especially loved to hear the other riders—most of them tourists who had never been on such a contraption—gasp in surprise each time the rotating tramcar passed over one of the steel truss pylons as it was pulled ever-skyward by the one-and-a-half-inch steel hauling cable.

When they got to the summit of Mount San Jacinto, Stephen and Barry exited the tramcar at the Mountain Station. With their picnic basket in tow and their blanket tucked securely under Barry's arm, the pair headed directly to the back exit of the building without stopping. Once outside, the couple descended the concrete path toward the forest. The cooler air at this elevation was a welcome relief from searing temperatures in the valley below.

They walked in companionable silence until they reached the end of the concrete, less than a mile from the Mountain Station. There, they came upon the Long Valley Ranger Station, and the rustic, utilitarian picnic area provided for tourists.

The park was crowded this afternoon and the last thing either man wanted today was to deal with tourists. Without a word between them, they both turned toward the westernmost trail and the route that would lead them to *their* spot—the craggy overlook where they'd first met 18 months ago—where they could share their picnic lunch in absolute private overlooking the Santa Rosa Mountains and the Salton Sea to the southeast.

Stephen had been hiking this very same trail on that chilly winter day 18 months prior when he rounded the final turn and nearly tripped over the lithe, handsome, younger man who was crouched low to ground trying to photograph a grouping of icicles suspended from the lower limbs of a mountain pine.

Stephen's life was unalterably changed in that single instant, and he could scarcely remember now what it had been like before Barry had become the best part of it.

He only wished … on today of all days … that they had met sooner. He also wished he knew what Barry was thinking as they made their way through the forest.

The two men sat atop their blanket a few feet back from the rocky crest of the mountain, their meal already laid out before them. While Stephen tore hungrily into the savory, deep-fried drumstick, Barry removed the plastic seal from the bottle of Hendrick's and filled two glasses he'd retrieve from the basket. He really *had* thought of everything, Stephen thought.

He passed one glass to Stephen.

"To us," Barry said as he raised his glass.

"To us."

They clinked their glasses together and drank.

The gin tasted of mild juniper berries, with just a hint of cucumber, against Stephen's tongue.

He couldn't help but think of Barry's thoughtful gesture—the picnic basket filled with his favorite foods, the blanket, this toast—as an olive branch. He had been certain earlier today, when Barry failed to show up at the Valley Station at their agreed-upon time, that his husband was still angry with him. He was relieved that Barry was still willing to drink a toast to their union.

"Thank you, Barry."

"For what?"

"For everything. For being you. For forgiving me."

Barry brushed off that last part.

"There's nothing to forgive, Stephen. You had a hard choice to make and you only did what you thought was right."

"Yes, that part is true. But I swore that I would never tell anyone about Ellie. I gave my word. Then I shared my burden with you and, in doing so, I forced that burden on you. That was never my intention. I just wanted to be honest with you. I needed to tell you, of all people, the truth."

Barry took another sip of his gin and swallowed.

"I admit I was angry at first. Not so much at you but more at the whole situation. At Ellie. And when I thought about everything you told me, I realized that you made the right choice—the responsible choice—the only choice that you could have made. What good would it have done to tell anyone else about Ellie? No one knew she was a threat until it was too late to stop her. Telling people now would only result in hardship and pain. And what would be point of that? Especially when there is nothing anyone could have done about it."

A tear slid down Stephen's cheek and Barry reached up and wiped it away.

"I'm glad you feel that way. I couldn't bear the thought of Ellie coming between us. She's already ruined so much."

"Yes, Stephen … yes she has. But you and I are together, here and now, and that's all that matters. Ellie can never change that."

Barry leaned over and kissed Stephen on the mouth.

After their love-making, the two men clung to each other atop the soft, flannel blanket. They were beyond caring if anyone stumbled upon them here, naked and intertwined. Their love for each other was all that mattered now.

Stephen looked over at Barry who suddenly appeared deep in thought, as though he was ponding some great puzzle and Stephen wondered what might be going on inside his husband's head now.

"Penny for your thoughts."

For a moment, Barry said nothing and Stephen thought that perhaps Barry hadn't heard him. He was wrong.

"Ellie is a name you don't hear very often anymore. Why did they choose to name her that?"

"Ellie is not really a name, Stephen. It's an acronym—E-L-E. It was Ferguson who first started calling her 'Ellie' and it just sort of stuck with the rest of the team. You know what scientists are like— most of us are just horny, middle-aged geeks who still have a hard time getting laid … and I'm sure Ferguson thought 'Ellie' sounded a whole lot sexier than 'ELE.'"

Barry snuggled closer to Stephen and smiled. "Well, I can certainly attest that you're always horny, but ever since I've been around you really haven't had to worry about getting laid."

Stephen smiled back.

"Isn't that the truth!" It wasn't a question.

Stephen rolled over and kissed Barry on the mouth. Barry's mouth tasted like raw almonds and gin, with just a hint of mint from the cheesecake they'd eaten earlier. Stephen would never tire of kissing this man.

He could also sense that wheels were still turning inside Barry's head.

"Is there anything else you'd like to know about her? She'll be here any moment."

Barry didn't respond right away but he furrowed his brow.

"So what does ELE stand for, anyway?"

"ELE is more geek-speak. It stands for *extinction level event*."

"Okay ... I guess that makes sense."

Barry paused before speaking again.

"Do you think it'll hurt?"

"No, Barry ... it'll happen so fast I don't think we'll feel a thing."

"Stephen?"

"Yes?"

"I love you."

"I love you too, Barry."

Just then, a brilliant, blinding flash lit up the sky to the east of the Salton Sea as Ellie—a 60-mile wide chunk of solid iron ore—entered the Earth's atmosphere at 38,000 miles per hour.

Stephen and Barry closed their eyes and clung to each other as the wall of fire engulfed them.

Subject 014: Feline

by Peter Saenz

Groggy. Red flickering lights fill my limited vision. Loud, unwelcome noise fill my ears. The sterile smell around me is unsettling. Unnatural. I can barely keep my eyes open.

Hungry. So hungry. I force my eyes to widen as far as they can go. I take in my surroundings. Between the one second beats of the strobing red alarm above me, I see that the normal color of the room I am in is white, almost florescent so.

I don't like the bright lights and noise. They anger me. I try to use my hands to cover my face and ears, but I feel a resistance. I look down and see that I'm strapped to a large metal table. FURY! White bands hold me to it at many parts of my body. I don't like it. I need freedom.

I growl, struggling against my bondage.

WHO DID THIS!? Who did this to me? I will kill them!

I can feel some of the tightness to my right claw slacken. Must keep struggling. Must get free.

My ears perk up as I hear the sound of many feet running in my direction. Panic. Must get free! Must get free before they are upon me!

Several men in white lab coats file quickly into the room. They are communicating with one another. I don't understand what is being said, but I am angry and scared. Will they hurt me? Why are they holding me here?

The largest man is yelling at one of the smaller ones. His face is turning red as spittle flies out of his mouth. The smaller man cowers, shaking as he reaches into a drawer for something. He takes out a large pointy thing. What is that? Vague half memories swarm into my head. DANGER.

I roar as loud as I can as several lab technicians shakily try to hold me down. I smell fear emanating from them. I look over and see that the smaller man is sticking the large pointy thing into a small glass vial. The middle section of the sharp pointed object he's holding fills with a clear liquid. The smell hits my nose. POISON!

I growl louder and struggle against my binding as the men continue to hold me down. I must get FREE! All grogginess leaves my body as I see the smaller man moving towards me. The sharp object he's holding shakes in his hand due to his high anxiety level.

I struggle harder. I can feel my right hand loosening even more as it finally breaks through the binding.

Just as the small man reaches me, I retract my claws as far as they can go and swipe at him across his throat. Crimson red blood streaks across the room and splashes on the far white wall. The small man grabs at his neck, stops moving for a moment, and then falls onto the ground.

The lab technicians holding me down stop their attempts of restraint and fall upon each other as they try to leave the room. The large man yells at them, reaching into his jacket. He pulls out a weapon of some sort. He fires it at the lot of them. The last two scientists fall to the ground as the rest rush to safety.

When the large man is done doing this, he moves to aim his weapon in my direction. I manage to use my now free claw to slice at the remaining bindings. Just as he is about to fire the thundering contraption, I leap upon him and bite into his face. He screams as we both fall downward. I'm relentless in my attack as I bite harder and harder into his flesh, not letting go until I finally hear a snapping sound. My mouth is flooded with his savory blood, which I try to gulp down. I delight in its taste. The large man stops his struggling and his body goes limp.

Far off I hear the sound of more feet coming my way, several times the number as before. I must escape.

I dash for the door, breaking its hinges as a catapult off of it into a new direction. I see other glass rooms similar to mine as I speed past them. Strange creatures are in each one, with funny writing posted above their sleeping bodies. No time to satisfy my curiosity. I must keep running. I must get away from these evil men.

I crash through a door and find myself outside. My senses go wild as the aromatic fragrances hit my nose and sounds of nature fill my ears. My moment of peace is broken when the loud noise of an alarm fills the open night sky as well. Off in the distance I see a large wall with men walking on top of it. I know I must get past it, and fast. My muscles stretch and flex as I use everything I have to race to my goal.

I hear loud, sharp noises coming from the men on the wall. All around me I see wisps of dirt dramatically shoot up into the air. A few times I feel painful stings on my body, but I keep running. When I reach the wall, I use the claws on my hands and feet to dig into the surface, using the leverage to propel me upward. I feel more painful stings on my shoulder and back as I finally make it to the top. One of the men there tries to grab me, but I grab him instead. I use all my strength to strike him across the face. Once I do, his head comes completely off of his body and falls over the side. I jump off of the wall after it, away from my prison, before any other human can try to restrain me. Once I land easily on the ground, I bolt forward as fast as I can go.

The sharp noises coming from the human contraptions keep me moving at a high speed. Within seconds the noises fade into the distance. I run past many trees and countless thick bushes, not allowing myself to stop until the men and their sterile den are safely miles behind me.

When I finally stop it's due to reaching the edge of a cliff. Looking over it, I see many lights spread out over the landscape below. Man-thing lights. Artificial. Unnatural. It makes a part of me cringe inside. My hearing picks up many sounds from the lights below. So many humans. So many of their contraptions. It is a huge jungle of sights and sounds. I look behind me and see the green nature I just ran through. It is more appealing than the bright noisy jungle below, but it is unfortunately also closer to the sterile prison I just escaped from. The bad men could come through the trees at any moment. My decision is made. I will make my way through the man-made jungle below. I will make it through to safety on the other side.

I follow the ridge line down the mountain. Once I reach the base, I see the man-made buildings in better detail. Before me are several boxed buildings. I sniff the air. They are man dens. I can sense several of them sleeping inside. Good. Sleeping men means safety for me. I just have to get past as many of them as possible before I am spotted. I race through the buildings on a strange wide pathway made of some sort of flat rock. I am too exposed. I will for my fur coloring to become dark, better to blend into the shadows. Looking down at my clawed hands as I run, I see my normal gray colored fur turn black. I flick my tail in excitement.

Pinned dogs smell my approach. They bark at me as I pass. Hissing in their direction, I am too focused on reaching safety to bother to make any of them my next meal. The blood of the bad man from before quenched my initial thirst. I will need to feed again, but for now, it can wait.

I continue running for a while when I pick up a new scent coming from one of the many man made dens. It is the scent of arousal. It is a new scent to me, but some instinct within lets me know exactly what it is. I hear fast heartbeats. The new smell of sex and desire intrigue me. I know I must continue running under the safety of night, but the scent of human sexual pheromones overtake me. I must find out where it is coming from.

My nose leads me to the den in question. I don't sense any dogs or other animals nearby. A tall fence blocks me from my destination, but I easily leap over it in silence. Landing on all fours, I notice that water is spurting from small man made contraptions along the ground. It lands in a scattered formation upon the grass all around me. I repulse from the wetness, quickly running over to a still dry stone area butted up against the den. The sound of the water contraptions muffle any small nose I make in the process. This close, I can hear the animalistic growls and groans at a much louder decibel. I follow the heat filled wailing to a window on the far side of the den. Peering in, I can make out the origins of the siren call that drew me here.

Inside are two male humans. They are nude and writhing around on a large plush bed. One is on top of the other, kissing and licking the human underneath him on a carnal level. They thrust and gyrate against one another at a steady paced rhythm. My heartbeat quickens and my senses go into overdrive. The urge to enter their den is intense.

I take one claw tip and use it to slice the flimsy netting covering the window. Once the new opening is large enough, I slip silently through it. My dark fur coloring still visually hides me from view. As I approach the men, the human on the bottom opens his eyes for a moment and looks at me as I loom over them. His facial expression goes from ecstasy to one of sheer terror. He begins screaming, which changes my feelings of arousal to one of anger. The human on top looks down at his mate in confusion. When he notices that his partner is staring at something behind him, the human on top turns around and looks at me too.

Unlike his mate, the human on top makes no sound. Try as he might, no sound is able to escape his throat. I can feel waves of fear emanate from him. This angers me all the more. I use my claws to swipe at the one on top, sending him across the room. The human remaining on the bed grabs a soft object from it, throwing it at me. My claws leave it in shreds. He holds his hands out in front of himself, trying to block me from seizing my prey. I swipe my claws at his arms, leaving deep gashes in them. His fragrant blood is now everywhere.

Off on the side I hear growling. Turing to see where it is coming from, I see the human I knocked to the ground. I notice hair beginning to grow out of every portion of his skin. He writhes around on the floor, spasming, as his body contorts and changes shape. His legs elongate and bend at an odd angle for a human. His ears shift upwards and become pointed. His eyes transform from round to slit. Curved claws appear on his now knobbed fingers. Finally a long tail erupts from his hind region.

I sniff the air. His smell is different. I know he is no longer human, but like me. My new subject looks at me with widened eyes. I give off the pheromone of dominance. The new creature lowers its head in submission.

Similar growls now come from the bed. Looking upon it, the

14

human there also begins to show the same feline manifestations. Within moments it too is no longer human, but one of my subjects. Smelling my aura, he lowers his head in submission as well.

I sense a human approaching outside. It is nearing the den. A female voice can be heard saying something in the man speak just outside. I must escape! I make for the open window and race out of it. Once outside again, I see the human in question now standing on the wet lawn. She is wearing round contraptions on top of her head and is wearing some sort of plush wrap around herself. Once she sees me she screams as loud as she can. My two subjects come bounding out of the den and tackle her to the ground. As they begin tearing into her flesh I notice many of the dens around us begin to light up. I growl at my subjects and they stop their carnage. The human female lay dead at their feet.

I make my way across the lawn, over the fence, and back onto the flat stone path once again. I begin racing along it, continuing my travel toward freedom. Looking back, I see my two subjects are still at a safe pace behind me. I hear a loud, blaring noise ahead. From its increasing pitch, I can tell whatever it is coming toward me. I decide to jump off of the main path and into some bushes. My subjects follow my example. I wait until the blaring noise is upon me. On the wide stone path pass several man vehicles with bright lights on top of them. They wail loudly as they zoom past, toward the direction we once were. When the loud machines are no longer in sight, I resume my run again. Looking up at the night sky, I hope the blissful darkness will stay in place long enough until I am finally free.

I pass many more man dens when I pick up the scent of another human and his animal. I sharpen my vision and see that they are just ahead. My ears lock onto the sound of the whimpering canine, as well as the man's aggravated sounds. Just as we are upon them the dog breaks free from the man and heads quickly down a side pathway. I hear my subjects behind me and can sense they mean to make after the dog. I growl at them, forcing them to stay behind me. As we run past the man, I slash my claws against his face. Several more man dens pass when I sense there are now three subjects running behind me, and not two.

When I see that the man dens have become sparse, I look up and notice the night sky has begun to lighten. Off in the distance behind me I can hear more of the man contraptions wailing loudly. As I make my way around the last batch of dens I stop my running. Before me I see light brown sand, and just beyond that an enormous body of water. It glistens as it picks up flecks of the now rising sun coming up over the horizon. The man machines continue to get louder.

Not wanting to go near the water, I and my subjects run along it instead. My fur coloring changes to match the sand we race over. As we run I notice humans starting to emerge from their various dens. The few that see shriek as we race by. I watch as they run indoors to safety. A few humans far enough away stop and point small boxed shaped objects at us, moving it along upright in the air before them as we pass. The objects don't make my skin sting, so I understand they can't be weapons. The man machine sounds continue to get louder.

Up ahead I see a forest of trees signaling the end of the sand and the beginning of a forest resting along the water's edge. Racing towards it, I hear a sharp screech. Quickly looking back, I see that one of my subjects is now lying face down in the sand. A large object is sticking out of its back. A few seconds later another subject screams out. Then another. Just as I leap into the thick bushes and trees ahead I feel a painful sting in my hind area. I continue running as best as I can but a dizziness in my head slows my body down considerably. After some time my back legs refuse to obey any of my commands and go limp. I use my front appendages to claw at the ground. I try to make for a large bush situated just before me. If I can make it under it

I might be able to hide from the humans who've managed to capture my subjects. Feeling the strength in my arms begin to slacken, I know I don't have much time as the sound of men can be heard not too far behind me. Just as I am able to feel the welcome bush at my fingertips, I feel another painful sting on my shoulder. A dumbness begins to overtake me as I lay helpless on the plush grass covered ground. Man shaped figures surround me but I can't quite make them out as my vision begins to blur.

"We got her Dr. Doyle, and the other transformed feline hybrids."

"Good, unfortunately they were seen by too many civilians. We're gonna have to scrap our research here and move our project overseas. Quickly, get her strapped in and on the truck. We have to evacuate the area before local enforcement arrive."

"Pretty good test run though. Your hypothesis was correct. The subjects CAN infect normal humans. Our allies in the Middle East will be pleased."

"First thing's first Colonel. Let's get Feline 14 and the others she infected to safety. We can continue our testing at the new locale."

"You heard him soldier! Get her and the others onboard ASAP! Be careful of her claws. Don't want any of you men getting infected either."

The humans continue to talk among themselves. As they do, I can feel my body fighting off the numbing effect they caused. Within a few minutes I'll be able to move again. I close my eyes and bide my time. Soon the man contraption they put me in will be dripping with their blood. I'll have more subjects to rule over and rivers of fresh blood to savor my ever increasing thirsty palate. Vengeance will be mine.

Inconceivable

by Simon Graves

June 5th,

Today is the day. Pete was humming to himself all morning. He even made me breakfast in bed! God, this is great, I feel great, Pete feels great, we're finally picking up our baby! Things are going wonderfully in the land of Chuck and Pete. It's been hard, on both of us, but now all that is over. I love Pete so much. I can't believe we've been talking about this for five years, dreaming about this for five years, caught up in the adoption process for such a long time.

I can still see Pete at the kitchen table, crying into his eggs when we first talked it over, when we realized that we were doing this. If we'd known how hard it would be. But we didn't. I'm so thankful for that. Today is the day.

We've been thinking over names. I want to call him Oliver, but Pete is set on Francis, his granddad's name. I think it sounds like a priest's name. Francis. Father Francis of the country parish. I would settle for Benjamin. Oh my god, I can't believe this is finally happening. Pete's in the shower right now. I bought him a special shirt for the occasion. Purple with white dots. He looks great in purple. I can't wait to hold him, to hold him holding Oliver, or Benjamin. Or Francis. I guess I could live with that. I can hear Pete still humming.

So, this is the plan. It'll take us 45 minutes to drive there, an hour if traffic is bad, an hour and a half if traffic is atrocious. We'll leave at 10:30, just in case, it's 9:30 now, so that gives us plenty of time. Is there anything else I need to cover? Pete usually just wants to wing it, but even he was pacing around last night, listing things we needed to take care of. Crib, check. Baby clothes, check. Cute little bear suit, check. Camera, check. Tissues, check. Oh, diapers, God I can't believe I forgot diapers, OK, we'll grab those from the store on the way home.

I'm tingling all over. There's still a part of me that is saying what if. What if something goes wrong? What if Oliver doesn't like us? What if they change their minds? I could dwell on what could go wrong for hours. I feel a bit sick. But, it'll be fine. It. Will. Be. Fine. God, Pete looks great in his new shirt.

I can't believe it. I can't believe it. Why? How fucking cruel? Pete's locked himself in his study. He won't come out. I can't get him to come out, and I'm so worried. He just stared out the window on the drive back. I can't even remember how we got home. What route did I take? He says he can't do this again. He'll come out of it, it'll just take time. I hope. We both want a family so bad. It'll work out. It'll just take time.

June 6th,

I can't focus at work, my appetite is gone, every time I try to talk to Pete he just snaps at me as if it's my fault. He actually asked me if maybe I'd forgotten to fill something out on the form. He apologized afterwards, but. We need to get away from this. I stare at the empty crib every time I go by the old study, even with the door closed. We need to get away from this kitchen, from these rooms. I want to go to the beach, but it'll make me too sad, I think. Maybe a city would be better. I think we need some noise.

We almost fought about it and then we both broke down. We're going next week, taking time off. We're flying to New York, we'll spend a few nights there.

June 10th,

Too much has happened. How do I get all this down? From the beginning. We came back and she was there, sleeping on the couch in the guest room. How'd she get in? What kind of person just—. I'm being harsh. Pete's right. OK. Slow down. From the beginning.

New York was bad. I tried forcing it the first few days but that was like pushing a body uphill. Pete's. Jesus. It not like I expected him to get over it in just a few days, but he could make some effort to help. It's not like he's the only one—. Goddamn it. My hands are shaking with how angry I am with him. He actually made me cry in Central Park in the middle of the day. I suggested a walk, some sightseeing. He grunted at me. We went. I suggested we go downtown and—. He made me cry on the street, in New York. Me screaming at him. Him just ignoring me. Jesus, God. I've never been so embarrassed. He sleeps the whole flight home. Tries to apologize on the drive back, as if he didn't have a chance earlier.

We get back last night. The crickets are going, it's nice, and I just stop out there for a moment to just listen, to take it in, something different. Different from New York, different from Pete. He just goes inside. Leaves my bag in the car. Leaves the front door wide open for me.

We didn't even know she, Julie, was there at first. I was in the bathroom, brushing my teeth for bed and I heard something fall in the guest room. I go downstairs, take a look, and there she is. Blankets lying over the bed, her on the floor. I can't even remember what I did next. Then Pete's there, lifts her up, checks her. She was so pale. Anemic, like she'd been starving herself, but she didn't looked starved, looked a little bloated.

Next thing that's clear I'm at the kitchen table, she's across from me, eyes on the table top, hands in front of her picking at each other, her eyes still red from when she came to and started bawling, terrified. Pete's making fucking chamomile tea for everybody. Hasn't even looked at me kindly for days, since—, and he's making us tea.

God, I'm getting nasty again. Pete's right, I was nasty at the kitchen table. Like a cop from TV. We should've called the police, why didn't we call the police? How did this only just occur to me?

Jesus, the way Pete was smiling at her, cooing at her when she burnt her fingers on the hot mug. Real sob story though. Poor girl. Stupid, but poor.

She still looks down at the table, at her hands, while she tells us her sob story. Pete is doe eyed at her.

Pregnant. Hand delivered by God you'd think by the way Pete reacted. WITHOUT EVEN CONSULTING ME. Just straight ahead, we'll take the baby. Oh, will we Pete? We'll take the baby, will we? What do we know about this girl? No chance of her being a drug addict, is there Pete? No risk there that the kid will be shriveled up and deformed. No need to know who the father is.

And here's the thing. Here's the goddamn thing. The girl was raped. Jesus. How can't either of them see that? I can understand her not

22

getting it, who'd want to admit that to themselves, but Pete's smarter than that, he should know better. God, am I the only one sane in this relationship. The girl was raped.

It's not that I don't want a baby. That's what Pete said. It's not that. I want a baby more than anything. With Pete. But not like this. This is wrong. He says we're helping her, but are we? What kind of family kicks their girl out in that condition? What are we getting here? I'm being so selfish here, but we have to look after ourselves.

Well. Apparently, she's staying. She'll be in the guest room. I admit, it almost broke my heart how relieved she was. Poor thing. I'll have to make sure not to take it out on her. Pete and I need to have a proper conversation about this. God, what a week. I need another vacation.

June 12th,

She reminds me so much of Kathy from grad school. Even how she giggles and tucks her hair back, Kathy all over. Julie's alright. God, I looked back over my last entry. I can be such a bitch sometimes. It's not so bad. Julie's great. I admit, I really like her. Still so pale though. We've been making pancakes. I can't believe it, but I think having her in the house is what we've needed, Pete and I. We had a big talk last night, Pete and I. Both had a big cry. Make up sex. Best in ages. I fell asleep with his arm cradling me. Wow. We're having a baby…again. I'm terrified something will go wrong.

We're taking Julie to the hospital tomorrow. It'll be fine. This is really making me realize I have no idea what a pregnancy entails. I'm nervous. Not as nervous as Julie though. Jittery girl. She'll be all right.

June 13th,

Doctor's went well, I think. I think Pete handled it. I don't know. I've been a bit out of it since this afternoon, maybe a summer flu coming on. The nurse gave us all some pamphlets to read and we sat around the kitchen table figuring it all out. Julie's a smart girl. She was doing political science for her undergrad when this all happened. I feel a bit sorry for her, she's got real brains, no wonder she doesn't want to keep the baby.

The stress over the past week has been phenomenal. Hopefully it'll be smooth sailing here on out, I've been having these dreams, I can never remember them but it reminds me of Gregorian chant for some reason, but lower, like the droning of a bagpipe without the stuff on top. How can a dream remind you of a sound? That's the only thing I can remember, but it makes me feel. I don't know.

August 3rd,

Things are nuts at work. I swear I can feel my pulse climbing as soon as I walk in there, it's like going for a run. We scored the big contract for AKL earlier in the year, and with James, who was handling it, going into hospital things are up in the air. I've had Tim Marshall from project management knocking on my door every five minutes. That would fine, well not fine but manageable, if that actually got the issues sorted out but it doesn't. I'll go over the same damn issue five times in a day and then he'll bring it back the next morning, and it's not even his fault. Can't just fire him to sort it out. I hate picky clients. James had this one in line, but with his cancer, AKL are changing their minds every five minutes.

I was worried all my time at work wasn't fair to Pete and Julie, but we had a chat about it the other night and it seems fine. They seem fine. Pete's cut hours from the nursery to stay home with Julie and take her to the doctor. I think he's been staying up with her at night too. I came home at a quarter to one (!) the other night and they were in her room chatting, her pale, him on his knee stroking her hand like she's terminal. I'd let myself be bothered by it but honestly I just have too much on my plate right now. Those two get along great, and it's not like I have to worry about Pete running off with her. I think once this AKL thing is done we'll need to take another vacation, just the two of us.

August 9th,

Jesus. I woke up last night. God, I almost threw up. I could swear someone was in the room with me, but not in the room, not at the foot of the bed like a person, but a pair of eyes staring down through the ceiling at me and speaking just below my hearing. God, the feeling, Jesus. Pete says it was the Thai chicken, but this wasn't food poisoning, I didn't throw up from poisoning, it was repulsion, fear, Jesus, down in my stomach this voice churning me up, making every part of me fucking shake to pieces. It was only once I was awake that I heard Julie crying and I mean really crying, begging someone, I could've sworn there was an axe murderer in the room with her but she was alone. So pale. Her eyes open and going everywhere but she couldn't see us. Jesus, what a night. Pete is the only one that was fine. I would laugh about the state of Julie and I the next morning if not for the dream. Fuck. Pete made us coffee and brought up the idea of a vacation again once this AKL is done. Two more weeks. That perked me up, but Julie. Jesus, she is down in the dumps. We've got another doctor's appointment for her soon, so hopefully that'll clear it up. I wonder if you can get pre-partum depression?

August 30th,

Pete said something weird the other night. Sent shivers down my spine. I haven't been able to stop thinking about it since. We were at the kitchen window, loading up the dishwasher, and he gets this look on his face. I don't know how to describe it. It was like if a dog had seen a ghost. Just pure fear. It only lasted for a moment and then it was gone and he went back to what he was doing. I asked him if he was alright and he smiled and said he was fine. OK, so I left it at that.

Later we were in the lounge, reading, and I get this…feeling, I don't know. I look up at him and he's looking up from his book, staring into the middle of the room, same look on his face. I call his name and I don't know if he heard me. He can't remember hearing me. Fuck. What he said next. It still makes me shake. I haven't been near a window since he said it even though it's nuts. It says more about Pete's mind state than anything else. It must be the pregnancy, he must be more stressed out than I realized. I've just been so caught up with work I didn't notice. Anyway. I guess…what he said next. So, he's staring into the middle of the room, so pale so scared, just like a little kid, absolutely terrified and I call to him and he doesn't say anything and then…Jesus…I can't believe this is shaking me up like this, I mean it's silly, it really is silly. "I can hear footsteps outside." Fuck. It doesn't make sense but I just wanted to spin around and run, just run, just get in the car and drive into the ocean, even though it's crazy, I mean there's no way he could hear outside, we were in the lounge, there's only the high windows there, someone would have to be jumping up and down, stomping up and down the lawn outside for Pete to hear anything. Maybe that's what scared me so much, it just doesn't make sense, and Pete's usually such a solid guy. I thought maybe we should turn on the outside light and take a look but I didn't, I don't know why, I just didn't, maybe because it's crazy, he couldn't have heard anything from where we were, anyway I suggested that maybe he should go back to work and that I could cut my hours as soon as this AKL thing is done on Friday and then he'd be fine. He just blinked at me and said, "No, I'm fine." Like at the dishwasher. It doesn't make sense.

September 18th,
I felt the baby kick today! I don't know if it's meant to happen yet,

but there it is. Man, I just looked back over that line, I sound crazy. I don't have to be paranoid about everything.

I thought things would even out after the AKL contract finished, and things have evened out, things have gone back to normal except they haven't. My hours are back to normal, Pete and I are taking turns keeping Julie company, that kind of thing. All the plants around the house are dead, I saw my mother last week and she says I'm thinner than I was and I had no idea, and I can't, this sounds horrible but, I can't help but smell rotting meat. Just sometimes. Sometimes around Julie.

I don't know what's going on. I can't help but remember what Pete said about the footsteps. I can't help but feel eyes. On me. All the time. And when I sleep they draw in and…go inside me, search through me, sliding over everything I am. Jesus, I feel sick every morning. It must be something like a chemical spill, it must be something like that, but why would that happen here? Here of all places?

I thought maybe I should ask the neighbours if they've noticed anything, but, it's the weirdest thing, we used to be on really good terms with them but now. I went over to the Jackson's on Saturday, just on an impulse, I just had to get out of the house, and I knocked and when Allen answered he was so rude, so abrupt, I don't know what it was. I asked him if I could come in and talk to him about some issues in the neighborhood and he just…well he practically slammed the door in my face. The Gupta's from down the street have gone too. I didn't notice them move out, but there's a for sale sign outside their house and no cars on the street. I just did it again, come on, Chuck, you don't have to be paranoid about everything. People move all the time and sometimes people have other things going on.

The meat though. That smell. It's really faint but I swear it's there. It's almost as if it's the tip of my nose that's rotting. Jesus, that's a horrible idea. Think happy thoughts, Chuck, How's work going? Work is fine.

September 30th,

So, a doctor came today. Not Julie's first doctor, just some guy. Pete says it's fine, says they met him when they went in for a check-up a few weeks ago when I was at work, but neither Pete nor Julie mentioned it then. Something about how this guy looked at me. Just for a moment I wanted to collapse and scream into the carpet. Is that insane? Yes. Things aren't going well in the land of Chuck and Pete.

He was an older guy. Close cropped white hair, grey cardigan, neat goatee, round glasses. Do doctors still make house calls? Does that even happen anymore? Maybe he rode a horse and cart to get here. Haha, that was meant to be a joke.

I have to admit, I took off as soon as I could. Just said I was going down to the store and sat in my car staring at the traffic on the north bound. Why that of all things? People throw themselves off the overpass there. I stayed out until 10, I don't know how I spent that time. Just sitting there I guess. The doctor was gone by the time I got back. Pete and Julie were dozing on the couch, Julie's head on Pete's chest. I went straight to bed, but couldn't sleep so I got up again at 2 and…I can't remember the rest. Isn't that odd? I can't remember the rest. I remember the stairs, stepping down the stairs to the lounge and then…waking up in bed the next morning, getting ready for work. That is odd. It is.

October 5th,

Ever been the third wheel? I swear Pete and Julie have developed some kind of secret language while I've been at work. I don't know. Maybe it's nothing. I feel tired all the time, maybe it's that, maybe it's the paranoia getting worse, because it is getting worse. I can't stand to look in a mirror now, even just side on. I'm afraid of my own shadow. What was I talking about? I sat down to write with something specific I wanted to talk about, but now it's gone.

I thought it was later than it is. The sun is just a bloody smear out the garden window. I thought it was dark already.

What was it? Pete. Pete and Julie. Bloody smear. On his cuff, on his shirt, on his purple shirt I bought him for when Oliver was coming to live with us. Why did I think of that? When was the last time we went on vacation? What am I talking about?

Eyes. So bright.

When will we go on vacation next? Perhaps we'll go after… after Julie gives birth to …

Blood on his cuff.

It makes more sense now. It's like I just needed to get away for a bit. The overpass is a bone color in the lights of the freeway. A guard dog. That's what Pete reminds me of. I've been struggling with it for days, 'what is it about Pete?' He is like a guard dog. Shoulders up all the time. Maybe Pete should have been a football player, a linebacker or whatever they're called. They go for walks sometimes, Julie and Pete, so that her feet don't swell, and he walks in front of her a bit, eyeing off the others walking in the street. I've watched them from the windows, Pete moving down the street like a guard dog, the Prince behind him. Why did I write that? The Prin—.

So, the blood on his cuff. They came back the other afternoon from the supermarket and Pete is riled. Something about an old lady, I didn't get the full story. A Jesus freak apparently. One of those crazies. She goes nuts at Julie for something. Imagine that, going nuts at a pregnant woman. I thought it sounded funny, but Pete had this dark look on his face. We would have laughed once, I'm sure. It was really weird. He starts talking about it, really going off about her and then he just stops. Clams up. Unpacks the groceries. I tried to press him for more, but it was like the channel had changed. "No, everything is fine," that kind of thing. Except for the blood on his cuff. Standing on tippy toes to slip the extra box of cereal into the cupboard and there against the purple, still wet, so thick that the pattern of the shirt was gone, smearing against the skin of his arm. I thought he'd cut himself. I don't know why I didn't mention it then. He hasn't got a cut on his arm.

Where was Julie during this? I don't know. That's strange. She's totally absent from my memory. It's like she's a grey figure. Transparent. Sliding in and out of the world. I have a headache. Time to go home and sleep, I think.

October 27th,

Stillborn. That's why I haven't heard a thing from the doctor, the first one we saw, in months. That rotting smell. They've both gone insane. They have to see it's not good for her, not good for either of them.

There's more too. Not Political Science for Julie. No record of her at the college. But there are records of her. I found them. It was the feeling in the back of my mind, a scratching there, pushing me to take a look. Enough time outside the house, enough time staring at the overpass and that did it. Julie. Never got her last name, didn't even occur to me. But I found it in her room. Julie Monroe. Nice name, but Julie Monroe didn't go where she said she did. Didn't go to any place around here. I found her though. I found out what she did to herself. Why she was so pale. The whole thing makes my brain shake.

She should have had bruising around her neck. This isn't making sense. I found her in a newspaper, real small, some kind of ritual, a girl hanging herself, being taken to the hospital brain dead. But it doesn't make sense.

And then the doctor. I called the nurse to get Julie's prescription refilled and she had no current records of her. She had older records from a few months ago and she asked me if it was medication for depression, and I said, "that's odd, is that a safe thing to give an infant?" and then the nurse said it was quite common after stillbirth, after the baby dies inside the mother. She must have meant someone else but I know she didn't. It doesn't make sense but I know it's true. Is this what it's like to be mad?

October 28th,

Chuck. Hello, Chuck. He can see you, Chuck, he knows what you are doing. He sees you.

October 29th,

Him. Him. Him. Him. Him. HIM. HIM. HIM. HIM. HIM. God. God Save me, GOD, I know what it is, GOD, I know it's HIM, it's HIM, oh God and I know. I know completely, God save me. I can hear HIS footsteps outside the window, in the room with me, in my head beneath my skull where he has been, God save me, please, God, please, save me from the devil.

Steamed

by David Wolfhaven

"Where ARE you bitches? It's pouring out here!"

"Relax, ReginALD. Trevor, wanted to stop by Whole Foods to get something to eat."

"Ugh. He's ALWAYS eating! I'm sure they'll have snacks at the spa, right?"

"Yeah, but, not the kind he likes, apparently. You know how he is. Everything, has to be ORGANIC. But, his clothes still scream homeless Hollister surfer...OUCH! Hey!"

"What?"

"Nothing. He just threw toilet paper at me. I didn't know they even MADE organic toilet paper. Huh. God, cell service sucks, over here. I can barely make out what you're saying. Something about a big dick in your mouth?"

"Ha. I wish. And, I can hear you just fine. I have Verizon. I told you Sprint sucks ass."

"Yeah. Well, at least my bill isn't over $100 a month. And, trust me, I can't wait to get naked. I've been super horny all week. This weather and the full moon, tomorrow, has me jizzed and jazzed."

"Just hurry the fuck up, will you?! I'm cold and I have to keep holding the door for these stout and wrinkled old men, in brown, hooded raincoats. Are you sure this isn't a monastery? Or, TATOOINE?! I'm not even sure I'm in the right place."

"Do you see a green door, with a hot pink light over it?"

"Yeah, I'm in front of it. My skin looks like Pepto-Bismol. How appropriate, since I'm already sick to my stomach."

"Okay. Well, look around. There should be an oval and gold sign above the buzzer on the right, that says: *Jack's Place*. See it?"

"No. I don'...WAIT. Hang on. It's on the ground. Ewww. It's all rusty, with one screw still in it! Probably like half the guys in there. I'm liable to get a disease BEFORE I even go into this place. I can't believe you talked me into this."

"Well, hello, it's MY birthday and you need to be shaken up a little."

"WHY couldn't we go roller-skating, or bowling, or to the Zoo, or something?"

"You mean, like rock climbing, which we agreed to do for YOUR birthday, last September? I STILL have that hole in my crotch."

"Biiiiiitch, that hole was there when you bought them, from FOREVER 21!"

"Ha. Bitch."

"And, anyway, it's your own fault for stretching out like that, to show off for that guy, who was SO ugly."

"Pssssh. Whatever. He's an extra, on CSI! I brought him home with me, didn't I?"

"You FOLLOWED him into HIS apartment building and pretended you lived there! Stalker."

"HA. And, it worked. I went through his mail when he was sleeping and everything. Did I tell you he had a subscription to *Better Homes And Gardens?*"

"Actor's. They're so easy to manipulate here," said Reg. "With their sinewy bodies and rippled muscles and blank stares..."

"... And, stupid tank tops and fake teeth. I can't WAIT for us to start film classes next month."

"Yeah. There's a kick-ass class on horror directors I want to take."

"DANG!" Miles shouted suddenly.

"What? Are you okay?"

"No. Yeah! I mean...dude, their parking lot SUCKS here. I saw this homeless woman almost get run over just now. This asshole was speeding and now she's drenched from the splash! Poor thing."

"Aw. Go lay down your coat for her."

"Boy, you're gonna get a beating, when I see you. This damned rain. I HATE it! If I'd known it was going to be like this, I'd have dressed warmer. My weather app said it was going to be partly cloudy!"

"Yeah. You never can tell here."

"Yay! Trevor's about to pay."

There was a loud clap of thunder and a blip of sheet lightning that lit up the sky, suddenly. The wind howled and made the traffic lights sway, causing red and green Freddy Krueger colors to melt and dwindle into puddles along the pavement. Reg turned half-clockwise and then counter, lifted his shoulders to his ears and contemplated going inside and braving the lonely stares of the other patrons. He put his hand on the cold, metal doorknob. Should he? Cars blared their horns in the distance and he heard tires screech and people scream, as if a roller coaster was being demolished. Reg bristled and felt a tap on his shoulder and jumped.

"FUCK!"

"OHMYGOD. WHAT HAPENED?" worried Miles.

"Ugh. Some dude just wanted to get by me. Fuck. My heart is in my throat."

"Was he cute?"

"MILES!"

"Whaaat? I heard it gets cuter as it gets later. We have ... eighteen minutes to get there and take advantage of the two for one special. Trevor! Hurry the fuck up. And, stop flirting!"

"I think I'm going to go home," lamented Reg.

"WHAT? Nooooo. Come ON, Reg, you PROMISED! THIS year, we are going to DO more. We all agreed. We came on and squished our hands together and everything!"

"I dunno, Miles. Harrison and Zelda are probably scared and cowering under the bed. I'm worried about them."

"Reg. Your cats are fine! Harrison is probably building a moat made of catnip and Zelda sleeps through everything. You spend far too much time with a feather toy instead of a battery-operated one, my friend."

Reg didn't answer.

"Reg? Reginald Davidson! Come ON. It'll be fun. We've all seen each other's dicks. Are you worried about that? We can each get a private room if you want. I'll pay the difference. I know you have a hard-on for Trev ..."

"MILES! Shut up!"

"What?! Oh, please. He didn't hear me. The boy craves attention. He's a Leo. Lord knows what manner of imperceptible chaos he's going to unleash on us next month for HIS birthday. UGH! If only we could get him to shave that ugly, long Hobbit beard of his.

Seriously, I don't understand the whole gay beard thing. I mean, there aren't any damn trees in this city to chop down, anymore. They keep building over the stellar views."

"Well ... I'm wearing his flannel."

"Ooooh. Somebody's in LOOOOOVE. Fucking lumberjack. Brillo bottom!"

"Shut up! It was the only thing I had left that was warm and clean, to wear. He probably won't even notice."

"You're probably right. I had to tell him THREE times where we were going tonight."

Reg turned away from the receiver quickly, closed his eyes and bent his head to sniff at the collar of Trevor's borrowed shirt. It smelled like vanilla and cinnamon and dogwood. And sweat. His groin started to moisten and thicken. Think about something else, he told himself. Think about Princess Leia. Think about the weird shit. Think about Bossk fucking her. Think of moist, Hostess cupcakes and the marshmallow ooze in the middle. The Ghostbusters siren ...

Trevor . Mmm. Trevor Mmmmaxwell.

Miles was still talking ...

."... Besides, we didn't move all the way from cold ass Minnesota last year to sit around and be his goddamn modeling managers! I mean, I KNOW it's a big city ..."

"I miss my family," softened Reg.

"I miss your family, too, Reg. And your mother always screwing up the holiday meals, like serving Thanksgiving dinner for Easter last year. Things take TIME. I mean, LOOK. Your transition to your advertising firm finally went through, without a hitch, even if it IS part-time, it's SOMETHING. The money and perks alone are SOLID. I'M working for a casting office, for *The Dance Team* and the kids LOVE me. I mean, sure ... most of them are brats and the mothers are nightmarish with bad perms. Trev's got six SOLID years on us living here. Just look at the meteoric rise he's had in that short of time. He's in the latest GQ! There's so much potential here to do your animation and my music. Your Dad would be so mad if you gave up already. My mother's already cut ME off."

Reg sighed again.

"Come on. Don't make me do the *Who's a fuzzy wuzzy Reggie-Bear?* routine in here in front of all these Russian women and their yippy dogs. My throat is sore."

"Yeah, I can only imagine from WHAT." Reg sort of half-laughed and blew raindrops from his lips.

"Theeeeere's my boy. Now, stop complaining. Damn Virgo. I swear, you're becoming that gay stereotype that complains even when he cums. Besides, LA needs the rain."

"Yes. But not down my back!" Reg shuddered and shook a large, wet glop from the middle of it.

"Mmm ... But how 'bout ON your back?" Miles chuckled.

"Not funny, whore. Now hurry up, please. My new sneakers are getting ruined."

"Let me guess. You're going to wear those instead of the flip flops they give out?"

"Hell, yes! And I'm wearing my underwear under my towel!"

"I swear I don't know how you can walk everywhere like you do. I couldn't LIVE without my car."

"The Metro here is perfectly fine. Look at how many problems you have with your Jeep all the time."

"The Metro is naaaasty. Oh. Except for the time that hot married dude sucked me off on the train, remember?"

"How could I forget? You tried to make me film it, " Reg grumbled. "Tonight is going to be a cakewalk for you. Ugh. We should've just gone to San Diego for Pride like everyone else."

"And still be sitting in traffic? No. Look. Nobody's on the road and everyone else is either out of town or inside jerking off online; making their thumbs purple from cruising stupid Grindr. NOBODY will be there. It's perfect!"

"Ugh. Ok. Well, HURRY UP! Two cop cars just went by. You know how paranoid I am about being out this late."

"It's only 9:45!"

"No. You know..."

"Oh. Because you're black?"

"Well ..."

"Reg. I may pass for white, but when my I.D. gets read by bouncers or employers—especially when submitting online, I'm a Mexican ... like everybody else in this town."

"You have a great name! Miles Martinez," said Reg with a rolled-tongue flourish.

"Oooh! Well, when you say it like that, it DOES make me horny, Papi. HA. We'll be there shortly. Trevor just cashed out."

"Hi, Reg!" Trevor interrupted, in the background. "I got you Sno Caps and ... Gummibarchen? Milesy ... what the hell are these? I thought they were bears, or somesuch?"

"They are," yelled Miles. "It's just their Flazehda packaging. Ugh. This boy. NOW he's making monkey faces at security. TREVOR!" There was a scuffle sound.

"Reg?"

"Yeah?"

"Reg, we'll see you, soon. Trevor is mooning you, now, and making his "Oh Yeah!" face, and nodding his head as he's getting into my car.

He heard Trevor shout: "I'm Tyler Durden!"

"Goddamn him and his perfect fucking ass. DON'T YOU GET MY SEATS DIRTY! Ugh. Omg, Reg," Miles squealed and huskily laughed, back on the receiver now.

" I can't wait to see him in a towel, for six whole hours. I doubt he keeps his on at ALL. Think about that, killer. HA. OK. Love You. See you, in like ... 10 minutes."

"Love you, too. Drive safe," cautioned Reg as he hung up.

He was instantly warmed by a smile threatening to spread across his face at the image of a naked, smiling Trevor doing his goofy, Scooby-Doo impressions once they got there. Over Miles' impertinent, impending insistence that everything had to be just so. Especially this evening. They all hadn't hung out since Pride last month when they had a huge, drunken fight over a guy at Here Lounge. He was always playing the hero and sacrificing his own good time to make sure everyone else was and he was sick of it.

He shook his head at the thought of gross, naked men at the spa, shuffling around, shiny and stretched out, like used condoms; their waxy skin and wrinkled asses jerking off, with their slovenly, protuberant erections.

The cold rain faded away for a moment. He ignored the sponge-like feeling between his toes. He knew his friends meant well. They were worried about him and his penchant for staying inside all the time; locked away like his namesake, paternal grandfather—sitting in the corner, eating butter pecan ice cream that he scooped out with an all open Swiss army knife he still had from the Vietnam War. Cleaning his pipe with the other mini-utensils, then his ears, then adjusting the volume from the missing knob on his old, black and white Zenith television—all in one, seemingly forward motion.

He sniffed at the memory, wiped off his misted iPhone on his chest and quickly pocketed it over his heart. He stepped down the steps to the side of the road to wait for the boys, did a bit of a hopscotch over the cracks and the mud and rain, and contemplated himself at a flower bed that was now a pool of water on the ground.

"Pansies," he whispered and tried to brush them free from the deluge. Staring at his reflection, he pondered the past. He shoved his hands in his Diesel denim jean back pockets and tapped at a puddle with his right Nike, magically made his image disappear and then reappear within seconds. He sighed at what he saw, which was partially obscured by the shadow of a tree. The branch of leaves made him look like he had an Afro instead of the inch-thick shaved look he was now sporting. Its' not like he was a bad-looking guy. He was an average, African-American male, just shy of six feet. He was only supposed to be five-five, according to the doctor's, as he was born prematurely, but his Dad was a giant of a man at six four and 235 pounds. In his heyday, his Dad was a running back with the Miami Dolphins, before an ankle injury shuttled them to his mother's native Minnesota. His mom still practiced sports medicine and traveled a lot doing lectures, leaving his father to run an automotive repair shop that her father co-owned. He had his mother's high cheekbones with soft, full lips, coconut-shell colored skin and his father's fat, wide chin; thankfully, without the butt dimple that his younger brother, Kent, got instead. Kids at school teased his brother and called him: "Fannyface." Kent got his father's pimpled complexion in spots, too. He was two years younger that Reggie and yet, was taller. And geekier. Yet, they shared the same eyes as their mother: Golden, amber orbs, which glowed in the sunlight, in the headlights of a passing car or when near an open flame, were surrounded by a slight, intrusive and intoxicating twitch of grey. Eyes he'd inherited from his Caribbean mother.

He sneered at the air. The rain was stopping now and he tucked his undershirt in to make himself look more presentable. He pinched his belly fat and moaned. His diet of Wendy's and Peanut Butter Crunch, while playing endless hours of Arkham City and other Playstation games, did little to curb his distracting indulgences.

"You got a Bagel-Belly, Buddy. B-B-B!" Trevor, would exclaim. "You should let me train you!" He took to wearing button downs now because he was developing an array of insecurity disorders that all gay nerds accumulate from time to time. Part of him used to not care. Part of him refused to believe that the lies of life weren't real. That is, until he moved here. Oh, this town.

Trevor. On his way, now.

Suck it in, fat boy!

Trevor's touch electrified Reggie. Behind his ears, his wrists, his ankles. Every ingrown hair was smitten. It's as if his feet sprouted wings, because he couldn't walk whenever Trevor was around. He would just be filled with adoration and glee and his joints developed a sort of rudimentary, psychosis palsy. His heartbeat flooded his ears and made him dizzy. He was always saying: "Huh?" when Trevor was around and Miles either rolled his eyes constantly, punched him, or laughed at him. He remembered the first time he'd seen him. It was the first day of the seventh grade. Trevor offered to buy him his lunch of pizza and orange soda because Robert Kirkwood, the school bully, literally turned him upside down on the bus on the way to school and shook the money free from his OshKosh's. Then, Trevor beat Kirkwood's ass after school and tied him to a traffic cone and let him sit in the busy, after-school parents' parking lot, while the other kids laughed and threw pennies at him.

He had to be sure not to stare.

"Trevor's just a big tease," Miles would say. "Sean Cody doesn't want him, because of his Neanderthal under bite and small dick. He smells nice, though."

He dreamily, Disney-cartoon smiled at the thought of Trevor in nothing but a towel hugging his hips and his gesticulating ass bouncing with every step, like bread rising in the oven. He hadn't seen him naked since he'd built up his physique over the past few years, since he'd been in Los Angeles, and tonight made him exceptionally nervous. Trevor was this skinny jock all throughout high school. Miles played in the band and Reg took art classes and was on the yearbook staff.

They all dreamed of moving to Hollywood to pursue their dreams, but Trevor was the one who escaped first. He skipped college and immediately moved to L.A. a month after graduation and took odd jobs, doing construction, which built up his physique. He'd seen Trevor in modeling magazines and ads for massage clients. Trevor sent them to him and Miles back home to entice them to move out here with him. But, the real thing? It was almost too much to bear.

He didn't realize he was still squeezing his stomach and he fingerpicked out a tiny lint ball, lifted it to his sight-line and squinted in the near dark. It looked like wet ink now as he rolled it between his fingers and conjured an image in his head of him unwrapping this *denim lint baby*, to perhaps make it into a pair of underwear, or a cock-sock, to hide his oncoming embarrassment. Images of Survivor and Project Runway flitted through his mind. "Make it work," he whispered through the rain and instead flicked off the annoying substance onto his jeans. I'll do push ups in between reading comics tomorrow, he thought.

A few minutes later, he heard a car honk and out bounded Trevor, in his direction, like a dog that had been cooped up for weeks. The ground shook with another loud, clap of thunder. Miles was yelling through the rain, which had started up again and was becoming heavier now. "I'm going to try and find a place to park! You boys go check in!"

And here was Trevor, beside him now, hugging him giddily and plying him with red gummy bears, between his teeth. Trevor went in for a teasing, transitory kiss, which Reg tried squirming out of. This playful embrace caused Trevor's short-sleeved, Junk Food T-shirt, with Thor emblazoned on the front, to ripple and stretch in the rain. It rolled up and brushed against Reggie's own belly skin. He almost fainted. He was so warm.

"Hey, Reg," said Trent and placed his thick, right arm around Reg's

43

shoulders. "Got you something." He shoved the remaining package of gummy bears into Reg's face.

"Stop, you APE! You know I hate it when you shove food into my face," Reg remarked and pushed himself away from Trevor, who tried not to laugh.

"Yeah, right," laughed Trevor. "Hey! Where'd you get that shirt? I have a shirt like that!"

"HA. This IS your shirt. You left at the bar after our tiff last month."

"What's a *Tiff*?"

"Our fight, remember?"

Trevor, *tsk*-ed his tongue along the roof of his mouth. "Oh, yeah. THAT. I'm over that."

"GOOD. I'm glad we could all come to a resolution and put it all behind us. Here's your shirt," Reg said and proceeded to take it off.

"Well, I don't want it now that YOU'RE wearing it."

Reg tried not to show disappointment. "Well, I can buy ..."

"HA relax Reg," Trevor retorted and threw a bag of nonpareils at him. "Here. And you can keep it. Looks better on you, anyway," he said and then smiled.

Reg tried not to smile back. He honestly didn't know WHAT emotion to project and, instead, looked around numb and shoved the chocolate in the other shirt pocket.

"I know you missed me, Bats. You kill that level with the Joker, yet?"

Reg didn't answer.

"Need my help," Trevor asked, then winked and rubbed Reg's shoulder.

"No. I solved it. It was awesome. Looks like you're spending all your free time in the gym these days, anyway. I've been following your videos on Instagram."

"Oi," Trevor suddenly shouted and jumped back like a caveman.

"Still employing an Australian accent too, I see."

Louder now. "OI!"

"You weirdo."

This remark, of course, made Trevor start posing in the rain and the water was turning his sky blue shirt darker with every plop. He didn't know if his armpits were wet from the rain or if Trevor had done push ups in the market aisle again. He continued to smile at Reggie, his under bite like a superhuman bulldozer scooping up phantom accolades wherever he went. His dazzling, blue eyes and Golden God authority was revered by all. This blonde model stunner held everyone at a standstill, as if at gunpoint.

Fuck. Trevor. I'd make a Pizza Hut salad bar out of you.

"Uh. If you bitches are about done being buffoon's, I'd like to get inside," extolled Miles from behind them. "I'm SOAKED!"

"YES. Let's DO this," yelled Trevor, who then peeled off his shirt and howled at the night before chasing them inside.

"Dude. These towels are so small," said Trevor. "I might as well not wear anything."

"Yes, you might as well," sang Miles behind Trevor's back; gum-grinning at Reg, mouth open and tongue out as if he were waiting excitedly for his daily medication, from the loony bin.

"The lockers are small, too. What'd they expect us to put in there?" asked Reg, securing his towel and lacing up his sneakers along the edge of the bench. "At least they have fun, rainbow colors to choose from."

Reg and Miles, both picked orange and Trevor chose green, because he said it was the "color of money." The boys rolled their eyes.

"Yes. How very PRIDEful of them," remarked Miles. "And, that Mario kid who checked us in is CUTE! I've never seen him before."

Trevor cleared his throat and then proceeded to take his towel off. He flashed them quickly, unknown if by accident or on purpose, and held it over his crotch and scratched himself there before proceeding to a nearby sink to check out his reflection.

Reg looked like his balls just got tased. He had never seen anything so beautiful in his life. Trevor had indeed blossomed into a full grown man during the years he was here without them. And, his dick wasn't THAT small. An average six inches. He was probably a grower. His impeccable and perfectly delectable physique made up for the jokes and insults Miles occasionally hurled at him about it. His muscles were expertly sculpted and the veins were so close to his tanned skin that you could actually see them working symmetrically with one other. Reg watched, as Trevor posed in the mirror and started squeezing imaginary blackheads on his nose. He is so gross sometimes (as boys are), Reg thought and yet, undeniably, Superhuman. What is it about him?

Trevor then resorted to smoothing his eyebrows down with his thumb and made sure his faux-hawk was just spiky enough in spots. He was hairless, except for his armpits, treasure trail and ass, which had just the right amount of Apricot fuzz adorning it. It was almost square. He would give up a million Christmas presents to be inside that ass. He imagined piping warm, vanilla icing on each meaty ASS-pect and licked his lips. He would have to shower with him, here tonight, at some point. He felt brave enough now. He felt himself starting to get hard and tried to put the lustful thoughts out of his mind and, instead, he and Miles affixed their locker keys around their ankles with a stinging snap and stood up to leave. Yes. The pain from the snap would help to ease the pleasure.

"You're starrrrrring," teased Miles.

"Ugh. I know. Look at him."

"I know. Your very own Aquaman. I wonder how much sex he really has?"

"Probably, a LOT!"

"Yeah, well, if they hadn't confiscated our phones up front, we could sneak a picture of him to blackmail him with. The boy is making BANK. He said he'd pay for me to have the air in my car fixed," said Miles. "I'll bet he has a sex video on his phone that he sends out to his gym *clients*."

"Oh, I'm sure if we asked him, he'd gladly show us."

"Yeah. He'd probably try to give us pointers on how to fuck."

"I think I prefer to indulge in the fantasy, for now," sighed Reg.

"Yeah, right, Romeo. Your bottom lip is practically shaking down onto your nipple. Ugh! I can't BELIEVE we couldn't bring our phones with us. I feel like I'm missing a hand! I've taken mine in the last two times I was here," complained Miles.

"Maybe they got sick of you taking selfies in front of the combination snack-slash-safe-sex machine," said Reg.

"And making videos of yourself," said Trevor walking over to them now.

Reggie complimented him. "Good one! I'm surprised his picture wasn't up front next to the register when we came in!"

Trevor cracked up, laughing.

"Oh, shut up you two. Good luck knowing all the secret sex *codes* that go on around here, without me," sniffed Miles and he slammed his locker and stormed off.

"Goddamn crabby Cancer," said Reg. "Ugh. Come on. We better keep an eye on him."

"Okay. Just not my brown eye. Ooooooohhhhhh!" bellowed Trevor and he guffawed. His chin punched out like a Pez dispenser.

"Ugh. You are such a *Tatum Potato*, said Reg.

"I LOVE Channing Tatum! You know he's bi, right? His wife is SO hot. Oh my God," remarked Trevor, not even paying attention to where he was going as he ran smack dab into a large, oscillating floor fan.

"Yo, Dude. At least have the decency to get my number first," he told the fan.

Reg, just shook his head.

"C'mon, Trev. Miles is probably looking to centipede himself into a lubrication pit by now. MILES!?"

They walked hurriedly through the locker room door and into a hallway that looked like a country home. Pictures of roosters adorned the walls and as they entered the main room, a red and white checker scheme flooded the place. Some of the walls were painted a pale, yellow and the other walls had a country-style wallpaper print on them that was neither green nor blue. Men in various red and black hunting outfits; some shooting at an imaginary prize, and others holding ducks in their hands, were patterned on it. There were a few, high-backed brown and worn, woolen chairs and a red and ripped leather bar with matching stools sitting in a corner to the left. An attractive, dark-haired, middle-aged, shirtless bartender was making drinks and tying cherry stems with his tongue, all at the same time, for two old, naked customers. Their bare fat asses were wrinkled and freckled, and pock-marked, and they slid over the red leather top of the barstools like a snack of melted—Swiss cheese—over a ribald tomato.

To the right of the bar and in the center of the room toward the ceiling was a wall-mounted color television playing porn, interspersed with cult horror movies. The sound was turned off. Next to that, on the right, was another long hallway with an exit sign above it, whose light was scratched and burnt out. The main lighting came from a smattering of cheap, assorted lamps, with no real rhyme or reason or theme that someone who might've been blind had placed around the room. Some didn't even have shades. About eight other guys were there, drinking and carrying on conversations with one another, and it seemed to Reg that they all knew one another. When he and Trevor entered, they all stopped talking and just stared at them for a moment.

"Ugh," said Reg. "I feel like I just stepped onto the *Roseanne* set."

"Yeah, dude," said Trevor. "It's like ... if my Grandma married my OTHER Grandma and they LIVED together."

Reg laughed and he thought he spotted Miles, when he heard a voice over the loudspeaker. It was Mario, the kid that checked them in.

"Hey, guys! Welcome to our first Friday of the month and grand reopening. Tonight's theme, if you didn't get a flyer or have been hiding out in your room all day, is: *Fright Night Friday's*." The voice stopped as if waiting for applause.

Reg pulled out his pamphlet that he had folded and sequestered under the elastic of the briefs he still secretly had on and read the four F-words:

JACK'S PLACE
Schedule:
Fright Night (All your favorite horror movies, under one roof,
ghost stories and séance room)
Fetish (Wear your favorite outfit and put on a comedy show
in the lounge for our less INCLINED guests)
Frisk (Cops and Leather. No chains, billy clubs, or guns permitted.
Edible handcuffs only. Gangster attire accepted)
Frat Night (Bring in your college I.D. for a super-sized discount
and free lockers, beer pong, and sports magazines)

There was a condom in a clear wrapper taped to the bottom.

Reg sort of was interested in the Frat night. They were obviously his type.

Trevor was scratching his bare ass and flirting with the two elderly men at the bar. They kept taking off their glasses, squinting at him, and squeezing his biceps. There were more guys entering from the locker room behind them and the crowd now and grew in size to about twenty-five, horny guys. The energy in the room was electric. More were heard in the hallway to the right, whose images and voices were hard to make out because it was so dark.

Reg moved in for a closer inspection and entered the hallway.

It was so dark all he could see were little slits of light from underneath the doors and also from the cracks in the door frames. They blinked to life by the moving shadows on the other side. A stoner would think he was trapped inside a dragon's ribcage or something. This must be where the private sex rooms are, Reg thought.

Moans and bangs emanated from behind the doorways. He thought he heard Miles orgasming from there, but he wasn't sure and shrugged it off. It made him too nervous.

He walked back to the hallway entrance and studied the road map of rippling muscles that prowled to life along Trevor's back. He had that ridiculous, triangular, V-shape and little brown marks that looked like a baby punched him on either side of his lower back, from where he assumed Trevor did sit ups on an Ab-Roller or something. The old men were laughing along with him, now.

Mario came on the loudspeaker again.

"So, for those true fanatics, if you're feely frightful instead of FRISKY, we are having Ghost Story Puppet Theatre in the room next to the main lobby in FIVE minutes. Normally, we have this in our séance room, but a pipe burst in there last night and it's blocked off. So, please be mindful of the *Keep Out* signs. It's not part of tonight's décor."

This caused Trevor to leap away from his aged admirers and when he saw Reg, he ran over to him.

"Oh, man, Reg, I gotta see this. PUPPETS!" He grabbed two robes that someone had placed on a couch next to them and hastily threw one on and handed the other one to Reg. "Here, Reg. Put this on."

They walked through the sex-roomed hallway and found themselves standing in the main lobby, on ugly, stained, and blush-colored wall-to-wall carpet, which once must've been candy apple red. A couple of gentlemen, who were making out in the doorway, blocked everyone. Was this the welcoming committee?

One, was short and Asian, wearing horn-rimmed glasses, and the other was a Ginger of equal height—in his 40s—with what must've been a nine-inch penis swinging between his legs. Reg nodded a friendly hello, to get by, humbly averted his eyes from the scene before him, and tried to keep up the pace with Trevor, who bounced bow-legged ahead of him.

Most of the other guys were Latin or older. Only a mouthful of guys were good looking and he realized that he, Trevor and Miles were the obvious "special guests" at the club, because they were the best looking. He was the only African American guy there as well and it made him feel special. He wasn't used to feeling this special, or looked at in this fashion. He never cared to notice, or was too busy being insecure about his weight, or what he thought was a bulbous nose. He *was* more comfortable just being alone. But where had that gotten him? Maybe Miles was right. Maybe he DID need to get out and explore his newfound, Hollywood neighborhood more. He certainly relished the attention he was receiving by a lot of the men here tonight.

"MILESY!" shouted Trevor. Miles had sequestered himself next to Mario and they looked like Bert and Ernie. Miles, towel securely fastened, was taller, thinner and paler than Mario, who was short, plump-muscular, and more tanned. He had a silver Jason mask on the back of his head, no shirt, ripped and black, oil-stained jeans, and he kept licking his thick mustache. He could tell that Miles was CLEARLY smitten, because Miles was QUIET. He chuckled to himself.

"Hey boys," Miles said, embracing them as he kissed their cheeks. "Mario, these are my boys, Reginald and Trevor. Aren't they cute?" Miles was smiling with his teeth pressed together and was playing with one of his two thin, gold chains along his stubbled chin. One had a cross on it. The other, a tiny padlock with his father's name inscribed on it. His father was a former janitor who had built his own multi-million dollar business from the ground up. He moved to Oakland after he divorced his mother and left him and his older sister, Mia, in Minnesota. Miles' father was shot dead, by a robber, when he was closing up the office, after working late one night. Miles didn't talk about it. And Reg knew better than to ask. He and Trevor went to the funeral about five years ago and no one said a WORD. The family all just cried and sang his father's favorite show tunes. His Mother, Domina, was especially grief-stricken and blamed herself—along with her depression and drug problems—as the reason for driving their father, Francisco, away. She had a hard time letting Miles go off to California. He and Mia still checked up on her but, things were never the same after their Dad died. They never caught the killer.

Mario shook both Reg and Trevor's hands with his left, which was sweaty, as he clicked on a G.I. Joe walkie-talkie with his right. "Hey, Antonio. We almost ready?" He had an accent! Aw. How cute, thought Reg. He was like this little, perfect lunchroom ice cream man. No wonder Miles was grinning. Miles searched for Reg's eyes and, when they locked, it was like a moment from *Clueless*—one of their favorite movies to watch while stoned. They pleaded, "PROJECT!" Reg nodded and smiled.

Antonio garbled back. "Yeah, bro. All set." Ah. So, he and his brother ran this place? They were a little young, Reg thought.

The lights dimmed and guys in various stages of undress came into the room, took their seats and waited for the show to begin. They had to sit in the back because Trevor was so tall. Reg could barely see anything and his tan folding chair was slippery and uncomfortable. Miles kissed Mario on the cheek and made his way through the bare-kneed isle and sat down next to Reg.

"God, girl. You're such a bottom. I thought you were Top Doggin' it these days."

"I am," said Miles and pinched Reg's cheek. Mario motioned, with a red, Darth Vader lightsaber for all to watch the makeshift stage, which sat on a large pool table and began to speak.

"Once upon a time, there lived a man named Jack Crawford Gale."

Up popped what looked like a felt figure on a stick that had blackened eyes and a beard. The puppet had blue swim trunks on and a tissue paper towel around his neck.

"Jack, inherited from his mother a tiny schoolhouse off of Fairfax Avenue. His mother was a teacher to young actors during Hollywood's heyday. He decided to turn the house into a spa, after the studios around town shuttered their offices for more profitable and sprawling locales, like Studio City and Burbank.

With no man and a large, empty space to fill, Jack decided to remodel it into what is now known as *Jack's Place*. He had a lot of ambition. His father was a salesman and taught him how to talk to people, how to woo them into giving him the money he needed. He even started dating one of the town's premiere, profitable bankers. He advertised in the backs of all the trade magazines, which were a hotbed, for the closeted, gay man. Many celebrities spent quality time here as well. Montgomery Clift. Tyrone Power. Rock Hudson. The Grand Dame, Joan Collins, even took a tour through here to see if one of her many husbands were cheating on her behind her bejeweled back. These famous men trusted Jack with their hidden lifestyle and Jack made it a point to only bring in the best looking men who catered to their every whim. Some were destitute. Some were just passing through on their way to the gay mecca that was San Francisco at the time. In the early 1970s, this place was really hopping. Sex, drugs, and liquor were prevalent and one could even sit out on the front stoop with a trick and a cigarette and make out openly, if they wanted to. Free love was apparent, and it made Jack undeniably rich and abundantly happy. Jack, had a handsome, compassionate ease and a way about him, which made you feel fulfilled."

The small puppet bounced back and forth along the cutout stage, at times holding building plans, cigarettes, or condoms, which he threw playfully into the crowd.

Reg elbowed Trevor who was still snickering over Mario trying to pronounce "Des-teee-tuuute."

"One day, Jack was partying with a group of friends in the Sauna and suddenly became dizzy and started drooling on himself. He had taken too much LSD and was having a bad trip."

The lights in the room dimmed as another loud roll of thunder bloomed in the distance. Trevor, "Oohed." Miles reached over and "shushed" him.

"It was the August 13th, 1974—a balmy, stormy night, much like this. The air conditioning was broken so all the guests decided to strip off their clothes and dive into the pool to cool off before heading out back to the sauna.

The little *Jack* puppet on stage dipped down and then reappeared and was surrounded by a bunch of other nude puppets that were skirmishing around and Muppet-bumping into each other. Reg figured Antonio was under the stage controlling everything and doing all the voices. Trevor couldn't stop laughing and Reg admitted to himself that Antonio was actually pretty good!

"Now, back in the day, this was the place to be seen and more importantly *un*-seen. There were no phones, no answering machines, no texting. No email. No sex aps. No Scruff. No Hornet. No Grindr. Just a man with a hard on and a dream. Outside the sauna and near the showers, several sinks were lined up and a HUGE wall-sized mirror would serve as a makeshift, steamy chalkboard you could write on if you liked a guy but were too shy to say anything. All you had to do was write on the mirror—or breathe on it and THEN write in the steam—your room number and what you wanted the other guy to do to you, or vice versa. Most wrote, "Jack Me Off," which was also a play on words, since Jack was the name of the place and the name of the MAN. Well. The day Jack almost overdosed, he found himself in a very precarious situation. He awoke in the middle of the wooden floor of the sauna with twelve men raping him and taking advantage of his body. He couldn't breathe and was choking on an orgy of their cocks as they pilfered his mouth and anus, one after the other, after the other. They were all high and drunk, of course—they were RAGING but, they didn't know Jack had a heart condition. He was forty-five, by this time and had no prior history of heart disease. He died on the dark, molding floor in the middle of them all orgasming and cumming on his lifeless body."

Some patrons in the room gasped. Some just ate their popcorn or sipped their drink. Reggie was aghast and Trevor looked scared. Miles patted his knee and got up to use to the bathroom. "I'll be right back," he said. "I gotta go take a piss."

Mario waited for the crowed to die down and made sure to have their full attention before he continued.

"They never found Jack's body. Some say he just made it LOOK like he died so he could join a group of friends up in Seattle. Others lamented that they all panicked and stuffed his body in the water heater near the old part of this building and that's why this place smells so bad. We've tried cleaning and disinfecting the vents but it doesn't take away the musty smell that I'm sure you all picked up on. It's not you."

Everybody laughed.

"We've even had mediums come through to claim his ghost still haunts the walls and changes the temperature of the shower, from frigid cold to scalding hot. Shoes and towels disappear all the time. The television changes channels all on its own, as well."

It was here that Mario paused and lowered his voice.

They say that if you write: "Jack Me Off" three times on the mirror, he comes to you to do your bidding. Or comes to kill you, just as YOU'RE about to come."

Trevor mumbled, "Yeah, right."

Miles gave him Blowfish eyes.

Mario continued. "We'll be giving tours, this Halloween of the grounds and the scene of the crime. We have a lot of work to do and are looking for volunteers to tidy up the place, so if you're interested in donating, please see Antonio. He'll be more than happy to help you."

Trevor exclaimed: "No wayyyy. They're just looking for more money so they can move more of their family members here."

"TREVOR," Reg scolded him and tried not to laugh. "You're lucky Miles isn't here to hear you say that."

Mario tried to end his tale by laughing maniacally but ended up accidentally dropping the microphone to the floor. It made a loud: "THUD." He picked it back up, clearly embarrassed, and said, "Well, that's our show, folks.

Antonio popped up from under the stage and waved all the finger puppets at the crowd and bowed. He had a cheesy grin on his face. Everyone applauded and started to get up.

"Dude," said Miles, who had returned and was tying his robe. "You gotta get your boyfriend to let us explore the old part of the building here tonight. It'd be so cool!"

"Ew. No, Trevor. It's MY birthday and we're going to do what *I* want. And, what I want to do is have lots of insane sex, with Luigi, over there.

"Mario," said Reg.

"Whatever. All I know is that he's got a Donkey Kong dick and I plan to be on it ALL night."

Reg looked at Trevor and Trevor looked perturbed. He could smell liquor on Miles' breath and instead of saying anything he looked at Reg and stormed off. He threw off his robe and ran all the way outside into the pool and made a large splash. Several men in there yelped and ran inside.

"Miles. I told you I wanted you to watch your drinking, tonight. I HATE driving your car. It's so low to the ground. I don't want to have to babysit you like I did LAST year when we all went camping. That was a disaster, remember? You almost burned off your penis peeing out the campfire. The s'mores we made later that night tasted TERRIBLE because of it."

"Ooooh, alright," said Miles and shook his fists at his sides. "Go tell your lunkhead of a boyfriend that I'll get Mario to give us a tour. But I want to do it NOW and get it over with! Gosh! You're both just so goddamned needy, sometimes."

Reg's face blanched and he tried to ignore Miles obvious, oncoming inebriation. He stormed off and walked up to Mario and pointed at Reg and then toward the pool, where Trevor was busy trying to climb aboard an inflatable swan. He then saw Miles pull a wad of cash out from under his towel, like a bad magic trick come to life, and Mario nodded as they started walking in his direction.

———————————

The four of them stood in front of a large metal door. They could barely see. Above it was a faded, green bulb surrounded by a black, metal cage, from which came a humming sound. Mario was rifling through a backpack and pulled out what looked like E.T. fingers with red ropes on the end of them.

"Here. Pass these out to your friends," whispered Mario and Miles inspected the trinkets.

"What are THESE," Trevor asked.

"SHH!" exclaimed Mario.

"They're a surprise, baby," said Miles through a drunken hiccup.

"They're something I make and sell online," said Mario, quietly. He was acting strangely and accidentally dropped the backpack on the tiled floor and quickly picked it back up again and looked around himself and into the dark corridors on either side of them. He was always dropping things. He fumbled with a set of keys.

"You guys have to PROMISE me you won't make a lot of noise once I let you in here. Everything echoes off the walls and I could be in deep shit if anything happens, like if someone gets lost or hurt up in here. My father owns this place and he'll fucking KILL me."

"We promise," chimed Trevor.

Reg hung the object around his neck. It was a flashlight on one end and on the other was what looked like a dildo.

"It's a dildo, Reg," laughed Trevor.

"Trevor, shut UP!" scolded Miles.

"Okay! Gosh! How do you turn this thing on?"

"Here," said Mario, grabbing the one around Miles' neck. "You have to press the penis tip for it to turn at the other end."

Trevor was excitedly doing the *Pee Pee Dance* and admiring his new toy. Reggie inspected his further. It was all a rather ingenious product. It had veins molded onto it and three soft ridges along the shaft and everything. It was flesh-pink, about seven inches long, and two fingers wide.

"Perfect size, eh, Reg," teased Trevor as he elbowed him in the arm. "C'mon. Let's do some ghost hunting!"

"Be very careful," said Mario. "There's glass and stuff all around. We haven't had a chance to clean it out yet." He took the ring of keys, tried to find the keyhole, and scratched the door, which made a loud screech. Miles' hands flew to his ears.

"Geez, man," said Trevor and helped Mario by clicking on his light so they could find the lock.

Mario shoved open the door and kicked away a few branches and leaves that had fallen through a broken skylight. "Fuck," he cursed to himself.

"What's wrong," asked Miles.

"I was hoping we wouldn't have to replace that," said Mario as he looked up at the light. "It's going to cost a fortune!"

There wasn't a lot of water from the storm, which surprised Mario and he was so horny being next to Miles most of the night, he grabbed Miles' hand and placed it on his cock, through his jeans.

"My GOD, Papi," exclaimed Miles. "How big is that?!"

Reg looked down as Mario's erection, which had pushed up through his waistline and pulsated at the top of his belly button. He swallowed hard and looked at Miles, who was blinking as he fell down on his knees.

"Nuh-Uh. Not here, *Action Jackson*," said Mario. "It's too dangerous."

"You're right," said Miles, huskily, and yanked Mario into the direction from which they came.

Reg stood frozen and looked up at Trevor, who peered up at the skylight. "Come on, dude," he said and grabbed Reg's hand.

They made their way through what was probably the old entrance and shone their penis lights along the cold, marble path. Reg was gratified he wore his sneakers and felt the tight squeeze of Trevor's right hand. He wondered if this was the hand he used to jerk off with.

"Look, bud. Up ahead!"

It was hard to make out, but there was a blue light coming from somewhere ahead of them and to the left. They heard what sounded like rushing water. Trevor quickened his pace and ended up almost pulling Reg off balance. His head fell right into Reg's shoulder blade.

"Whoops. Sorry, buddy," said Trevor and put his arm around Reg's waist. He guided them to the light and looked in.

It was the moonlight cascading in from another skylight—an unbroken one. This time, from what Reg could gather, they were in the clothes check room next to the shower. There was ripped, red carpet on the floor covered with cigarette butts and beer cans. It reminded him of the day after the Oscars when he would walk outside of his apartment and down the street, past the Dolby Theatre, to the Hollywood & Highland train station to go to work and meandered through all the refuse littered on the ground as workers dismantled the extravaganza.

Vines and dead flowers littered the hallway as they pushed on through. Trevor kept a steady grip on Reg's waist all the way.

"I want to get to the showers," said Trevor. "I'm all sweaty and gross."

"You're not going to take a shower HERE, are you," questioned Reg, shockingly, as he picked some dead leaves from his robe.

"Why not? This could be our own little moment in paradise. We should follow the flow of water, as I'm sure it will lead to a drain somewhere," Trevor said and winked.

They passed their lights across the floor and along the walls, and when they crossed streams Trevor bellowed, "Don't cross the streams, dude!"

Reg jumped and looked shaken. He had forgotten where he was, suddenly and could still feel Trevor's arm cuddling his waist.

Trevor guffawed. "Relax, buddy, I'm just playing. It's a Ghostbusters reference. Duh!"

"I know Ghostbusters, butthead."

"Oh, wait! Here it is. Look!"

They followed the trickle of water that had grown larger now and sure enough, they ended up in the middle of a set of open, old showers with a drain in the center.

"Holy fuck. JACKPOT!"

Trevor threw off his robe and bounded over to one of the showers, stark naked. He looked up at the head and then down at the silver knobs. "I wonder if they'll work?"

"Maybe we shouldn't," cautioned Reg.

"Aw. Come on, buddy. Look where we are, right now! We're never going to have another moment like this."

He walked up to Reg, poked him in the chest. He traced his finger down to Reg's waist and untied his robe. "Take this off. Underwear, too."

Reg's eyes bulged out as he felt Trevor's own bulge brush purposely against his side, as his friend walked back toward the showers. With a few quick, wrenching turns, a low rumble shook the wall tiles, and out sputtered a thick, brown gunk. Trevor had wisely stepped aside for this and waited for cleaner water to start shooting out from the head.

Sure enough, after a few moments, hot water was gushing out and steam started to fill up the room. "Wow. This puppy still has power!"

Reg did what Trevor told him to and took off his robe and pressed down on the hard on in his underwear. He didn't have a HUGE cock, but he was an impressive seven inches. He closed his eyes and though of wildlife after-birth and his father's Penthouse magazines he used to jerk off to get his mind off the blood flow that was impregnating his oncoming embarrassment.

He looked at Trevor washing off the refuse of the night. He was all blue and as he walked toward his friend, he peeled off his underwear and bravely stepped right next to Trevor—who had started a shower for him, too. Trevor smiled down at him. His teeth were an electric, Smurf blue, and his cerulean blue eyes were masked by the moonlight and appeared ALL blue. There was no albumen in them, it seemed. He looked at Trevor, from head to toe and admired his physique. He looked like *Dr. Manhattan*, one of his favorite characters from the Watchmen, and he was sad, suddenly, at the remembrance of fitness guru, Greg Plitt, who died, tragically, last year from a train accident.

"What's the matter, buddy? You look sad."

"Oh, nothing. I'm just worried about Miles."

"Miles can take care of himself, dude. I'm sick of him always going off without us and coming back drunk. He's on a downward spiral and he's getting fat."

Reg looked down at his stomach and tried to cover himself. The steam did little to cover his erection, but the memory of Greg and the pondering of Miles' whereabouts, softened his stiffening wood.

Trevor, while washing his armpits, noticed his discomfort and said, "Don't worry, dude. You have a great body. I keep asking you if you need me to train you."

Reg sighed. "I know. And thanks. I think I'm about ready to give up the ghost, as it were. Ghosts from the past that are holding me down. And my sugar addiction. Ugh!"

"There you GO! You know what ELSE you need?"

"What?" asked Reg as he twisted his nose up at him like Mowgli scouting the *Man Village*.

"SEX," exclaimed Trevor and he turned down the heat from the water to let the steam calm down.

Reg noticed that Trevor was hard and he DEFINITELY wasn't a grower, but he didn't care. It was all he could do not to drop down to his knees and suck him off, right there.

Trevor shut off his shower, walked over to the opposite wall and began brushing away leaves that were stuck there.

"What are you doing?"

"You'll see," said Trevor. "Come here, hot shot."

Reg walked over to Trevor, being careful not to slip, and made sure to pick up Trevor's and made sure to pick up their robes, and he hung them over the opposite shower head. The robes looked like two invisible men in their robes, hovering in the windy air that had suddenly kicked on.

"That's weird," Trevor said when he heard the vents turn on, and the remaining steam started to be sucked up into them at a ferocious pace.

"Yeah. That IS weird. It's probably Miles fucking with the controls to try and scare us. What's up?"

Trevor kept brushing away dead vines and dirt until he found what he was looking for. A gleaming, unbroken mirror.

He gasped.

"What's the matter, Reg?"

"I know what you're going to do."

What you were hoping he'd do …

"Oh yeah?" asked Trevor as he smiled and looked at Reg through the mirror.

"Don't," cautioned Reg.

"Why not? Come Onnn. LIVE a little. Besides, it's just an old ghost story to make people come back to this place. None of that stuff ACTUALLY happened. There's no such thing as OOgah-Boogah!"

The white bathrobes swayed in the breeze and the cuffs met and touched, in the air, for a moment. The pipes creaked and moaned.

Trevor splayed out his hand in front of Reg's face, touched the tip of his nose with his index finger, and then moved it to the mirror. He put his finger on the glass, looked at Reg's reflection and said to him, "This is what I want you to do to me." And the he wrote, three times:

Jack Me Off
Jack Me Off
Jack Me Off

Reg coughed and began to choke suddenly. Trevor looked shocked, swooped him up into his strong arms and started to carefully pat him on the back.

"Are you ok, buddy? Arms up." His naked body pressed against Reg's. Trevor's penis slid in between Reg's legs as he set him back down. "What's the matter? Isn't this what you want?"

Reggie stammered. This was all a dream. It HAD to be! He was going to wake up any moment to the sound of Harrison, his black, Siamese cat, batting down his vintage, Star Wars action figures to wake him up at five in the morning so he could eat. He felt snot bubble out of his left nostril and he squeezed his eyes shut.

Wake up ... wake UP ... WAKE UP!

He opened his eyes and wiped his nose with his wrist. Yep. Trevor was still there, embraced and beaming down at him.

"Come on, dude. I won't hurt you," Trevor said and planted a kiss on Reg's full lips. His beard tickled his teeth. Trevor lifted Reg up off the ground a little and his rigid cock immediately sprang to attention and rubbed Reggie's taint. So, this is what being a bottom feels like. He didn't care. He was in the arms of *THE MAN*. He was parting his lips, now, to take Trevor's full tongue. This was going to happen. FINALLY.

Trevor tried forcing his cock inside Reg's puckered and pulsating hole.

"You're so tight, dude."

He opened his eyes again and when he did, he noticed out of the corner of them, that a copper-colored light had suddenly appeared in the reflection of the mirror from a room behind—and yet also somewhat beside—the showers. He couldn't see through the haze of bliss and middling, meddling fog.

Trevor groaned, set Reg down, got onto his knees and started sucking on his stiff, thick cock. Reg felt Trevor's wet Faux Hawk, between his fingertips. His hair was so soft. He had always wanted to run his fingers through Trevor's hair. He bent down and sniffed it, then yanked it a little roughly.

Trevor moaned.

He was trying to make sense of everything—trying to enjoy the sensation of Trevor sucking him off. Trevor's mouth was licking his balls one by one now and then he began to tongue his ass.

They both groaned.

What, he wondered, had happened to the two bathrobes?

Reg was orgasmic. He thought of the free condom that was stuck to the flier they gave out before the puppet show. He had put it in the left pocket of his robe. He hadn't bottomed since high school, when he'd been fucked by a teacher's aide that he had a mad crush on.

They were both on the edge of completion when, suddenly, there was the sound behind them. Something moved. Trevor sprang up and and they both, defensively and nervously, looked around.

Reg wiped off Trevor's chin and give his long beard a soft yank.

"Fuck, your dick tastes good. What was that?"

"I dunno. But look," said Reg, pointing at the light which was looming larger behind the showers. The steam had fully dissipated now and they could make out where the source of light was coming from, which was a doorway that was built in to the wall that led to another room.

"Come on, Bats. Let's go investigate!"

"Treeev. I dunno. I think we should leave."

"No. C'mon, man. When are we going to have another opportunity like this?"

"We should go! I'm worried about Miles."

"I'll let you fuck me in there if you come with me right now."

Reg couldn't breathe. His premature, elongated eyeballs hurt. He tried to act manly and crossed his arms and brushed free from his mind all the train-wreck euphemisms and all of the times he shouted at a stupid, horror movie victim, who was about to get massacred on a movie screen.

He was still rock hard.

"Okay."

"Fuck yeah," said Trevor, hungrily.

What is that music, Reg thought? Did Trevor hear it?

They slowly walked to the source of light and as the music got louder, it sounded like disco.

"You hear that," asked Trevor. "It sounds like Carly Rae Jepsen!"

He DID hear it.

The boys walked, hand in hand, and entered the room.

There, in front of them, were fifteen naked men. Writhing and laughing, they kicked their feet in a whirlpool next to the sauna and splashed each other. Ten of them had some form of facial hair.

All of them were in various stages of sexual exploration.

Trevor gasped. "Holy God, I'm in COLT heaven."

None of the men appeared to notice them standing there. It was as if they were transported through time. Everything had a golden-beige glow, like a J-Lo CD cover, and champagne bottles were strewn about everywhere. It turned into a full on orgy within seconds.

Trevor walked right into the middle of the action and started jerking off. The ghosts came alive at the sight of him and, one after the other, they piled on Trevor, until only his head was seen poking out. The music got louder and more ferocious. Thrash metal, now. Nine Inch Nails? More like: *Nine Inches, NAILED!*

You let me violate you …

The lights became more blinding now. Reg felt sick to his stomach. Someone was grabbing at his ankles and pulling him into the melee. He felt a cold suction on his cock, suddenly, and he was so worked up he blew his load right there. He heard Trevor cumming too.

They came together after all.

Trevor had almost completely vanished in the frenzy of figures and when Reg realized what was going on, it was almost too late. He sprang into action and clawed at the monstrous mold and found Trevor's hand, yanking him free after three forceful tugs. He was near exhaustion.

Trevor was lethargic and Reg dragged him over to the shower and turned cold water on the both of them. The icy cold water shook them to their cores and they both exclaimed; "HOLY FUCK!"

They had their backs turned to the orgy, and when they finally looked up from the shroud of water raining down upon them, they saw that the mountain of men had conjoined themselves into a cacophony of heads and arms and penises; their faces angry and resembling Edvard Munch's *The Scream*.

They both took their cue from the specter and started screaming at the top of their lungs. The giant ball of men suddenly melted onto the tile and, where once there were fifteen men, there was now only one coming up out of the floor.

Reg knew INSTANTLY who it was.

Jack Crawford Gale.

The figure raised its hands up and out of the tile floor. It pulled itself up out of what appeared to be quicksand. But, it wasn't quicksand. It was STEAM. Reg found their robes and shoes on the ground, grabbed Trevor's wrist and yanked him out of the room as quickly as he could.

Their hearts thumped in their ears as they tried not to slip on the wet tiles.

Don't look back. Don't look back!

Reg and Trevor found the corridor through which they had entered and went for the metal door. It was LOCKED!

They screamed and pounded on it.

"Help! Help!" they shouted at the top of their lungs. Trevor tried kicking the door but ended up bruising his knee in the process. They turned and there stood Miles and Mario.

"I TOLD you guys not to fuck around! I ..."

There was a slice-suction sound and Mario dropped to the floor. His whole body had turned purple in an instant and his eyeballs burst in their sockets.

Miles screamed and covered his mouth with a clawed hand.

Jack had assimilated himself into the Mario's body and overheated it from the inside. Slowly, he reformed himself and leaked out of Mario's large ears. Part of Mario's brains came out with him.

Miles leaned over and vomited.

Trevor and Reg carried Miles under their shoulders and ran to one of the boarded up side rooms. Trevor crashed through the door with ease while Reggie held onto Miles.

"Fuck. Fuck! FUCK!" Trevor shouted.

Once they were inside, Reg laid Miles down on a wooden bench. They appeared to be in one of the old locker rooms. He could see an assortment of names and phone numbers here, and pictures of dicks, carved into the walls. *1972. Abel was here.*

"What do we do, what do we do," cried Trevor. Reg had never seen him so unhinged.

Miles sat up. Trevor brushed back his hair and felt for a fever.

He was okay and coming out of it. "Look for ... look ... for ...," he stammered.

"What? WHAT?! Look for what," Trevor shouted.

Miles shakily stood up and began slapping himself in the face.

"Miles, stop it," yelled Reg.

But, just as Miles had sunk into despair, he had brought himself back with equal force and jumped up and began barking orders.

"Go through the lockers. Find anything that will pry open the door or that will get rid of the steam! The steam is where he gets his power!"

Trevor and Reg looked at each other and then at Miles. They couldn't believe he resurrected himself so quickly and were secretly worried that he had been possessed. He must not have been as drunk as they thought.

"Go! GO! I'm fine! I'll keep a lookout!"

Trevor and Reg ransacked the room and, just as they were about to give up, Reg yelped and Trevor ran over to him.

There, in an open locker, were 3 old hair dryers. Trevor was clued into what Reg was thinking and tossed the other one to Miles, who was beside them now.

"Look for an outlet," said Trevor, hurrying.

They all scrambled and searched for an outlet. They heard a shuffling coming toward them and knew it was Jack, reforming himself again.

Trevor yelped, again and called them over.

"I found one! Here! Give me your hairdryers. Let's pray they work!"

The outlets were on the far side of the locker room and on the opposite side of the entrance door. The shuffling grew louder and, before they knew it, Jack was advancing on them—a seven-foot figure, now, made entirely out of steam.

They could almost see right through him to their escape!

All three of them screamed and turned on their hair dryers. The dryers sprang to life and for a moment, the boys inadvertently posed like Charlie's Angels. The hair dryers were white, with long snouts and short handles, with the words *Con-Air* written on them, in black. The cords, thankfully, were unnecessarily long.

Jack's mouth opened and he screamed again, a loud, dinosaur shrieking sound. His mouth sank down all the way to the floor, this time scraping against the tile. He hissed and swung a long, misty arm at Trevor, who ducked and jumped at the chance to advance on Jack and catch him off guard.

Reg and Miles ducked at Jack's other threatening arm but weren't as agile as Trevor. It sliced across Miles' arm with a crude burn. Miles screamed in agony but bravely kept on him.

Jack tried once more to dodge the heat from the dryers and formed into a cloud above them. But it was too late.

The three friends stood on the bench and backed the specter toward an open air vent. They seized the opportunity to force him into it and snapped the vent shut.

They hung the dryers—that were still on—around the vent's open edges and took off running toward the door. This time, the door slid open with ease due to the change in air pressure caused by the warm dryers, and they fled into the night.

Breathless, they found themselves outside the club. There were fire trucks everywhere. And people from the neighborhood stood on their front lawns inquiring as to what was going on.

In the confusion, the boys snuck out a back entrance gate and ran to their car.

"Fuck! My keys and phone are inside," shouted Miles.

"Fuck your phone," Trevor and Reg said at the same time.

"And, I've got your keys," said Reg and produced them from his robe pocket. "I didn't trust you driving."

Trevor roared with laughter and exclaimed, "Oh my God! You Go, Boy Scout!" and lifted Reg up in the air and swung him around and kissed him full on the mouth in front of all the onlookers.

"Oh my God. You guys FUCKED," extolled Miles. "OHMYGOD! You whores!"

"Shut up Miles," said Reg with a newfound authority. "It was bound to happen sooner or later."

"Yeah, Milesy," said Trevor. "Don't be jealous that you can't handle all of this."

Miles winced in pain and massaged his arm. Trevor took the tie from his robe and twisted it over Miles burn and wrapped his arm like a Mummy.

"Ouch, buddy, this burn looks bad," said Trevor. "We should get you to the hospital."

"I don't need a hospital. Ugh. Poor Mario. Antonio must be beside himself. We owe it to all of them to let them know what happened. That thing is still in there!"

"I know," whispered Reg. "But all I want to do now is go home. We can contact them in the morning. We could be charged with trespassing … or worse—murder!"

"You're probably right," said Miles. "But promise me, we call them when they open and then, the cops, first THING. Maybe they'll think Mario slipped and cracked his head open. Or got electrocuted somehow."

"I promise," said Reg.

"I don't want to take showers for the rest of my life," exclaimed Trevor.

"You already smell like you don't," said Reg and punched him softly in the gut.

They all walked to Miles' car and Reg got in the front to drive.

"Miles," asked Reg and looked at him in the back seat through the mirror. He shuddered and shook. Trevor was in the front, next to him, with his hand on Reg's thigh.

"What?"

"Never again are we going to do what YOU want for your birthday."

"Noted," grumbled Miles as he sank into the back seat of his car and rested his head against the window.

Trevor looked at Reg. He went in for a kiss and instead yanked the rearview mirror off the front of the windshield.

Reg screwed up his face and whispered: "You ass!"

"Hang on a minute," said Trevor.

He looked at the mirror and blew his hot breath on it.

"Trevor! I will fucking kill you, I swear," bellowed Reg.

"Trevor, knock it the fuck OFF," yelled Miles, from his backseat stupor. "Fucking Johnny Bravo wannabe."

"Hang on," Trevor whispered and laughed. He looked directly into Reg's eyes. "Do you trust me?"

Reg nodded. "Of course."

"Okay." Trevor huffed on the mirror, again, wrote on it for a moment and handed it to Reg.

It read, "Take us home, baby. Take us home."

Reg laughed, started the car, put Trevor's hand on his crotch, winked at him and said, "You got it, boy."

Then, he peeled off into the remaining night.

Moonlight
by Patrick Raith

It's as if I've been asleep for a week. As my eyes slowly begin to flicker open, what feels like of their own accord instead of mine, the shape of her face becomes apparent to me as my vision focuses. The already feral, icy brilliance of her eyes seems to absorb the gathered light from the outside window making them shine like a pair of stars in the dark.

I try to lift my arm from the floor at my side, and it feels as though it weighs several hundred pounds. The look on her face, briefly of concern, becomes a relieved smile and I watch as she turns her gaze in the direction of my slowly rising hand and then back to my face. Almost, though not quite to her face, maybe her chin, I could at least see my fingertips before she snatched up my hand and clasped it softly in her own. I found it strange that she was so gentle with me now when before the few times she had touched or grabbed me she had been so strong.

Maybe she was trying to be gentle with me now? I didn't know.

"Slowly," she whispered, the soothing sound of her voice entering through my ears and into the cavern that was my skull, each repetitious echo resonating through every part of my body commanding it to rest. The grip of her hand, which no longer feels ice cold, lessens and I can feel my own hand slowly returning to its place on the floor. I blink several times, despite the fact that my vision is already crystal clear, before I begin to speak.

"Where," I manage to choke out of my scratchy, sandpapery throat before I cough several times, the acrid deluge of bile erupting into my mouth. The whole world seems to spin and I feel the nausea start to take hold before I swiftly roll to my side, opening my mouth in a spray of the most disgusting smelling vomit I have ever experienced. I feel her still holding me as she did before I woke up, her gentle yet strong hand circling against my back as I watch the rest of the regurgitation gather at the cement floor in an ever growing pool of nasty. It felt as though everything within my abdomen was being squeezed and pushed up into my stomach and further still, my head screaming all through it as though it were clamped between an ever tightening vice grip.

"I am sorry that it is like this," she whispered to me before she gave a light chuckle. "We do not usually speak of these moments that occur after the turn. We, all of us, endure this our first night."

"What..." I began to ask, through gasping and regurgitating, "the fuck...is this?" Strangely my body did not seem to spasm nor did I wretch as all of it came up out of me in waves. The vomit literally seemed to expel itself from my body as though it were alive, a repulsive entity entirely unto itself, desperate to escape from inside of me. The gentle massaging of my back from her hand moved to the side of my head, her fingers gently combing through my hair.

"It is everything from inside of you before from when you were human," she answered. "We have no need of food as the humans do. Our stomachs do not contain anything any longer, and so you no longer possess the bodily functions of a human being." She stopped as I gave one last spew, the agony of my insides being rung out replaced by a growing feeling of relief and an odd sort of emptiness. "Should you ever try to consume human food, water, anything that is not blood," she began, "this shall be the result." I wiped my mouth with the back of my hand and noticed the absence of the previous weakness in my limbs.

"Yuck and noted," I replied as I sat up and pressed my back into her, her arms encircling and drawing me closer. I felt the cheek of her face against the side of my head, her taller frame completely encompassing mine, making me feel protected and safe. I took a deep breath, allowing her scent, a strange mixture somewhere faintly between lilacs and how the world seems to smell, no matter where you are, after it rains, into my lungs. Even now, so close, I could not hear any sound coming from her at all.

I did not feel the breeze of her breath over my ears or across the skin of my neck and I noticed there was no feeling of rise and fall from her chest. "Ara?"

"Yes, dear one?" she answered. I felt my own breathing, tense and anxious, though the normal accompanied feeling of my pounding heart was absent.

"You're...not breathing," I answered as I slowly drew my hand towards my chest.

"No," she replied, "I am not." My hand stopped, inches from my breast. I didn't need the proof of what I already knew, that my own heart too was not beating, and yet my hand hung there as if it had a mind of its own and it was unsure of what it should do.

"Why am I?" I asked, feeling the surrounding dry, stale air continue to enter and escape my lungs. Ara tightened her arms around me and I felt her chin rest over the top of my right shoulder.

"You are only doing it out of habit," she explained. "This was a mandatory series of movements essential to your once human survival." I felt her smile through her voice. "Since the moment you entered this world you have done so. In time you will grow more accustomed to the new way of your body." I sighed and looked away from my hand and towards the window. I had absolutely no idea where we were.

I had been attacked that night and chased away from the club my friends and I had gone to by the only other vampire I had ever seen. The last memory I had of her face was the horrifying, bestial look on it. I had never before in my life been looked at with such scorn and complete hatred as she had done before she chased me into the warehouse next door and began the twisted game of cat and mouse. Naturally, being human, I lost, and when she found me she nearly ripped my throat out with her teeth. The last thing I saw was Ara tear through the center of two large, steel doors as though they were plastic.

"Um...where are we now?" I asked as I gazed around the room that we were in.

The walls were unfinished drywall, the skeletal stripes of chalky scented joint compound glowing almost fluorescent in the unlit space. The silvery trail of light from outside, illuminating everything, fell from the window of the unfinished room into a glowing pool upon the dirty, concrete floor I'd woken up from. What I'm guessing must be dust, as I've no fucking clue what else it could possibly be, floated on the lunar light, looking less like a debris filled moonbeam and more like a galaxy of spiraling asteroids made up of god knows what. I'd never before been so in awe of something so simple, and yet here I was staring at dust.

Jesus. It's only fucking dust.

"A housing development, several miles from where I found you," she answered. "After Rachael fled, I gave you my blood." Her hand played with several strands of my hair. "You were beyond, there was no life left in you, yet even still I was able to bring you across." I closed my eyes and sighed as I gently shook my head.

"I don't remember a thing after that psycho took off," I replied and then stopped as I realized she'd said a name. "Wait a minute," I pushed forward and away from her, onto my hands and knees. I crawled a few steps before I rose, kneeling into a crouch, turning to face her. "Rachael?" I asked confused. "You knew who that was?" Ara's expression was that of stone, unwavering and apathetic.

"I did," she answered, "I do," her tone apologetic yet the look on her face unchanged. "She was once my fledgling, long ago, though I set her free into the world. Always she was the most jealous and ill tempered of any progeny I had ever made."

"Riiiight," I said, irritated at how easily she seemed to brush aside the fact that I had just been through an extremely traumatic experience. Oh, and nearly murdered. "So, you dumped her then?"

"Aya please," Ara sighed dejectedly, though I wasn't sure if it was from annoyance or actually feeling guilt at what had happened. Either way, I wasn't having any of that.

"Hey, it's not like I'm any stranger to being dumped by my girlfriend or anything," I replied thinking of how only hours ago I had spent an awkward portion of my night with my friends around *my* ex. The night had honestly gone from shitty, to awkward, to whoa, to what the fuck.

I recalled how elated I felt when my friend Katherine had introduced me to Ara hours ago, and how terrified I was. Ara was, quite literally, the most beautiful woman I had ever seen in my entire life, and I had absolutely no idea what interest she took in me whatsoever. I didn't think much of my appearance, though I've never thought of myself as ugly, maybe just plain. Being biracial, I looked more Asian, like my mother is, and I shuddered as I thought of how pale my skin had been *before*…all of this.

"So, is your psycho ex-girlfriend always this nice to the new women in your life, or am I some kind of exception?" I demanded. I was starting to feel like a bitch, but I was angry and I had every right.

Only now did she frown as she closed her eyes. "I am entirely responsible for everything that has happened to you, and I did not even give you the choice of this."

"Then why?" I demanded, growing angrier still. "You don't know me. You didn't know a goddamn thing about me before tonight." I stood up, towering above where she sat on the filthy, concrete floor, my head filled with questions. "Is that woman going to come after me again?"

Ara shook her head. "No," she answered, "she would not dare." I narrowed my eyes at her, not remotely convinced, and she closed her eyes and nodded. "You doubt me."

"Someone just tried to rip my throat out tonight," I screeched, my voice growing ever louder, "with her teeth. I would have died Ara, if you—" I felt my voice halt as my mouth stopped moving altogether. My body stood in place, still as stone.

"You *did* die," Ara said solemnly, rising to her feet, her eyes staring holes into mine. My body suddenly was my own again and I closed my mouth before Ara took a step forward and reached out and touched the middle finger of her open hand to the notch below my throat. "Your life as a human no longer remains. You are vampire now, and you can never again go back to what you were."

I swallowed as she drew her hand away from me, and I gazed up the three inches she had on me into her pale, sylvan face. The once carefully side-tied chignon that her straw-colored hair had tonight when I had been introduced to her, now fell past her shoulders in golden streams seemingly brighter where they hung over the dark, hunter green coat that trailed past her. The locks seemed almost as white as the moonlight that reflected off of them and it was if her face were the center of an otherworldly, silvery nimbus.

My body began to freeze up again, this time from the conflagration of emotions I was engulfed by. The full realization of what had happened to me, the reality of it all, slammed painfully into me at full force. I felt my lip quiver and I bit down on it. I would not cry. A small smile spread across her face as she spread out her arms.

"Weep," she began, "if you must. Scream. Tear apart this dwelling if you wish. Anything," she said as she clasped my hands. "And when you are ready, Sano Ayaka, I shall still be here with you."

I shuddered as I held her hands. "Please," I whispered, realizing that I should have known better than to ask while I was trying not to lose my shit, "would you just hold me?" No sooner had I asked did she take me into her arms and I buried my face in her breast, the folds of the fabric of her coat stabbing into my eyelids. What was I going to tell my mother, or Christopher? They were the only family I had left.

"You cannot tell them anything," Ara answered me as though she had heard my thoughts. My body shook from my silent sobs that I couldn't seem to stop. I was surprised by the sudden sensation of the tears cascading down my cheeks, and mortified when I saw the bloody splotches they left on the concrete floor at our feet. I immediately thought of my best friend. "Or Mika," she said, again answering my thoughts. "You are going to have to let go of everyone from your human life," she continued. "That is just the way of things. You will come to be glad of it, in time. They are safer left to their ignorance."

I took a deep, ragged sigh, my body still shuddering even as the air escaped my body, while I wiped the bloody tears from my face. I wasn't going to think about that right now, I decided. That was a bridge I was going to worry about crossing later. I closed my eyes tightly and tilted back my head, my face looking towards the ceiling, before I opened them again. My new vision frightened and equally intrigued me. I could see each and every crack in the ceiling above, insignificant or deep, every speck of dirt or dust, and all of the fingerprints, fresh or days old, stamped or smudged into it. My eyes followed a blade of light trailing toward the wall and down to the window below.

Letting go of Ara's hands, my head turned along with the rest of my body towards the window. I glanced back at her and she nodded. "Go on," she coaxed, and I turned and walked towards the portal to the outside and the night, my footsteps echoing throughout the unfinished dwelling with an intensity and sound almost entirely foreign to me. I let myself sigh deep and loudly, the sound of my steps drowned out by the boom from the echo of my breath as it bounced around the room. I stopped dead in my tracks waiting for silence.

"Fucking A," I whispered to myself before I turned, yet again, back to Ara. "What is up with my ears?" I asked.

Grinning, she gave a soft chuckle bringing her hand up to her face to hide her mouth in her laughter. "Your senses are far more than they were in your human life, though especially now since you have only just become a vampire. The first few days you shall feel an almost unbearable hypersensitivity, though it will eventually fade," she continued. "It will take time for you to adjust to how strong they are, though when you do," she stopped and smiled in a flash of teeth before, in a blur, she vanished from the spot where she stood and, in a silent instant, was suddenly standing at my side. I gasped as my head snapped to my right where she stood, smiling warmly at me.

"How did you **do** that?" I demanded, my wonder turning candidly to almost childlike glee. "Teach me how to do that!" Ara suddenly burst into laughter, surprising and equally delighting me into my own, and motioned towards the window. Following her gesture, I continued forward, my arms swaying in the pendulous momentum of my stride, when I caught the glint of something towards the floor. I looked down at my hand and realized it was only my tiger's eye ring's golden band glinting back at me as it reflected the moonlight from beyond the window glass.

I hesitated before I slowly raised my hand toward my face; the already present optical effect of the ring's stone somehow managing to appear even more dazzling as I gazed closer. Holding my hand in place, I deliberately pushed my vision and felt the muscles in my eyes not exactly straining but definitely focusing themselves in a way I was completely ignorant of and not yet used to. I nearly jumped out of my skin, dropping my hand to my side, realizing that even when I had stopped and held my hand still, my eyes had continued to look closer.

And microscopic vision, I thought to myself, *eye zoom*. I would have liked to have laughed aloud at that last bit but I was feeling more and more anxious by the second.

I finally reached the window, trying to be as silent as possible on the way to it and failing as the sound of my shoes on the concrete continued to sound like the beating of drums. Outside, presumably behind the house, I saw a massive, towering willow tree. Its catkins glinted like silver dollars under the moonlight while its branchlets slowly swayed in the breeze that took hold of them like the hair of a massive sentinel.

Leaning my head against the glass, stupidly, I sigh again. The boom of the sound of my breath bouncing back and forth off of the windows and my face is almost deafening. I recoil all the same, still not used to the sound, and feel Ara's hands on my shoulders as I reel backward into her. The real shock arrives when I turn to look back out of the window and it's just as I'm placing my hands against the glass that I notice how different they are.

81

Pale doesn't even begin to describe how they appear, almost glowing, in fact, they're so light in tone. My fingernails, longer and definitely sharper looking than they had ever were before, due to my meticulous habit of keeping them filed short, are glass-like, their smoothness reflecting the moonlight.

"Holy crap," I gasp as I raise and turn my ghostly hands about examining them, testing the sharpness of my fingernails against my fingertips. I wince at their dagger like feeling before I gasp, shocked and completely unprepared for what I see next. I lean forward and watch as the bit of my reflection that I am able to see in the window manifests as a ghostly twin of what my face once was. I watch the image staring back at me bring its hand to its face just as I do mine. I feel my expression crumple before I whirl around to where Ara stands, now in front of me. "Ara," I begin, feeling my voice give as I choke out her name, while her hand reaches for and caresses my cheek gently.

"This is not permanent," she says reassuringly and I give a shuddered sigh of relief as she smiles back.

"No?" I ask anyway, growing more and more afraid of what it is I now look like and dreading my next meeting with an actual mirror. I feel the fingers of her hand trail across my cheek and towards my hair, combing through it and past my ear repeatedly.

"Not exactly," she began and my heart sank again. Smiling in reply to the dread on my face, she leaned forward and pressed her lips to my cheek. "You do realize that you have just completed an extremely dramatic metamorphosis?" she asked. "You are a newly made, fledgling vampire," she grinned impishly at me, "it is only natural you should look like a bit like a corpse, is it not?" she giggled at how mortified my reaction was as my mouth hung open in shock. "This is all a process, pet, I assure you. Never fear."

"If you say so," I muttered, my gaze falling downward to my feet. I felt her finger under my chin, lifting my face back up to meet her eyes.

"I do say," she said, entirely serious now, "which leads me now to what next we must speak of."

"Okay?" I didn't like sound of where this was going as evidenced by the tone in her voice. I had the distinct feeling that she was going to say something else that I was not going to like.

"When we leave this place," she began, "when you encounter humans for the first time, as you are now, as you inevitably shall, you are going to feel a great and terrible feeling of hunger." I said nothing. I had known this part was coming. I wasn't expecting I would be told that I could turn into a bat or that I would need to find a coffin to sleep in during the daytime, but the part about drinking blood? Well, that I did.

Ara waited a moment for me to say something before she went on. "You must understand this. You will, quite literally, smell the blood inside of their bodies. You will hunger to the point of great pain within and you will immediately feel the compulsion to kill, to feed, anything to end that feeling inside." I nodded though I still said nothing as she looked quizzically back at me. "Are you not afraid?" she asked.

"I'm terrified," I admitted. "I don't want to kill anyone," and I truly didn't. I did not feel what she was talking about yet, hungry, but I knew that there was definitely *something* there, waiting.

Ara smiled and put her hand on my shoulder. "I know you do not, pet," she replied, "and that is not something that we do." She walked up to the window and traced her finger across the glass. "We do not kill humans nor do we do anything else that would draw attention to ourselves or our kind."

I nodded to her back, though making eye contact with her mirror's image, glad the "vampires cast no reflection" bullshit was exactly that. I watched her reflection smile back at me.

"Come."

The moment I opened the door and stepped outside, my ears were assaulted by the nocturnal cacophony that was the night. Immediately I threw my hands to my ears and spun around, about to dart back inside were it not for Ara blocking my path. Solemnly, she shook her head and did not budge an inch.

"Focus your senses, fledgling," was all she said before I felt that same feeling of puppet strings connected to my limbs, tugging me back around to face the open yard ahead of me.

I knew that it was her, it had to be, controlling me and I didn't dare ask how or why. That much, my thoughts I mean, I had control of during this and I honestly was afraid of what the answer would be or just what else she would tell me that she could do to me. Slowly, of my own accord, I stepped off of the small, raised concrete square that stood in for a porch and onto the dark, construction machine rendered ground below.

"Ookay," I whispered to myself before taking a deep breath and continuing forward. A crowded shopping mall, a full theater, a busy restaurant, none of them or remotely of the sort had anything on the chaotic symphony of everything, all at once, that I was experiencing. I felt Ara's eyes on me from where she still stood in the open doorway of the house, though I heard the sound of her voice as though she were just over my shoulder, whispering to me.

"Hear only what you wish to." Frustrated, I gritted my teeth in reply, stopping the raising of my hands at the sides of my head, resisting the urge to clamp them over my ears.

"I hear *everything* Ara," I growled back at her under my breath, knowing full well that she would be able to hear me.

"Pick something Aya." I heard her voice whisper to me once more. "Pluck it from the air and focus upon that and only that. Silence the rest. Be in control."

I took a deep breath and began to concentrate. I felt my senses, completely out of my control, as the network of chaos that I heard surged and bellowed into my ears. I felt my focus, entirely shaky and difficult to grasp, bounce from sound to sound. There were crickets chirping one second, the noises of traffic steadily moving: its sounds of horns and tires squealing one moment, engines accelerating the next, and so much more. It was almost too much for me.

Come on, god damn it, I screamed inside my head. My body trembled at the passing of an airplane, high enough to be a speck on the night sky, yet roaring as though it were just over our heads. Next was the horn of the coming train along with the clanging of the railroad crossing block nearby.

I sucked in a deep, pointless breath of oxygen while slowly closing my eyes, feeling the gathering mass in my chest where I held it. Slowly, I lowered my hands to my sides, exhaling, feeling a gentle breeze race past my face and through my hair. I let my concentration rest on the sound of the wind, pushing away all interruption of anything else, and I followed it in the direction of the willow tree I had glimpsed earlier before from inside of the house. As I listened it felt almost as though I was the wind itself, the breeze my hands touching different parts of the tree I heard as I raced past: the catkins amongst the delicate, shaking leaves in the swaying branchlets, the rough, course feeling of its bark along its several trunks.

As the breeze began to fade and die down, I began to search for another to focus on before I heard the next sound, or rather *sounds*. I grew excited as a familiarity began to form and return while I felt the confusion diminish and I let the multiple noises gather together in my hearing. The commotion came also from the tree, from *within* it.

I listened, focused entirely on that one spot, now effortlessly ignoring the sound of the presence of the returning wind that caressed my face. I heard a shuffling, followed by a scratching of skin or hair coupled with a light thumping against the tree, though when these brief noises ended I noticed the new, constant one. It was similar to the thumping sound of earlier, though more vibrant and organic, like a drumming, quite constant and rapid. I focused deeper and realized that I could make out three sources of this beating sound among the discordance made up of each.

"Heartbeats," I whispered to myself. "They're heartbeats." I smiled widely and spun around to look back at a very pleased looking Ara. "I can hear them in there."

"Yes," she replied, now stepping off of the porch and making her way toward me and taking my hand. I closed my fingers around hers and let her lead me around the unfinished, cookie cutter modeled home, through the area that would one day be a front yard, and out into the black street. I gazed up into the sky, marveling at the passing clouds that obscured the vastness of what loomed above us and the many celestial bodies presently upon it.

"Can we fly?" I asked or rather blurted out what I wondered next.

Ara smiled before she leaned in towards me and pressed her lips to the side of my forehead. "You are far too young to," she answered. "One day though." She stopped abruptly, as did I. I glanced past her, uncertain of what had caused her to stop.

"What is it?" I asked. Ara stood frozen, nearly a statue.

"Humans," she answered. Hearing the very word elicited a mixture of feelings within me. Excitement, anticipation, and fear were what I felt first, and before I realized what I was doing next, I felt my now preternatural sense of hearing focus and race forward past the sounds of dead leaves swirling through the street ahead, over the swaying branches of trees, and into a room within another unfinished home. I took two hurried steps, my legs preparing for an all-out run, and pulled free of Ara's hand.

"Aya! Wait!" I heard the sound of her protests behind me as the night seemed to become a world of blurred colors, lights, and wind. In only seconds I found myself at a large bay window. Staring inside the dimly lit front room I could hear the sounds of several people within talking amongst each other and the echoes of their footsteps. Turning and looking past the window frame, I saw the front door and prepared to dash towards it and inside. As I turned to bolt for the entrance, I felt a jolt shoot through every part of my body and I fell to my knees, overtaken by that familiar feeling paralyzing every inch of me.

Ara quite literally seemed to appear out of thin air, several feet in front of me, the blast of wind upon her arrival exploding past my face and drying my eyes. Our eyes locked for a second before she was suddenly, just…just there, she was so fast. Standing before me, her hand fastened around my arm as my body seemed to stand on its own upon her touch. Looking into her now wide, almost hysteric eyes, I knew I had crossed a line. I was afraid, truly afraid, for the first time since I had woken up and come to.

Watching her mouth barely seem to move, the words nearly inaudible, I was still able to hear her say, "Do not make a sound," before we walked together to the large window, her hand still clamped on my upper arm. Inside, although empty and not entirely finished, it was extremely large and would likely serve as a living room to its future inhabitants. The room's light that had pulled my attention to the window earlier came from the glowing mass of embers and dancing flames at the center of a completed fireplace, a man in dark clothes crouched next to it.

The growing feeling I had noticed before, when Ara had told me of the hunger, roared from below as it tore to the surface the moment I saw him. The light from the flames illuminated his already bronze skin as he turned and made his brown eyes look as though they were two glowing pieces of amber stuck into his face. As he sifted through and poked the red hot kindling with a firehook, I watched as he bit and chewed on his dirty fingernails. Normally I would have been entirely disgusted at the gross, and what I could tell from him, manic looking habit, I instead was wondering what he smelled like or if his skin was as soft as it looked.

"Aya," I turned my head towards Ara, my eyes not wanting to leave the man I had been staring at, whom I was thinking had to be in his mid-twenties. I felt that little tug of control she held over me pull my gaze to hers. Surprisingly, I felt myself struggle against it, for once, despite the futility of it all.

"I want to go inside," I whispered as our eyes met.

"If we enter that house," Ara replied solemnly, "you will kill those people." I felt her hold let go of my body before my head snapped back to the window and the man inside. Straining to listen, hearing the cracking of the fire, the man's ragged breathing, the sound of his fingernails shuffling through his curly, mousey hair as he scratched his scalp, I did hear the sound of others.

"There are two more of them," I replied, squinting as my eyes scanned the room. To the left of the fireplace was a wall that ended at an archway that lead out into a hall, stairs beyond leading to the upper floor ahead of where the front door was.

"Four," Ara corrected before I turned to look at her. "There are five people inside of this house," she nodded to the window. "That man there, two more men, and a woman upstairs," she glanced up at the windows above us on the second story, "Though I can hear five heartbeats in all."

"How in god's name is that even possible?" I blurted out, louder than I would have liked. My head snapped back to the window as the man's own head shot up and jerked in the direction of us. Before I had a chance to react to my stupid mistake, Ara grasped my arm and yanked me close to her body. The night again became a whirlwind of color for a brief moment as I found myself pulled from the spot we had been standing at the window to behind the corner of the house, past the front door. "Shit," I whispered as I collected myself and shook my head.

Ara put her finger to her lips motioning for silence before poking her head around the wall. Even before the door opened I could hear his hurried footsteps approaching from inside. The sound of the door made my body go rigid as the coming breeze from the opposite side of the house brought an equally disgusting and stimulating bouquet of alcohol, cigarettes, body spray, and sweat. Ara's grip on my arm tightened as I felt my eyes grow wide, my body fighting with every bit of strength I had to pull away from her.

"No," she whispered, and I felt the full force of her influence upon me then. From inside the hunger thrashed against me and screamed, my own mouth wanting to scream out loud with it, but I remained rooted to where she held me. The feeling was beyond claustrophobic, the almost alien, primal feeling inside like a pinball bouncing around my solid statue of an unmoving, uncooperative body.

The sound of two footsteps over the cement step seemed to calm the ravening feeling inside as I listened, my ears only for him. The door creaked as I heard the sounds of his body shifting, not moving from the spot, and his attempting to not breath too loudly.

"The fuck you doing!" I flinched, somehow, at the surprise of another voice, also a man, from inside the house. Ara stood staring at me though I knew she was listening just as I was to the now two people closest to us.

"I heard something, dumbass," the man hissed back. "You think I'm doing?" Ara's arm squeezed tighter as the sound of the door opening wider followed the conversation.

"Just get the fuck back inside!" came again the voice of the second man. "Quit fuckin' around or Mertes is gonna get pissed!"

The sound of the man at the door chuckling came in reply to the threat. "Mertes can fuckin' blow me."

"Just get the fuck up here," the man inside ordered, each of his words growing further away as I listened to the sound of his footsteps retreating from the foot at the top of the stairs inside. Ara's grip lessened though her body showed no indication other than alert.

The man outside sighed against the sound of the creaking of the door. "Bitch-ass bitch," I heard him mutter under his breath, though perfectly audible to the both of us, before the sounds of his footsteps retreating back into the house ended with the door shutting behind him. My body tenses at his departure, my insides on fire as the hunger screams for me to chase after them both.

I contemplate for just a moment the idea of trying to get past Ara when she breaks the silence, interrupting my mutinous thoughts.

"Those people have someone," she began, pointing upwards to a window above us, "someone they have taken." My eyes widened at the revelation.

"Like kidnapped?" I asked and she nodded. "Then we have to help, Ara."

Ara looked down from the window, her face expressionless. "Do we?" she asked. "And why, pet, do we have to help?" I hesitated for a moment, kicking myself for blurting out what I was feeling, blaming the hunger for my outburst. So I said the first thing that came to me when I asked myself why just as she had.

"Because," I said, "it's the right thing to do."

Ara smiled. "The right thing to do." She looked up at the window again and stared for a moment before looking back to me. "This is not how I wished to teach you to hunt, Aya," she replied as she led me towards the front door, "though if there are innocents within being held against their will, I will not allow it."

I watched as she reached for the door handle, my anticipation growing as the hunger within made me want to push past her and

90

smash through the door. The knob turned several times in her hand though the door refused to open. She smiled. "He locked the door."

I frowned. "Should we try the oth—" I stopped as she twisted the doorknob again, the sound of the metal locking mechanism grinding and giving a metal popping sound before she pushed open the door. "Or not," I smiled, still secretly wanting to race past her and up the stairs several feet in front of us.

Ara returned my smile and I fought not to turn to mush at how lovely she was. I also wondered if vampires even could blush. The endearing look that was all for me melted down to all seriousness as she placed a finger over my lips. "Now," she began in a voice just barely above a whisper, "I want you to be as silent as you have ever been, and to follow me inside." I nodded. "When we reach them, you are to do nothing until I say to."

"Yes," I said in as convincing of an agreeable tone as I could while I tried to think about the very thought of actually coming into contact with blood. I thought of how squeamish I was, of how sickened by it had always been. I began to remember the metallic, coppery smell it had and how it reminded me of pennies.

It was all I wanted now, to go inside to tear off their heads and gorge myself on the fountains that were their ruined necks.

"Come," Ara ordered and I followed her inside of the house. The air this time was damp, musty, and I wondered how long these people had been here or even if they were squatting. Ara took the first step up the stairs, not a sound to be heard upon her ascent. I followed, sucking in a breath and holding it, and took my first step as lightly as possible. I winced as the step gave the tiniest of groans, hoping that I had only noticed it because of my new hearing. Watching Ara continue instead of turning around to chastise me as I feared, I continued upward to the next level and to the sounds of voices.

Ara stopped in the small hallway flanked by two doors to our left and another further, straight ahead. I poked my head around her shoulder and gazed at the flickering light from underneath the door ahead of us as shadows moved across it on the floor. The voice of the man from outside erupted into laughter and I heard the sound of a muffled cry. My stomach tightened at the sound of the newest sound, the owner sounding weak, subdued. I couldn't stand it any longer and dug my heels into the floor before I shoved and bolted past Ara, the hallway becoming a blur of dark shades of color as my new found speed catapulted me forward.

It wasn't two steps past her before I felt arm shoot after me, her hand clamping shut around the back of my neck upon impact. I sucked in a breath through my open mouth as I fought not to scream against my body's protest to continue my rampage into the next room as well as against the pain of her fingernails digging into my neck where she held me, effortlessly in the air. The world seemed to bob up and down for a moment before I realized that Ara was walking forward as she still held me above the ground. She stopped and I heard the door of the first room to our left open.

My body swung as she whirled around and placed me on the floor inside of the empty room. Ready to pounce right back at her, now completely in the throes of my hunger, I stopped as soon as I saw her face. It wasn't so much the look she gave, mixed of annoyance and caution, but more so the two red glowing orbs staring back at me from where her eyes had been.

"Do-*not*-follow-me," she commanded; each word feeling as though it were a shackle fastening over each of my wrists and ankles. A woman's shrill scream shrieked from down the hallway. Ara's head snapped in the direction of the pleading cry before she was gone in a blur, the sound of her vastly accelerated footsteps stomping across the hallway.

"Don't do that!" the woman's voice pleaded. "Stop hurting him! Please! Let us go!"

Wanting to chase after her, I screamed in frustration as the feeling of the compulsion held me inside of the room. I raced to the wall at the end of the room past the doorway, still another barrier of this cage I was stuck in yet closer still to where Ara had flown towards. I placed my hands against the wall, and then the side of my head, straining to hear what was happening. I jumped back, startled, from the wall as I heard the sound of the door exploding at the end of the hallway as well as three male voices in reply.

"What in the fuck!"

"Shoot that bitch!"

The brief sounds of guns firing, their bullets assaulting the walls beyond, rang out through the house. I stared back at the open doorway and felt the muscles of my eyes strain, as though entirely in reaction to the chaos, and I suddenly saw several paths within the air outside of the door ripple and cascade as though they were water in the wake of several glinting cylinders sailing past.

I can see them, I thought as I watched several more packs of bullets sail forth through the air, almost completely oblivious to the sounds of crashing and screaming from beyond the hallway.

"Get this crazy fucking bitch off of me!" screamed the voice I had heard earlier from the steps. His struggled roars became desperate, shrill screams that ended in a sickening snapping sound. Another man's scream, whose it this point I could not tell, rang out followed by the sound of frantic footsteps stomping closer. I saw the shadow of the figure racing down the hallway before I heard the impact from behind that had sent him to the floor. I looked down at the floor of the hall just outside the doorway where I could make out the head of the man who had been knocked to it.

It was the man from the fireplace who had come outside earlier.

The sound of deliberately slow, loud footsteps came from the room from which he had fled, and I watched his head quickly turn to look over his shoulder before he cried out and frantically climbed to his feet. I stood, completely frozen, my body feeling as though it would surely explode, as he flew inside of my room and flung shut the door.

It happened before I even had time to think of doing it. The echo from the impact of the door slamming closed would be heard by no one as I already had rushed up from behind him, his surprised scream the new sound to echo throughout the dark, barely lit room. My arms found him in the way of my right slithering past his own, clamping it down against his waist as I hooked it around the opposite side, spooning the back of his body against the front of mine while my fingers dug into his ribs.

My left hand shot up from underneath his left arm and curled past the back of his head in a sort of half-nelson before my fingers coiled around that mass of curly, greasy brown hair. Yanking his head to the left, I give him the brief opportunity to scream once more as my own mouth seemed to open on its own before I dove into his neck. The shudder of his body as my fangs enter his flesh becomes a seizing as I ever so slightly pull out, my mouth still clamped over him in a sickly, wide open kiss. The deluge of his lifeblood that explodes into my mouth, even before I begin to greedily suck more forth, screams like waves hitting the shore, *it* the waves and me the shore.

After I take the first swallow, I feel my eyes roll back into my head before they close. Every cell within my body, beginning at my throat and downward further, quickens to a mix of satiation and ecstasy as my body burns like never before in my life, the screaming of the pained hunger from before entirely absent. The feeling of holding him against me, restraining him, seems just as gone as the feeling of my standing there in the room with him. We're one now. A rapid drumming beats against the inside of my ears as I continue to drink, wanting to swallow him up entirely. I don't even hear the door open.

"Aya, let go," I hear Ara tell me to do. My hands continue to grip him tightly against me, my body doesn't respond and I don't want it to. The drumbeat continues to pound, though it begins to lose a bit of speed even as it echoes inside of my head.

"Aya," I somehow manage to hear her again. "Aya, you must stop now." But I can't stop. This is all there is right now, it's all I want. The taste of him, better than anything I had ever before savored, the feeling inside, better than any sex I had ever experienced. *Don't stop. Please, don't stop.* The drumming slows from a steady, even pace to a weaker, struggling beat, his breathing coming now in shallow gasps. It is in this moment I realize that it's his heart.

"AYA!" I feel the force of her will in her scream and its influence upon me as my eyes suddenly snap open, focusing immediately on her sad, forlorn expression. "You have to *stop* before you *kill* him."

Let him fucking die then.

Who gives a shit about trash like him anyway?

He's just food.

It's just food.

"You mustn't," I hear her barely say in a mournful whisper. Her words reach me, I hear them, and I understand them, but it's too late and we both know it. His body has gone limp in my arms, the sound of the drumming of his heart stopped completely. I open my mouth, the link is broken, and I recoil from the still body which slumps to the ground in a lifeless, empty heap.

I look up from the corpse and at Ara, feeling my eyes widen as I return to myself and realize what's just happened.

"Aya," she begins but stops. I fall to the floor, faster than the remaining drops of blood from my meal, or was it my eyes? Once again, I take hold of him, scooping him into my lap. *He was a person, not an It*, I think to myself. He was someone's child, or brother, or friend—he was a life, perhaps not a good one, but still a life; a whole other, entire universe of individual consciousness that I had just snuffed out as though it were an insignificant nothing.

My body racked with the coming sobs as I combed his hair gently with my fingers before I pulled his body against my chest and cried, rocking back and forth as I did.

"I warned you," I managed to hear her lamenting over my sobs—whether it was aloud or magically in my head, I did not fucking care.

At that moment I didn't care about anything anymore.

The Blood of the Willing

(a modern day mythological horror story)

by David Berger

1200 BCE—A temple deep beneath the earth, at the edge of Tartarus.

The cold obsidian blade parted the skin with no effort, and the blood trickled down the supplicant's arms, puddling below, soaking into the hungering earth. Lying on a stone altar etched with arcane runes of lost magic, the young man's body oozed life until his eyes closed. No scream. No struggling. He gave himself willingly to her, and once empty, his body shriveled until only a husk remained. Twenty other supplicants—men, women, and children—standing around the altar, raised blades to their throats, spoke the phrase, "Díno ton eaftó mou eléfthera." *I give myself freely*, and then slashed their throat. Each body crumpled, its life flowing into the earth.

Fleet-footed Hermes flew into the cave, his winged caduceus in hand. The snake-entwined staff pulsed with energy as the god made ready to stop the goddess' ritual.

"By Zeus' command, halt! What you do here is heresy!" He raised his staff.

The High Cleric ignored the god, put the blade up to his own throat, and recited the final sacrament,

"O Atë, daughter of Eris, to you goes the blood of the willing,
O Goddess, to you goes the power of life,
To you goes the power over us all.
When once again you rise,
You prepare the world for discord,
Who in turn incites the world to war."

Muffled thunder rumbled above, Zeus' censure for such an inhuman act, and Hermes moved to intercept, but the High Cleric's hand was swifter, and with his blood spewing forth, he fell on the altar. Hermes felt Atë's presence growing, so he departed, returning to Olympos despite his fear of Zeus' wrath at his failure.

Atë was a voracious goddess, and she who was Obsession was not easily sated. The ritual, now complete, would bring power to her—for a time. Then, the ceremony would need to begin again.

Time had its way of hiding the past until it was ready to emerge again, and the gods would fade into memory. Order and chaos would be all that remained.

2015 CE—New York City.
The city of New York in the 21st century bore the weight of its

populace: crime had become the stitching that kept the city together, paranoia kept those threads taut, and the blood of the innocent had dyed them a fearful crimson. This, coupled with a perpetual haze of smoke and exhaust, suppressed the desire for most people to rise above and find a better way. Day to day life meant simply existing in a pungent pond of still water for most, and while some managed to transcend this, most were the mosquito larvae in this stagnant liquid— their life brief and unfulfilled.

Apex predators in Manhattan consisted of business executives and lawyers, each trying to devour as much of the rabble as their bellies could handle. For the executives, their gluttony came in the form of mergers and acquisitions, buyouts and takeovers. Lawyers had an appetite for the wounded and scared, the innocent and inexperienced. At the other end of the spectrum, mundane humanity scurried about, from job to home and back again, taking whatever they were given to survive. The city had provided for them as it would for any scavenger or cockroach, remnants to feed on and corners in which to hide. Filling the great divide was the rest of the world, the inhabitants who didn't quite have the power to make change, but also didn't flit about with primal survival instincts guiding their path. They strived simply to wake up every day and find some sense of purpose. It was into this stratum of society where the gods would have found their place.

Within this existential maelstrom, order met chaos, each vying for dominance.

Marjorie Edison, corporate attorney, sat on the subway, handling one of her colleagues on her Bluetooth phone. An elderly Japanese woman sat next to her, glaring, and after a few minutes, tugged Marjorie's coat and gestured for her to talk softer, but the attorney swiveled away and continued speaking.

"Oh, it was nothing, Gerry. Some bag lady here with sensitive ears." She turned back to the woman. "You can switch seats."

Screeching to the Lexington Ave./63rd Street stop, the car doors flew open, and Marjorie pushed her way to the exit. Somehow, despite the activity of the station, her voice managed to transcend the din, and afternoon travelers scowled as she brushed past them.

"I hate people." She was still connected to Gerry, and her Jimmy Choos clacked on the concrete. "Yes, I *wanted* to work in the city." She rolled her eyes. "Just tell Stevenson not to get his low rise briefs in a twist. I'll be there in a minute."

At E. 63rd Street, she crossed Lexington and disappeared into the corner office of Edison, Stevenson, and Powers. Giving a casual wave of her ID to Curt, the security guard, she stepped onto the elevator, sliding her badge into a slot on the wall, leaned back, and exhaled as the doors closed. She'd be in her penthouse office suite soon enough, she thought, and then she could deal with *real* issues: taking apart people's lives bit by bit, penny by penny. As the doors opened, her administrative assistant Mandy handed her a double espresso.

"The mayor's on line one about the demolition of the apartment buildings on the south side, you have a 10 o'clock with Mrs. Chen, and Mr. Stevenson…"

"Nice of you to make it in before noon, Marj."

The voice emanated from a man with the build of a football player not quite in his prime anymore, wearing an Armani suit tailored to bring out his shoulders, and hair gelled so solid that any high-pitched sound might shatter it.

"What did I say about your briefs, Carl? You lurking in the halls again?"

He huffed and walked with her toward her office.

"Let me deal with the mayor before you give me shit about

whatever it is you want to give me shit about today. I have a ten o'clock in…" She checked her watch. "About eight minutes."

"Fine, my office, a.s.a.p."

She brushed him away as she was picking up the phone.

"Good morning, Mayor. Let's talk."

On the south side of New York near Tribeca, half a dozen hard hats gathered in a trailer in a vacant lot next to Regency Oaks Apartments, a complex slated for demolition to make room for a law office.

"All right, boys, we're waitin' for the go-ahead to start smashing." The foreman, Artie McDougal, sat back in his worn office chair swigging back some stale coffee.

"Thought we had the green light for this months ago." Tom Mazzati, the assistant foreman, finished shoving an Egg McMuffin in his mouth.

"Tommy, it's those corporate muckety mucks. One minute everything's fine, then next it falls to shit. Some lawyer for the building owner wanted to go over the relocation plans. Don't know why the residents are whining. They're being moved into a brand new place across town. Indoor swimming pool. Right next to a Starbucks. Not sure what they have to complain about."

The phone rang. Artie tapped his fingers against his thumb and rolled his eyes at Tommy as he listened to the voice on the other end. A minute later, he put his hand over the mouthpiece.

"The law office got a phone call that someone was still inside the building. They're bringing down someone from Social Services. It'll be about an hour."

The rest of the men groaned and took off their hard hats. Three went outside for a smoke. As soon as Artie hung up, he headed for the door, tapping Tom on the shoulder.

"Let's go see what's happening. Maybe we can get this whack job outta the building before Social Services gets here. We don't have all day."

When they got to the fifth floor, Artie crinkled his nose.

"What the hell. Something burning up here?" He nodded to Tom to follow him.

The scent led them to an apartment at the end of the hall.

"Geez." Tom covered his nose. "That stinks. Never did like incense."

Artie knocked. "Hey, you in there, we gotta demo this building some time today. You can't be in here."

He knocked louder, and the door moved, letting more of that pungency escape. Pushing it open further with his foot, Artie looked inside, but he could hardly see anything due to the heavy cloud of henbane and hemlock. At the back of the living room, a small bowl sat with flames peeking over the edge and a silhouette lingered behind it.

"Hey, didn't you hear me knocking? You can't be in here. We're knocking this building down." He moved closer, but then, he couldn't.

Tom got to where Artie was standing, but then he, too, couldn't move.

"What the hell? Why can't I move? Tommy, can you—"

"No. Did we step—"

The ethereal figure turned, and a woman with her head covered held a censer etched with runes on the outside. She blew the smoke and a pulse of energy washed over them.

A gravelly whisper said, "You are of the willing."

They said nothing. They also didn't try to free themselves.

"You *are* of the willing." The whisper gave way to a soft laugh.

She seemed to glide across the floor to them, and when she lifted her head, her eyes were crawling with maggots. Both Tom and Artie didn't have the will to move, but when she peered inside them, she felt their fear.

"You won't need *that* anymore." An ancient hand reached up to

Artie's and Tom's head, and she caressed their temple. "It is time for her to feed. Bring them."

In unison, they replied, "We are of the willing."

Leaving the building, they didn't look any different.

"You wanna grab some lunch? I could go for some pizza." Tom patted Artie on the back, and they joined their crew in the trailer.

Across the street, sitting on the brick steps of a brownstone, a homeless man in his early 30s wrapped himself in as much of *The New York Times* as he could, his head topped by a ragged gray knit hat. An untrimmed auburn beard rose to the top of his cheeks leaving room for eyes that had witnessed more than their share of life. These eyes watched as Tom and Artie left the building. He looked back toward the doorway and squinted out of curiosity. He'd been watching the building for days, noting who entered and departed, and these two men had been the only ones to do so since the building had been evacuated.

• • •

When someone interrupts a meeting of the partners at Edison, Stevenson, and Powers, he or she does so with reasons like a stock market crash, an unsuccessful merger, or a maybe even a family crisis. Marjorie reclined in her chair in the boardroom listening to Gerry discuss strategies for an entertainment law case when her assistant Mandy tapped on the glass wall just outside. At the second tapping, Marjorie raised an eyebrow, her silent gesture for, 'This had better be worth the time you're wasting.'

"Forgive the interruption. You have the foreman from Regency Oaks on line 2. He says it's urgent."

Letting out a controlled exhale, Marjorie excused herself into an outer office. The remaining partners and their assistants took bets on whether or not she was going to eviscerate whoever was on the other end of that phone call. All was normal until Marjorie's shrill voice almost shattered the glass walls.

"What? Look, I don't care! I need that building down by the end of the week… Do you know how much money delays cost? We have a deal with the mayor… Whatever. Take care of it."

She walked past her assistant, who averted her eyes. The young woman returned to her desk without a word.

"Thank you, Mandy. Apparently, the working class needs permission when to fix problems… or wipe themselves." She closed the glass door as abruptly as the hinge would allow.

"There will be some *delays* in the demolition of Regency Arms." Marjorie lowered herself into her chair, her palms on the table edge. "Edison, Stevenson, and Powers stands to make quite a tidy sum once that office building goes up. As you know, we had to relocate the residents to *reasonable* accommodations, which thankfully didn't cost that much. It's amazing what you can do when you buy out the management company and remove their rent-controlled status. When we offered relocation to an older building across town, with a dilapidated pool, the residents were more than eager to accept our offer."

"Of course, many of them who worked locally will have to increase their commuting costs and change how they lived their lives. Not sure that was an equitable arrangement."

"Gerry, not my problem. At least they have a roof over their head." She crossed her legs. "Fortunately, you were in the minority of the vote. We can't always be on the winning side."

He sat back and crossed his arms, his glare receiving no comment from her. The meeting finished an hour later with Marjorie returning to her office.

"Mandy, if anyone needs me, tell them I'm unavailable."

• • •

Tom pulled in six from the group waiting outside the trailer and told them he needed a small crew to reinvestigate parts of the building, looking for anything out of the ordinary. Even though they weren't trained inspectors, he said, their observations might see potential issues with demolition. The six men seemed willing to take this on. Tom suggested they check the fifth floor first.

As they moved down the hall, the only light came from one window by the stairs, hazy incense causing them to cover their mouths. This time, the door at the end of the hall was opened just enough for them to walk inside, and the same fire-filled brazier blazed on the table. They stepped forward to investigate and realized, a few steps in, they couldn't move. Before they knew what was happening, the shrouded figure turned, blowing more incense at them.

"You are of the willing." By the end of the sentence, the gruff voice had stopped their struggling.

She glided over to them, gently touching their temples, lifting her maggot-filled eye sockets toward their faces. From beneath the folds of her gray cloak, she pulled six obsidian daggers, handing one to each. Returning to her place behind the table, the men faced each other in pairs, and in monotonous unison said, "We are of the willing." With swift strikes, each opened the other's jugular vein and carotid arteries. Their heads lolling forward, the bodies collapsed, their warm blood flowing over the carpet. Exsanguination took a few minutes, and the red liquid pulsed into the carpet fibers. Desiccated husks crumbled into dust—the feeding had begun.

After the lunch break, Artie sent another six to check on the first crew, saying Tom hadn't heard back from them. Tom sent the rest of the men home, saying that they weren't going to get anything else accomplished that day. When he was asked about the others, he told them he had already sent them on their way.

• • •

Back in the brownstone doorway, the man took swigs from a bottle of water offered by a passerby, a rare act of kindness in an otherwise selfish city. Licking the moisture from his lips, he rocked a little, his eyes locked on the glass doorway leading into the Regency Arms. A woman joined him on the steps. She unwrapped a sandwich that already had bite marks, her gnarled fingers clutching it like an owl with a field mouse. Her gray eyes followed his across the street, never moving her food far from her mouth.

"Whatcha watchin', Ricky?" She took more small bites.

He sipped again. "Something ain't right over there, Sophie. I see people goin' in that building, but they ain't coming out."

"Maybe you fell asleep."

"Something ain't right. Just ain't."

Sophie shoved the last bite into her mouth and folded up the wrapper, putting it in her pocket. Ricky handed her his bottle, and she took a sip.

"Thanks, Ricky. I'll be back later. Lemme know if your mystery unfolds."

Ricky nodded, adjusting the newspaper. A breeze picked up, making him shiver. With Sophie gone, he undid his makeshift newsprint blanket and crossed the street to take a closer look through the door of the Regency Arms. Down the dark main corridor, he saw nothing, but he kept squinting inside. No light or life of any kind could be seen.

"Something just ain't right." He murmured as he wiped the exterior dust from the window with his palm. He resumed his perch on the brownstone's landing, putting the newspaper back over him in layers.

• • •

Hidden by fog, the sunrise went unnoticed, and Marjorie looked out over the city from her office, her jaw clenched. Mandy tapped on the door.

"Unless you're here to tell me that the Regency Arms is now debris, I'd suggest you not bother me with anything else."

Mandy pushed the door open an inch.

"Ms. Edison…"

No response prompted her to push the door open another inch. She knew she was taking her safety into her hands.

"Didn't I just tell you—"

"I'm sorry, but there's a Mr. Mazzati on line 1. He insists on speaking with you. He says it's urgent."

"Who is he?"

"The foreman at the Regency Arms."

Marjorie didn't bother turning around. Within arm's reach was her phone, and she put it on speaker.

"Ms. Edison? This is Tommy Mazzati."

She cringed at his thick Brooklyn accent. *Neanderthal,* she thought.

"Yes, Mr. Mazzati? You insisted—"

"Yeah. Listen, it's gonna be a little longer on this controlled demo. We've gotta check some structural issues out before we set up the charges."

"How long is a little longer? It's true what they say: time *is* money."

"Uh, a coupla days. I'll keep you posted." Click.

"He did not just… Nevermind. Mandy!"

"Yes, ma'am?" She cupped one hand over the other against her chest.

"Get the partners in the board room. One hour."

. . .

Even by midday, the fog hadn't lifted, and Ricky hadn't noticed any activity by the construction trailer. This time, when he approached the door of the Regency Arms, he detected something he hadn't smelled in a long time. The brass doorknob turned easily, and when he stepped inside the foyer, he stood a little taller. A distant memory was rising, and he couldn't quite place it. Voices from outside made him hide in a corner away from the door, and six workers came in and headed for the stairs. He overheard their mutterings of having been asked to do some weird stuff, but this seemed off even to them. As soon as the door to the stairwell closed behind them, he returned to his stoop, careful to make sure no one saw him. Hours passed, and Ricky noticed that no one left the building.

Around 3 p.m., Sophie returned, pushing a cart filled with assorted remnants: balls of yarn, old books, a wool cloak with frayed edges, a half-filled bottle of olive oil, and other sundry, discarded items. With care, she placed the cart next to the stoop, looking all around before sitting on the steps with Ricky.

"You're lookin' spooked there, Ricky. What's got you so on edge?"

First, he looked at her, and then he looked back at the door.

"There's something there. Inside. Like, in the olden days. You remember?"

"It's been a long time, Ricky. I ain't as clear-headed as I used to be. Don't have all the wisdom." She tapped her head.

"Six workers went into that place in the morning. They didn't come out. I stepped inside, just for a moment, and I remembered stuff. Stuff I ain't thought about in a long, long time."

Sophie pursed her lips. "Things that come back need to be put down."

. . .

The partner meeting was more of a misnomer. It was less about the others contributing to the conversation and more about Marjorie railing on about how they needed the land from the Regency Arms and other properties to expand their foothold in Manhattan. With the firm growing, and with prime real estate at a premium, she had prompted the others to buy out rent-controlled apartments since the buildings were older. When Eric, a junior partner, commented that Marjorie was just preying on those who didn't have the means to live elsewhere by moving them to rat-infested tenements across town, she made it a point to remind him that new buildings for the law firm benefited them all. He wasn't convinced, and his last words before leaving the meeting were that she was sowing the seeds of discord.

"And that, gentlemen, is the best way to lose a junior partnership. Sayonara, Eric!"

Gerry turned in his chair, his fingers laced in his lap. He was one of the few partners in the room who wasn't afraid of Marjorie, and she knew it. They were equal partners in the firm, and she had no control over his future, unlike Eric, who'd be lucky to work as a court-appointed lawyer anywhere on the eastern seaboard.

"He's not wrong, you know. If you're not careful, you're going to piss off the wrong person, and then there won't be anyone to save your size 4 behind."

"So nice of you to be so concerned about my behind, Gerry." Marjorie smirked. "But, don't you worry your pretty little comb-over about it. I have this under control. As far as those people whom we've moved across town… well, I'm not worried about being sued."

"You thrive on conflict, don't you?"

"Oh, Gerry, you have no idea."

• • •

Two days passed, and Ricky decided he'd go back inside. Whatever he'd started to remember had faded once he left the building, and that didn't even concern him as much as what his gut was telling him. Why the building remained unlocked made him a little curious, but he took advantage of that to climb the stairs. By the third floor, he had to stop. Pulses of memories swirled into his mind, and he gripped the handrail to keep from falling down. Something in this building had lured him in. Ricky reached the fourth floor and had his hand on the door from the stairs when a sharp pain rifled through his arm and into his head.

"I'm—I'm not ready…" He barely got those words out when he decided it was best to leave the building for the time being.

He walked over to Rockefeller Park, looking out over the Hudson River just before sunset. Distant memories of another river he used to see flashed into his mind, and he patted his head with closed fists.

"What am I tryin' to remember? It's almost clear when I go in the building, but when I leave, it goes away."

Another itinerant man like Ricky sat down next to him. He looked over and smiled. His face, a bit leathery for a twenty-something, was covered with stubble, but his blue eyes looked like the sky. He wore a secondhand Oxford under a moth-eaten brown cardigan and ripped khakis. Street life had been especially rough on him.

"Hey, Percy. How've you been? Haven't seen you in a few days. I was worried." Ricky put his hand out on the bench.

"Aw, I've been good, Ricky. Real good. Just helping out a friend."

He took the hand and closed his around it. "I've missed you." The two sat quietly for a few minutes looking out over the river.

Percy leaned his head on Ricky's shoulder. Ricky turned and gave that 'what did I do to deserve you' smile.

"Something's comin', Percy. Something bad. Something from way back."

"It's not like the old days when you could up and battle the dark things. We're just not like that anymore. What're you gonna do, Ricky?"

He squeezed Percy's hand and then kissed it. "I have to try."

"Do you have to go right now, or can you stay a little longer?"

Ricky put his hand behind Percy's head and pulled their lips together. The kiss lingered, and then Ricky lowered his arm around Percy's shoulders.

"I can stay a little longer."

• • •

A few hours later, six workers stood unable to move, wisps of incense curling around them.

"You are of the willing." The shrouded woman uttered, her feet not touching the floor as she moved around them.

One of the workers shifted and his face twitched, his hands clenching and unclenching. The incense hadn't quite taken hold of him. His breathing came in fits, and through his spasms, he choked out the question, "What—What do you want?"

She placed her cold, aged hands on his cheeks and raised her face to his. He shivered and teetered, but despite his best efforts, he couldn't break free of the paralyzing incense. Her maggot-filled eyes met his, and his pupils dilated. Her mellifluous voice had an eerie lilt.

"I want you to give yourself to me. I want you to be willing to offer your blood."

His body convulsed as he resisted her influence, his eyes flitting around the room. His feet stayed planted on the floor while she used her finger to lift his chin. All he could see was the ceiling, and he didn't have any control over his body. She gently stroked beneath his chin until she felt his struggling diminish.

"It's all right. You want to offer yourself to me."

Tears trickled down the sides of his face as he whimpered. He continued to clench and unclench his hands as she stroked beneath his chin.

"I need you to be willing." She raised the censer emitting the gray smoke, its meandering tendrils caressing the sides of his face and swirling around his head. Her fingers continued to stroke the soft skin over his trachea.

"You need to relax and relinquish your spirit to me. Be willing."

She placed an obsidian dagger in his hand, but he wouldn't hold it. The maggots in her eye sockets squirmed faster, and a guttural growl escaped her cracked lips. She held the handle of the dagger against his palm, but he splayed his fingers. Her mouth next to his ear, she whispered something in a forgotten tongue repeatedly until his fingers closed over the handle.

She added, "*You* are of the willing."

He raised the dagger, but she could see him resisting. As long as he did as she asked, she would be satisfied. The dagger was at waist height. In front of his chest. Then, it stopped. His hand shook. It was then she felt a presence. Behind the worker, by the door, was Ricky, his arm extended. He was repeating something, in that same forgotten language, that intercepted her power. Once he realized she was aware of him, he quickened his words, raising his voice a little. The man dropped the dagger and gasped.

"Run. Now!" Ricky's voice had an imperious quality it hadn't had in a long time.

The man scrambled out the door of the apartment. Ricky lowered his arm and stood tall.

She hovered back a little. "We meet again. You can have that one. The others…"

The other five workers said, "We are of the willing," and made two dagger slashes, each on his own carotid and his jugular. Their bodies collapsed.

"No! Witch!" Ricky gritted his teeth.

With a wave of her hand, she pushed him out the door which then slammed shut as she replied.

"I'm not done, *Kírykas*."

Herald. Ricky hadn't been called that in… eons. He pounded a fist against the door, and it felt more like cold stone than wood. Growling to himself, he returned to his stoop, but instead of retreating under his newspaper blanket, he glared at the building's entrance.

"I remember now, Äte. I'm not as strong as I was when we last met. But, now I know."

• • •

In her office, Marjorie sat back, her eyes exploring a Rubens painting that took up most of the wall behind her desk. A gentle smile grew on her face when her eye caught a certain detail. *Poor Paris*, she thought. *He didn't really know what he was getting himself into.*

"Mandy." Even though she hadn't raised her voice, the sound reached its intended.

The young woman appeared in the doorway.

"Any updates on the Regency? Has Mr. Mazzati called back?"

"About an hour ago. He said he was having a few staffing issues."

Marjorie swiveled in her chair, still smiling.

"Call the partners. We need to end this."

113

. . .

Percy found Ricky pacing in the brownstone's doorway, his face locked on the Regency Arms. When he reached the top of the steps, Ricky saw him holding his hat, wringing it.

"She's back. I knew she would be."

Percy leaned against the balustrade. A breeze picked up, waving Ricky's auburn hair. His blue eyes seemed to brighten with electricity, but it could have been the sunlight playing tricks.

"What will you do? It's been so long. If she's taking the willing, can you stand up to her?"

"I have to." He wore the tattered clothes of a homeless man, but his bearing had become much more confident, almost regal.

Percy joined him, putting his hands on Ricky's shoulders. He then took Ricky into a firm embrace, muttering.

"I'm afraid for you, Ricky. Be careful."

Stepping back a little, Ricky took Percy's face in his hands, smiling, and landed a gentle kiss.

"I'll do what I've gotta do… *Perseus*." These words prompted a more passionate kiss, one like they had shared in an age now gone.

"I'll stand by you."

Ricky shook his head. "This ain't your fight. It's mine."

They turned to shuffling footsteps.

"It doesn't have to be, Ricky." Sophie joined them both.

He pulled her head closer and kissed her forehead.

Over the next two days, no one had entered the apartment building. Ricky, who had been joined by Sophie and Percy, sat fixated on the glass doors. Sophie played with her necklace, a tiny owl on a thin copper chain.

"She's plannin' her endgame. I can tell."

"Ricky, what's yours?"

"Sophie, I'll know it when I need it." He was wringing his knit cap.

Percy hooked his arm through Ricky's and leaned against his shoulder.

"Too bad your father isn't here."

"He didn't do anything then, Percy. He wouldn't now." Ricky squeezed the man's arm against his side.

• • •

At midnight, Marjorie's BMW pulled up to the darkened building. At the sidewalk, she looked up and down the street before going up the front steps. The glass doors had a sign from the construction company warning against trespassers. She pulled it down. The door was unlocked. Unexpected, but convenient. Without electricity in the building, she pulled out her cell phone and shined it along the wall until she found the door to the stairwell. It clicked shut behind her, echoing in the empty space. High heels clacked against the old marble steps, like the sound of a ticking clock. Pale moonlight through the fifth-floor hallway window provided an almost sentient luminescence. Under the door at the end of the hall, Marjorie saw shadows move, and a wry smile spread on her face. The brazier flickered inside the apartment, and the ethereal figure behind it moved to meet her guest. With her heels, Marjorie towered over the shrouded woman who reached up to touch her face. Worm-filled eyes met those of the corporate attorney, a woman of power and means, and the shriveled figure spoke in her rough voice.

"The time has come for those most willing to give of themselves."

Marjorie's face went blank when she heard footsteps and voices in the hall. Gerry, Carl, and the junior partners, about fifteen in all, had apparently gotten her message about something holding up the demolition. They filled up what would be the living room, each one holding his hand over his mouth.

"What the hell is this, Marjorie?" Gerry stepped forward. "Who's that?"

Marjorie turned. The only light in the room came from the flames, and her face was in shadow. "She's the one who's held up the demolition."

"Lady, you're in for it now." Carl laughed through his hand, his comments directed at the shrouded figure. "I don't think you know who you're dealing with. You don't mess with Marjorie Edison."

"You're right," the voice replied. "You don't."

Billows of incense surrounded the partners, and they found themselves stuck like all the others. Some tried to pull their feet free from the floor, others tried to turn, but their efforts were fruitless. When the incense took effect, they stopped struggling, their eyes glazing. Marjorie walked among them, smirking, her fingertips brushing against them. She returned to her place before them, but her smirk diminished when she saw them resisting. Their bodies quivered, and their breathing became erratic.

"Not this time, Atë." Ricky's voice came from the doorway. With both hands, he was holding a gnarled and winged wooden stick, two serpents slithering up and down its length.

"I told you he would return." The haggard woman snarled.

"Indeed you did. Time hasn't been kind to you, Hermes."

When he heard her speak, Ricky's eyes widened. He hadn't heard that voice in thousands of years.

"I should've known you were behind this, Eris. Like mother, like daughter."

Marjorie took a few steps closer to him.

"She's done so well, too. The time of the gods is over, trickster.

This last group will not only satisfy my daughter's thirst, but it will strengthen *me* as well. The blood of the willing—"

"They're not willing." A voice came from the hall.

"Ah, who'd you bring to help you, Kírykas?" Marjorie noticed someone move into the flickering light. "You brought *her?*" She laughed.

Sophie put her hand on his shoulder. "Things that come back need to be put down."

Atë's incense cloud passed the others and lingered around Ricky and Sophie.

"Your magics won't work on me."

"Perhaps not, but it will work on *them*." Flames blazed from Marjorie's eyes.

Moving her censer around the immobile group, Atë muttered the ancient words,

"To me goes the blood of the willing,
To me goes the power of life,
To me goes the power over us all.
As I rise,
I prepare the world for discord,
Who in turn incites the world to war."

The partners ceased their struggling. Ricky and Sophie incanted words of their own,

"By Olympus, We bring you strength,
By Olympus, We bring you power,
By Olympus, We bring you spirit.
Take hold of our offering,
And it will set you free!"

117

With two voices invoking the power instead of one, the partners regained some ability to move on their own. Atë shoved away the table where the brazier sat and exposed an iron cauldron filled with blood. Dipping her hands into the thick liquid, she held them up, the blood dripping down her withered arms.

"Eíste próthymoi! Tha dósai to aíma sas se ména!" *You are of the willing! You will give your blood to me!"* Her rough voice echoed down the hall.

The eyes of the partners became maggots, and they replied in one voice,

"Eímaste próthymoi!" *We are of the willing!*

With fluid movement, they sliced open their throats. A pile of corpses drained into the carpet, the blood moving toward the cauldron. Once the bodies had desiccated, Marjorie stepped through their remains toward Ricky and Sophie.

"You should have remained silent, and all would have been fine. Atë would have had her fill, and then you would have had another millennia to wait for her return. Now, I need to dispose of you both. You truly are homeless, aren't you? Not even Olympus could help you. Pathetic."

Ricky was on his knees, tears streaming down his cheeks, and Sophie was trying to get him to stand up. Marjorie only had a few feet until she could reach them when someone ran through the door and toppled her.

"Like all monsters, you must fall!"

"Percy!" Ricky reached out, but he was weakened.

The once-slayer of Medusa and Cetus had Marjorie on her back, bashing his fists into her, when they all heard a slicing noise and then a thud. Percy's head rolled toward Ricky, and the fallen hero's body fell away as Marjorie stood. Atë held the bloody dagger.

"How ironic." Marjorie laughed.

Ricky pulled away from Sophie and landed by Percy's body, cradling the corpse. His cry of remorse was loud enough to shake the walls. He took hold of his caduceus with blood-covered hands to use every ounce of power to blast Marjorie, but nothing remained. Atë and Marjorie were gone. The cauldron and brazier, also gone. No remnant of their battle lingered.

Hermes had once again lost Discord and her daughter. Kneeling by Percy, Ricky put his hand on the man's chest. The other hand reached for his caduceus, and he touched Percy, releasing his soul to Hades. Having performed his last task as *Hermes Psychopompos*—the Conductor of Souls—Ricky's only place to go was his stoop. Sophie followed, bringing Percy's head so she could place it in her shopping cart that held the bits and pieces of the past.

Wrapping himself in newspaper once more, Ricky wept.

The Angler
by Michael Manschot

"It's so great to see you again, Chip!" Aunt Marge exclaimed while sipping her 4th margarita.

It was the start of summer and I was back home in Texas visiting my family during my vacation. It was a Friday night and just like every Friday, since I could remember, my parents cooked a big southern feast. And like most Fridays of my childhood my Aunt Marge and Uncle Ruben were over. We were sitting at the kitchen table as they gave me "buzzed small talk."

"It's good to be back Aunt Marge." I smirked; only replying just to keep her happy.

It really was good to be back. I missed my small hometown where everyone knew each other and you could look out your window and see trees for miles until you reached the road. That was one of the major things I missed after moving to California for school. The weather may be perfect in California and the people may be beautiful but I never felt the isolation I needed to come down from a hectic day.

You would think being a gay man in his early 20's that California would be a dream come true. I could see that being the case maybe a decade ago, however, times are changing. Surprisingly friends and family have always supported me in my hometown. Sure Texas is a Red state but I've found that we tend to be a "Live and Let Live" type of folk.

"Look at you, all big and brawny like your Uncle!" Aunt Marge nudged Uncle Ruben, who looked ready to pass out. "You must be having those California boys hootin' and hollerin' just to get your attention!"

"Well, I'm not having much luck. Between class, the gym, and my studies, it's hard to really concentrate on anything else."

"Don't let too much time slip by hunny! You can only be young and beautiful for so long. Then when you actually realize that the time for love doesn't present itself and you gotta make time, well, then it may be a lot harder for you to find someone." She paused while taking another drink of her margarita and then continued, " Maybe you should try wearing something other then those plaid button ups, show off them muscles!"

Aunt Marge had glossy eyes that could barely stay open behind her 1950's cat-eye glasses. She had dark maroon hair that she curled every day and violet eyes. Her face was tan and you could tell she spent a lot of time outside. My parents would always tell me stories of Aunt Marge in High School and how she was the rebel of the school. Even though she was respectful and followed the rules, "her mouth would always get her in trouble" my parents would say. I always admired that about my Aunt, if something was wrong she would say it. She was a beauty in her own right, a real southern belle. I didn't expect our conversation to go this deep.

I didn't want to think about it.

I nodded my head and politely excused myself to the bathroom.

It has only been two semesters since I've been home and yet the house still stays the same. As I walked to the bathroom I passed by our living room that has not had a new piece of furniture in it since I was 11 years old. Walking through the house I never thought about the beauty of it all. Nostalgia, that's what makes a home.

I got into the bathroom and looked into the mirror. I only had two beers, which were making me tired. I brushed by hair back with my hand. I couldn't help but think about what my Aunt told me. I'm an attractive guy. I was at a 6-foot height, played football in high school, was able to keep my fitness up. My hair is always nicely combed and who can forget my "precious root beer eyes" as my Aunt used to call them. I laughed at myself and again realized why I loved my Aunt. She found a way to make everyday brown eyes special.

There was a scratch on the window. It was loud and sharp. There was no doubt that this was caused by something…or someone. I stared at the window for a second. The window had a small white curtain with sunflowers printed on it. This too was an artifact of my house that has been around since childhood. I slowly started making my way to the window. I pulled back the small, sunflower-printed curtain and looked out the bathroom window, afraid of what I might see. There was nothing. I was relieved and reminded myself that it's been a while since I've been in Texas. There are rats, birds, snakes, and rabbits running around all over the property. The idea of any of these animals causing the noise gave me comfort.

"Chip!" my mom yelled from outside the bathroom door.

I was startled at the volume that my mom had said my name.

I opened the door to see my mom in the hallway waiting for me. My mom had her brown leather purse over her shoulder and keys in her hand. She was my Aunt Marge's sister. You could tell they were related but my mom had her natural brown hair color, didn't curl her hair, and never wore make-up. I guess my mom was the tomboy of the sisters.

"Your father and I are taking your Aunt and Uncle home, I don't think they are capable of driving."

"Why don't they just stay the night here?" I asked.

"I offered, but your Uncle needs to take his medication and your Aunt left Gilbert outside."

Gilbert was my Aunt's pet goat. She brings him inside every night for fear of coyotes getting to him. My dad walked past my mom helping Uncle Ruben keep his balance. Aunt Marge walked by and gave me a big hug and kiss.

"Rest up Chip, Sunday you can go to church with me. Uncle Ruben decided he's not a member of our congregation anymore. I'll need your help praying for his soul." Aunt Marge winked. "And I know you aint going to confession out in California so we'll get that out of the way too."

"Yes Ma'am," I smirked.

Most of the guys in California knock religion, but I find comfort in it. Maybe it's also the memory of going to Sunday school every Sunday with my classmates. People always ask me, "Why do you go to church? Don't they judge you for being gay?" I was lucky enough to grow up in a church that focused on doing good and loving others. My church told us what we could do to be better people and to help people. We didn't focus too much on the "What not to do" and "hellfire" sermons.

I said my goodbyes and watched everyone leave the house. I followed behind them and locked the door. It was getting dark out. The sun was setting on the trees and I finally felt relaxed. I didn't want to go to bed and started making some coffee. I grabbed my favorite coffee mug with different colored roosters on it and put in two squirts of creamer. After the coffee was done I poured it on top of the cream and let it sit. I grabbed my coffee and made my way to the back porch.

Walking past the bathroom I saw a strange light coming from under the bathroom door. The light had a faint purple/blue glow. I opened the bathroom door and saw that the glow was coming from the bathroom window. I made my way to the window, the same window that had scared me moments before. Pushing the small sunflower curtain away from the window I saw that the glow was coming from the forest outside. It was a faint glow that almost seemed natural. If the glow had been on the skyline I wouldn't have had a second thought about it but because it was coming from in-between the trees it peaked my interest.

I found myself staring at it for longer than I should. There was a sense of calm coming from the glow.

There was a loud knock on the door.

I jumped.

I made my way over to the front door thinking my aunt had left something behind. I opened the door and saw our neighbor Gretchen standing in the doorway. Our neighbors aren't like the neighbors in California. When I say Gretchen is my neighbor I mean she is the next house you run into when you drive a mile past my house.

"Hey Ms. Gretchen," I said.

"Hello Chip, good to see you made it home safe from school."

"Thank you, ma'am."

"Listen Chip, have you seen Tommy around?"

Tommy was Gretchen's 10-year-old son.

"No ma'am I haven't. Did you check in the woods?" I pointed to where the purple glow was coming from. " I saw some lights coming from there. Wondered what was causing it but it could be Tommy messing with some of his friends."

We turned around to look in the woods. There was no lights, no more glow; everything just seemed a little darker.

"Thank you Chip, do you mind if I go take a look?" asked Gretchen. Here in Texas you want to make sure you let someone know before you go traipsing around their property.

"No problem Ms. Gretchen. Do you want me to go with you?"

"No thanks hun, I'll just go get Tommy and get out of your hair."

"All right, let me know if you need anything!"

Ms. Gretchen left as I closed the door.

I made my way to the back porch. From the back porch I could still see the woods from the side of the house where Gretchen walked into. I heard a faint voice come from the opposite side of the house. I couldn't make out what it said and wasn't even sure if I really heard something.

There it was again!

It was as if someone was whispering "I….."

I got up and walked to the opposite side of the house along my back porch.

"Tommy is that you?" I waited a moment for a response.

"Tommy your mom is looking for you, she looks real worried."

I reached the end of the house and saw nothing. I turned back around and about dropped my rooster mug as I ran into Derek.

"Shit!" I yelped.

"Whoa!" Derek said laughing.

"What are you doing?" I asked in a panic.

"Sorry! We heard you just got in town and wanted to swing by to surprise you."

Derek stood there, a little shorter than me with his blonde faux hawk. Derek always dressed like a model of our small town. I think it was to set off his 'class clown' persona. Derek was my best friend all

126

through school. He was straight and played a huge role in my 'coming out'. I owe Derek a lot for helping me through my dark times.

"Jeez man!" I laughed. "Surprise or kill me?" It suddenly hit me that Derek said 'We'. Derek and I have been friends since grade school. We both played and caught bugs in the back yard together when we were little. We joined the football team together in high school. It was really good to see him but I felt the panic come back when he said 'we'. A normal person would have let it slid but my anxiety has me clutch on to small details like this.

I heard a noise come from inside the house and saw Brad walking out my back door. My heart dropped. My throat swelled up and my anxiety kicked my stomach in.

"Hey Chip." Brad said with a half smile.

Brad was my high school ex, my first love. They say you never truly get over your first love, I think they're right. I had no intention of seeing Brad again. He was too much of a distraction from the real world for me. Brad was just as tall as I was, had black spikey hair and a goatee. Growing up in the south I think it was Brad's 'heavy metal' appearance that really got me hooked. He was different from the typical guy in my town. Brad was the nicest guy with the most dangerous smile.

"Hey Brad." I said after what seemed to be like an eternity of glances.

"Uh oh!" shouted Derek, "I sense some awkwardness!" Derek was being a smug ass as always.

Brad hit Derek in the shoulder.

"Hey Chip, mind if I raid your fridge for snacks?" Derek said in an obvious attempt to leave us alone.

"Sure man." I responded still a bit dazed.

"It's good to see you again, Chip." Brad said as Derek went back into the house.

"Thanks, I've been hearing that a lot today." I hope I didn't sound like an ass.

There was an awkward pause.

"How's California?"

"It's pretty great, couldn't be happier." I smiled, trying not to make it obvious that I was lying out my teeth.

Another awkward pause, I knew I had to say something.

"Look Brad, I'm sorry the way things went down."

"You mean leaving town without telling anyone?" Brad said in a more serious tone.

"Well, my parents knew." It was a bad time for a joke.

"I didn't." Brad looked disappointed and hurt.

"I know I owe you some answers Brad and I'm sorry if what I did didn't make sense to you. I promise you one day I will explain everything and how I feel, but I'm really just trying not to think or stress about anything. My parents don't know this yet but I may not be able to go back to school."

Brad looked up at me surprised. I could feel my eyes watering. "I have been so stressed this whole year with school and my personal life that I stopped caring about what happens in class. I snuck in soda bottles with vodka in them and went to bed as soon as I would get home from school. I know I need help and that's why I'm home. That's why I'm not my usual outgoing warm self."

I felt as though the conversation was getting too personal and too messy. I needed to end the conversation so I wouldn't have to explain anymore of my problems.

"I'm sorry Brad, but..."

Brad, wrapping his arms around me and pulling me close to him, interrupted me. I haven't hugged anyone in a long time. The hug was tight and warm. I felt his chest parallel to mine as my heart fluttered. I didn't want to admit it but this was the first time I felt relief since the beginning of the semester.

"I missed you." Brad said in a cracking voice.

Was Brad crying?

Derek came out the back door again with a bag of chips.

"What I miss?" Derek said shoving an obscene amount of chips in his mouth. Derek looked at me then glanced at Brad. With his mouth full Derek said, "Looks like some gay shit."

I let out a half sigh half laugh. Leave it to Derek to say something semi-insulting to lighten up the mood.

"Well Chip" Derek began, "I wanted to swing by for a quick sec to say hi with Brad and so we can make plans for later. I'm about to head out to take my brother back his truck, but I heard you were in town and thought we could make a stop to say 'yo'."

"How bout it Chip" Brad turned and looked at me, "maybe we can go bowling tomorrow night, have dinner, and you can give me that talk you owe me?"

Derek made a face as though 'talk' may have meant something else.

"Sure, sounds good" I said.

A loud BANG came in from inside the house. Something fell inside, something big. It sounded more like a break. Whatever it was that made the noise seemed to have been dragged for a short bit as well.

All three of us jumped and looked inside the screen door.

We stood for a moment in silence.

"The hell was that?" Derek said, breaking the silence.

"Sounds like something fell" said Brad.

"I haven't been home in a while but I don't know what we have that big that would make a noise that loud." I added.

"Should we go look?" said Brad.

I don't know if it was the loud California city living or the relief of being home but I wasn't fazed by the loud noise.

All three of us found ourselves walking through the hallway where we heard the noise. Brad was in front, I was in the middle, and Derek was behind me grabbing on to my sleeve.

"Dude chill out." I told Derek.

"I am chill, man," Derek said defensively. "I just don't want us to get mauled by a mountain lion.

"More like a Black Bear," said Brad.

"That's comforting," I said.

"Actually it should be, black bears actually aren't that aggressive…" Brad stopped talking looking into my room.

The window was open. Everyone was silent.

"Did you leave your window open?" Brad asked turning back to look at me.

"I don't remember," I said. I knew I didn't open it but I wasn't about to get freaked out over nothing, it could have been my mom anyways. She always liked to air out the house. "I think we're all good." It was probably the wind blowing a door shut." I knew that was a lie, I was just emotionally exhausted and ready for bed.

"Sure thing man, let's bail Brad, my brother is waiting for his truck.

"Alright," Brad said, taking one last glance in my room.

It made me feel good that Brad was there, he wasn't pissed, and he cared about some strange noise.

All of us were walking to the front door.

"Hey, did you guys happen to see any strange lights coming from the woods on your way here?" I asked.

"Like aliens?" asked Derek. I wasn't sure if he was serious.

"No, Derek, like a weird glow. Almost like a purple fog low to the ground."

Brad looked confused. I hope I didn't sound dumb.

"Ok Chip, where are the drugs?" Derek asked jokingly.

"Never mind," I said sighing.

Derek opened the front door, turned around, gave me a firm handshake and a 'bro' hug. Derek started walking towards the car.

Brad stood in front of me, "Well… I guess I'll see you tomorrow."

I couldn't help but get lost in his black eyes. It felt like staring up into the night sky at night – stargazing. I could always stare at Brad in the eyes because everything else seemed to fade away within seconds.

"Sure thing, unless I happen to ditch town again" I said smirking. Brad didn't think it was funny. Another terrible time for a joke. I need to come up with another coping mechanism. "I'm sorry, you know I was just playing…"

Brad grabbed me by my hands and leaned in. He kissed me on the lips. This was a huge deal. Derek has never seen me be affectionate with another man. I always avoided that just in case it would make him uncomfortable. Brad's kiss was firm and meaningful. The kiss lasted longer than I was comfortable with but I didn't want it to end. Brad let go of my hands and leaned back. I could see Derek standing by his truck with the biggest smile on his face. Derek proceeded to bend his knees and slap the air in front of him, I think he was smacking an invisible ass.

I guess Derek wasn't uncomfortable with that.

Brad walked away from the house into the truck with Derek. As I watched them get into the truck and reverse out of my driveway a sense of dread came over me. All of a sudden the loud noise, the glowing lights, the faint voices in the back yard started running through my mind. I wished Derek would turn the truck around and they came back to sleep over, like the good ol' days.

They weren't coming back.

I turned back around into the house and locked the door. The house was quiet. The sun was officially gone and darkness flooded the house. I walked slowly down the long hallway back to my room. I stopped in the hallway. There was something on the floor that I didn't see earlier. In front of my room there was a large scratch on the floor. It was one singular scratch that made a straight line from the hallway wall to the inside of my room window. I tried to think really hard if this was something that was already there. My anxiety started up a bit. I walked past my room and looked inside.

Chills ran down my neck. My bedroom window was now closed. My focus shifted from the bedroom window to the same woods seen out the bathroom window. The strange light was back. What's going on? Who closed my window? Maybe one of the guys closed it.

I knew that wasn't true.

What made that scratch? When I was attending therapy I learned not to dwell on things, it makes anxiety worse, I brushed it off and contemplated when is it healthy to brush things off and when is it ok to dwell? I guess I'll bring that up next therapy session.

I decided it was time for bed; I had enough of today. I walked into my room and slipped off my boots. Man, I love that feeling of your feet on a hard wood floor after a long day. I exhaled and unbuttoned my plaid shirt. Across from me was a full-length mirror. I glanced at my body and started moving my hands from up my side to my chest. They say in therapy you have to accept yourself before letting anyone else in. Before California I was always so shut off and afraid. As I glanced here shirtless looking at the hard work I put into myself I realized that leaving home and coming back was a good thing. Being isolated in California gave me no choice but to accept myself. All I had was myself.

My eyes went from the mirror to the window next to it. I thought of how embarrassing it would be if someone saw me rubbing myself like a teenage girl. Out of the window I saw the purple fog still lingering in the trees. It looked so magical like something out of a fairy tale.

Someone was coming out of the fog. My heart skipped a beat. Based off of the silhouette I could see it was Derek. I laughed at myself for expecting Brad to appear through the shadows like the end of some romance novel. I was relieved it was Derek. This whole night left me so confused and lost, but with Derek I felt home. I slipped my boots back on and put my flannel back on unbuttoned.

Did the truck break down?

I walked out the room, down the hallway, and out the back door. When leaving the house the warm breeze billowed against my chest. In California the nights can be pretty chilly for a Texas boy, this warmth gave me comfort and added on to my feeling of "home."

I began walking toward Derek who was staring into something in the woods. Was Brad in the purple fog?

My cell phone rang.

Mom was calling.

"Hey Ma" I answered the phone.

"Hey Chip, I wanted to let you know we stayed a bit at your Aunt's and Uncle's house but we're heading back now."

"No problem, Derek and B…" I stopped not knowing how my mom would react.

The phone was silent as I continued walking to Derek.

"What about Derek?"

"Yeah, he came over to say hey."

I reached Derek's side. Derek continued looking into the woods without acknowledging me.

"Didn't he leave already?" mom asked.

"No he's still here."

Derek began walking into the woods.

"Hunny, I just saw Derek and your old friend Brad when we stopped at the gas station." Mom replied.

There was a bit of silence.

"Chip, listen to me very carefully."

There was an awkward silence, but I could tell something was wrong.

I felt a lump in my throat. What is going on?

"Have you been hearing strange noises?"

"What do you mean?"

"This is going to sound strange Chip, but have you been hearing someone calling you in the distance?"

I didn't know what to say, but I knew exactly what she was talking about.

Mom continued, " OK hunny, go inside the house and lock the door. Can you do that Chip? ... CHIP! I need to you to tell me you are going to go inside and lock the door can you hear me..."

I dropped the phone as I felt something grab onto my leg. I couldn't see anything but the purple fog made it's way around my feet. I panicked and let out a yelp. Every time I tried to pick my foot up it sank lower and lower. I couldn't see through the fog but it felt like a belt was wrapped around my leg. Every movement made the belt tighter. I tried to scream but the pain ran from my foot up to my leg. I let out a shriek.

"HELP ME!" I screamed. "DEREK!"

I tried again to free my leg out from the grasp of the unknown. I looked into the forest and saw a dark figure approaching me. I couldn't make out what it was but did not want to stick around to find out. I tried not to look but I couldn't help but notice the massive size of this lanky figure.

Come-on Chip, one stronger tug and run like hell. The figure was approaching. The figure must have been 8 feet tall, probably taller because I could tell the figure was hunched over, looking straight at me. I couldn't see its eyes, which terrified me. You can tell a lot from eyes, you can tell motive, emotion, danger. All I saw was darkness in the figure.

I breathed in and held my breath while I forced my foot out of my boot. I felt and heard my foot pop. There was a tree next to me that I was able to catch myself on. I lowered my foot on the ground to run but immediately fell to the ground. My foot felt as though there were tiny shards of glass inside and any pressure was causing immense pain.

I was shaking, crying. My problems seemed so minuscule at this point. I wanted the grief of getting kicked out of school, I wanted the jitters Brad caused me, I wanted to be anxious because at the end of the day it's what I knew. I did not know this creature.

I turned to look at the stalking figure. It changed. The black figure had a definition in its face that was not there previously. A smile that encompassed half of its face. I turned back around and scrambled out of the trees. A strong grip came onto my left foot. I turned back and there was an arm that came from the ground, grabbing me. This was not human. I quickly jumped on the only working foot I had. I jumped one more time to get to another tree for some balance. When I hit the ground an arm shot out of the earth and grabbed onto my foot, this time my broken foot.

I've never screamed so loud in my life.

The figure began emerging from the trees.

"HELP! SOMEONE PLEASE HELP ME!"

I felt hopeless. I was sobbing. I was scared.

Sounds of branches snapping, leaves rustling, and bark bending filled the air. I turned to look at the figure to see it was now dragging me across the earth. I noticed that the figure was now diminishing into the ground.

"NO!" I yelled.

It was going to take me down with it.

"NO!"

I saw the headlights of a car pulling into my driveway. It was my parents.

"MOM!" I screamed.

The creature was pulling me underground. I was terrified. My surroundings began fading into black as the earth was engulfing me.

As I was being dragged lower and lower into the earth I looked up and saw multiple figures in the treetops. These shadows were all staring at me, watching like a pack of animals.

I saw a quick glimpse of my father running out of the car into the house.

The terror set in strong. I couldn't mutter a word.

All I could think of was where is this creature taking me and what is he going to do with me when I get there?

Unholy Matrimony
by Daniel W. Kelly

They're here. Right on time!

Noreen didn't even give the couple a chance to ring the rear entrance bell of her wedding shop. She'd been waiting at the door, peering through the glass panel until she saw two forms materialize out of the dark. She immediately let the two men in; they brought a chilly breeze with them.

"Quick. Quick! Before anyone sees you," she whispered.

As the husky couple passed her, the much heftier of the two, who had to weigh near three hundred pounds and had a bald head, thick beard, and hoop earrings, said, "No one in their right mind is coming around this dark place."

"I'm sorry." Noreen closed the door behind them and peered out for any sign of life. "The bulb is burned out. And honestly, it's probably for the better that there wasn't a light on. All the shops are closed at this time of night but I still worry that you may be seen."

The other man, noticeably younger with a full head of hair and a kinder face, was full-bodied in a stockier way that didn't yet bring to mind obesity. He smiled and said, "If you're this worried, then we really need to repay you for actually coming face-to-face with us."

They must spend their entire lives being paranoid about people despising them, Noreen thought. She outwardly offered them her biggest, most comforting smile. "Of course. I simply have to handle situations like yours secretly like this. This is a small town that doesn't support your kind of wedding."

The two men glanced at each other awkwardly.

"But I do! I *do*!" Noreen said then they all laughed at her choice of words. "I lost my husband several years back, and I sure don't want to spend eternity alone. Everyone deserves to be together until death do them part." Noreen shook a pondering finger at the older, bearded fellow. "You look so familiar."

He nodded. "I grew up in this town."

Noreen's jaw dropped. "Last name Winston! But your first name was—"

"Was," the bearded man said. "But I go by Presa now."

"Okay," Noreen said. "Presa."

"And I'm Terry," the younger man said. "The one you spoke with on the phone."

"Right. Right. But you didn't grow up here," Noreen said.

"No," Presa answered for him. "We met in the city we live in now."

"You're Kelly's older brother, right?" Noreen asked Presa. "She had a lovely wedding! But you weren't home for that. And she moved away. Is she back in town for your wedding?"

"I'd had a falling out with the family for years," was Presa's only response.

Noreen shook her head. "Just not right. Family is the most important—"

"We've patched things up," Presa said brusquely, a tone that fit his persona, making it hard to determine if he was annoyed by her comment. "And the family is completely supportive of my marriage."

"I'm sure they are," Noreen said. She chucked the more approachable Terry under the chin. "Especially when you brought home such a handsome, sweet boy. The girls in this town would line up around the block to get this lucky."

Terry rubbed Presa's back. "Well, this lucky guy didn't have to line up. And he's going to look amazing in a tux."

"Of course," Noreen said. "We'll get to them last. I keep the men's clothing down in the basement. It's not exactly as complicated to choose tuxes for men as it is for a woman to decide on a wedding dress. Unless you're going to wear pink tuxes. Then I'll have to special order them."

Again the men exchanged uncomfortable glances, and Noreen thought, *Stop trying to be too "cool" with them or you'll offend. They need to trust you.*

"I even have a groom/groom cake topper selection I can get from one of my suppliers!" Noreen made her eyebrows dance excitedly. "Come. Let's go into the bakery so we can do cake tasting first."

She took each of their hands (shutting down the wandering of her mind to where their hands may have been recently) and led them through the dimly lit shop. The long shadows and silhouettes of mannequins and wedding dresses encroached on the walking space.

Terry giggled and tapped Presa's shoulder. "It's like a bunch of ghost brides rising from a cemetery."

Noreen glanced at him sharply.

"Sorry," Terry said sheepishly. "The city we lived in is big on the supernatural, and we use humor to keep things light."

Your friend doesn't seem to find humor in anything, Noreen thought. Out loud she said, "I find light in God. He'll always show you the path to righteousness. You shouldn't dabble in that occult evil."

"We definitely don't dabble," Presa said.

The way he left the comment dangling, it felt to Noreen as if he was implying something else. But it was a conversation she definitely didn't want to continue. She branched off between the mannequins and led the men into a large professional kitchen lined on one side with glass fridges. Finally, she was able to turn on overhead florescent fixtures.

"It burns! It burns!" Terry giggled, holding a hand over his eyes.

"Quite a playful young spirit you have on your arm!" Noreen said to Presa.

Presa may have actually smirked. His thick whiskers made it hard to tell. "He keeps me feeling alive."

Terry peered into the well-lit display refrigerators. "These cakes are amazing. Do you design them all?"

"I have bakers," Noreen said. "But that's just a portion of the designs we have. There's a whole binder full of possibilities. Flowers. Rainbows. We even have a disco themed cake!"

"Now you're on our wavelength!" Terry joked, sitting on a stool Noreen offered at a big wood prep table.

Presa sat on a stool next to him and Noreen took a stool across from them. She opened the binder and spun it around. "You can look at these for starters. There are plenty of choices, but we can also come up with unique ideas together. My guys can make anything."

As the men flipped through the pages, Terry doing all the "oohing" and "aahing," Noreen went to an industrial refrigerator in the back corner of the kitchen and pulled out a tray full of plates holding different cake slice samples; it was a tray she'd made up especially for them. She then grabbed plates and forks from a cabinet and drawer, respectively, and brought everything to the table.

"So what's your poison?" Noreen asked. "Red Velvet? Buttercream? Lemon?"

"Devil's Food," Presa said, his thick eyebrows seeming to dip evilly in the center.

Noreen raised her eyebrows in opposition. "Wow. That's unconventional for a wedding cake."

"It's an unconventional wedding," Presa said.

Noreen nodded. "You're right about that. But would you like to sample any of these other flavors? I have delicious chocolate cake samples here." She pointed with a fork at square pieces on the tray. "Chocolate mint. Dutch mocha. There's even s'mores cake. So delicious. You really must try this one."

Presa refused the forkful of cake she extended to him. She leaned back on her stool, trying not to show her frustration…or her discomfort with him.

"We just really have it all planned out in our heads," Terry said. "And he's set on an all chocolate cake."

"Oh. Then this one right here is for you. It's death by chocolate," Noreen said. "Here, try."

"We're sure it's perfect," Terry said. "We're both trying to lose some weight so the tuxes won't need to be refitted right before the big day."

"Oh, but one little bite won't hurt." Noreen held her hand under a fork of death by chocolate and moved it forward, hoping one mouth or the other would bite. Both men stared at her blankly. She shrugged and shook her head. "Okay. You want death by chocolate. But if you hate it on the day of the wedding, there's no refund."

"Why don't you just take us down to the tuxedos?" Presa pushed.

Noreen stared at him hard and fought not to swallow the lump forming in her throat, concerned it would make her appear nervous.

"Maybe we'll be up for a taste when we're done," Presa finished.

"Yes. Maybe you will." Noreen closed the binder of cake designs. "And we can pick out the look you want as well. I just don't want you two to get all bridezilla on me at the reception!"

Terry smiled. "You watch the show?"

"Of course!" Noreen felt the warmth returning to their exchange. "I'm a wedding planner with a wedding shop! It gives me good tips on how to deal with that kind of insanity."

"Me and Dodd used to watch it religiously," Terry said.

Noreen's forehead tightened.

"My previous partner. He...drowned," Terry said after glancing over at Presa.

That sure was defensive.

"I'm sorry," Noreen said. The silence that followed was somehow... creepy. And it must have been power of suggestion, because Noreen could swear she got a whiff of ocean...or...fish. "But you have this big guy now, right? And he loves you."

Presa just shrugged.

This is getting weird. The drowned one hits a nerve. Why? What if they killed him so they could be together?

Noreen shook the thought from her head. "Now come. We'll go down to the men's shop and find you both tuxes that will make you look stunning."

"I'm amazed that you actually sell tuxes," Terry said as they followed Noreen through the shop.

"I cover as many bases as I can," Noreen said as she turned on tranquil, ambient lighting in the next room they entered. Finished in wood and adorned with imagery of grape vines, it looked like an upscale liquor store. "You can even do some wine and champagne tasting later."

She led the men diagonally across the room to a door in a far corner. Opening it, she stepped aside to let them go first.

"It smells," Presa said.

"It's a basement," Noreen said from behind him. "It's a new addition and hasn't been fully renovated yet."

"And it's dark." Presa leaned into the doorframe, feeling for a switch on the wall.

There was an echoing clank as a thick wine bottle struck the back of his head and didn't even crack. Presa's huge body was no match for gravity. He left a trail of cacophony behind as he disappeared down the dark stairwell.

When Terry turned to see what had hit Presa, Noreen smashed him across the face with the same bottle. Now it did shatter, for Noreen used even more force, fearing Terry might try to fight back. His face was sliced in numerous places and simultaneously saturated in deep purple liquid as he soared backward, following his fellow sodomite down the staircase.

##

Noreen waited patiently for them to awake, savoring the moment when they saw where their disgusting attack on the institution of marriage had led them. She fought to ignore the stench, which was so much stronger down here. If the big fat one was able to smell it from the top of the stairs it might start permeating the shop soon, so this ceremony couldn't have come at a better time. Although, she wasn't sure what she was supposed to do with all the bodies after the task was complete. She knew her guardian angel would tell her.

She looked at the two of them, battered and bruised, tied in upright positions to a support post in front of which she had centered the altar. She felt just as battered, having had to drag then lift their deadweight into those positions. At her age, she hadn't been sure at first how she'd found the strength, but she had shamefacedly reminded herself that her guardian angel gave her all her power.

She slapped Terry across his youthful but lacerated face with a sterile rubber glove from the kitchen so she wouldn't make contact with his possibly diseased life fluid. "Wake up! It's your big day."

Terry's lolling head lifted. His eyelids, covered in drying blood splashes, peeled apart and fluttered.

Noreen smiled excitedly. "Hi! We've been waiting for the runaway bride. Or are you the groom? It's so hard to tell with you deviants trying to destroy tradition."

Terry laughed. He actually laughed. "So you've learned all your lines."

Sweat pushed at Noreen's pores. "What's wrong with you?"

Terry snickered. "Guess I'm just nervous. It being my wedding day and all."

Noreen felt her face heating up. *Why is he acting like that? Why is he saying it's his wedding day? And why do dead bodies smell like rotting fish?*

"Love muffin. Wake up." Terry looked over at Presa. "Yo, dog! Wake up!"

Presa's eyes popped open like he'd been awake the whole time and just pretending to be asleep. It almost made Noreen recoil, and she felt like dead fingers were touching her neck. She swiftly stepped aside so she could make sure nothing was directly behind her—hadn't come alive to get her. *Ridiculous thought.* She was merely moving aside to allow Presa to see who was present for his wedding.

It had just been her imagination. The bodies of Presa's mother and father were still propped up in a single pew that sat behind her—a pew that was usually used as part of a front window display in the spring.

She had to avert her gaze from the pale faces of the man and wife while acting as if she was looking upon them, for even though it had only been two days, they were starting to look…and smell…their age.

Presa didn't even flinch.

Maybe he's in shock?

"Remember Mom and Dad?" Noreen asked. "They rushed right over when I called them to tell them you were coming to plan your wedding. They insisted I not say a word to anyone until they got here. Very hush hush. Perhaps they weren't as accepting as you thought. Maybe a little ashamed to let their neighbors know the mockery you were making of God's blessed event."

Presa fidgeted on his feet as he tried to escape the thick rope that pinned him to the post. "I thought you didn't recognize me until I got here."

"A special friend told me who you were," Noreen said then couldn't help antagonizing him. "You don't seem too upset to see them like this."

Presa shrugged. "I figured they were already dead by now. They kicked me out of the house when I was still a teenager. I ended up having to suck dick for money to survive."

Noreen's knee-jerk reaction was to gasp, after which she immediately kicked herself inside.

"Oh yeah," Presa said. "It was hell on earth. Just the way my folks and people like you want it for people like me.

Kicked him out? But they supported his deviance.

"But eventually," Presa continued, "I made my way to a collapsing city and got a job as a dockworker. And I watched the city get worse and worse. Whores. Killers. A whole child sex slave ring."

"I don't care about you or your city of Sodom!" Noreen barked. She lashed out and kicked Presa in his man parts, which wasn't easy for her tired leg.

His only reaction to the hit was a smile…finally. His voice wasn't even shaking from pain when he said, "This isn't about me. It's about the monsters and horrible worlds your kind create when you rob people like me of our humanity and banish us to vile places."

"But it didn't work in our city," Terry interjected. "Men like us came in and fixed it, got rid of all that misery and made it a beautiful safe haven just for us. Well, with a little help from some unexpected evil. But sometimes, it takes evil to fight evil."

Those are the words my guardian angel used when he told me I needed to break a commandment to rid the world of this filth.

"Shut up!" Noreen screamed. "Both of you! We are here to perform a ceremony that will send you where you belong for eternity!"

"We're already there," Presa said.

Noreen stumbled backward as the two men seemed to morph… or melt? Flesh seemed to disintegrate. The heads of both men, who were tied back to back to the post, turned in her direction, their grins getting bigger as lips and facial skin simply disappeared.

She screamed when the back of her legs bumped into something. The body of Presa's little old father thumped to the floor beside her… and brought her foot and calf down with him. She cried out in pain as her knee crashed to the floor, putting her in a kneeling position. She looked back to the altar to see that both husky men had trimmed down drastically. So much so that the ropes holding them up slipped right off…along with clumps of flesh that plopped wetly on the floor.

Ocean rot assaulted Noreen's nostrils as she struggled to get her leg free from the deadweight of the daddy corpse. *This can't be happening! Is this a test?*

Presa and Terry dropped to the basement's dusty, dirty floor. They were both rotten in numerous places, large chunks of their flesh and some appendages completely gone. Their skin was a rainbow of colors—pink, blue, green, yellow, purple. Something slithered out from what appeared to be a huge hole in Presa's posterior, which was exposed because his pants had fallen to his ankles. Noreen thought the black slimy creature was a snake, but when it began to squirm in a little puddle that had leaked out of Presa's orifice, she realized it was an eel.

Noreen yanked until she felt a pain shoot up her leg. But she was free. She grasped the pew in order to get herself off the floor. It shook and nearly tipped over. The mother corpse crumpled, her forehead clocking Noreen in her head. She was crying now, but managed to get on both feet.

"Don't leave," Terry said as politely as ever from where he was doing a pushup off the floor. "We need you here to be our witness. To give us away. To be our surrogate mother for the mother/son dance. Till death do you part."

Some sort of multi-legged crustacean Noreen couldn't even identify crawled from one of Terry's eye sockets and fell to the wet floor, where it was almost immediately smacked around by the struggling eel.

Much like the crustacean, Terry was crawling as well—right toward Noreen—because his legs were completely gone. He was only feet away from her as Presa was busy picking his damaged bulk off the floor with the one thick arm he still had. His other arm was simply missing right up to the shoulder and was nowhere to be seen in the basement.

Noreen screamed and ran, feeling just how badly the daddy corpse had hurt her leg. Maybe even fractured one of her aging bones. But she ignored the agony as she stumbled for the stairs.

She could *hear* the sloshing of their naked bodies as they shuffled (or dragged?) along the floor.

"Till death do you part!" Terry spat. It sounded like a gurgle, as if he had water in his lungs.

"Stay away from me!" Noreen screamed. She tripped up the steps, the harassed pain receptors in her leg stabbing her directly in the brain.

She practically crawled up the stairs, sobbing with terror, wondering what had gone wrong, where her guardian angel was, and how he could have exposed her to the true face of their evil and not protected her.

She was amazed at how quickly she reached the top of the steps, which seemed much creakier than usual. The noise completely jangled her nerves…and drowned out her auditory detection of how far or close the degenerate demons might be to her.

All the moisture had been drained from her mouth and throat. It made the liquor still spilled on the floor at the top of the steps look deliciously satiating. She grasped the doorframe to avoid slipping in the liquid, which was adding a vinegary smell to the sea stench. She attempted to swing the door closed but didn't give it enough power. She didn't pause to rectify that. She just kept going. She staggered from one display of bottles to the next, causing them to clank together noisily.

Reaching the other side of the room, she leaned heavily on a full wall wine rack. About to push through the nearest swinging door, she grabbed at the neck of one of the horizontal wine bottles. It would serve as a weapon…again.

The bottle slipped from her shaking hands and shattered. The crash was echoed…by *two* drowning voices calling "Till death do you part!"

At the door at the top of the basement stairway, the corroding version of Terry was dragging its way into the room. The larger and more erect Presa was right behind and actually tripped over Terry's leg stumps. Noreen seized the opportunity to run from the room, although it was without any bottle weapon.

The bright light in the kitchen was a relief, its beckoning white brilliance warming Noreen's soul with a promise of safety. Without hesitating, she hobble-ran to the drawer that held all the knives. She didn't even care that the metallic jangle might draw attention to where she was as she yanked the drawer open and reached for cutlery with a double-fisting plan.

She screamed as the room went black and she was jabbed by a blade in the darkness. She grabbed the first two knives she could get her hands on and groped her way around the table at which she'd been marketing (poisoned) wedding cakes not an hour ago. Her already aching knee slammed into a chair. Her hip hit another. And then there was the sound of the metal door swinging open from the wines & spirits room.

"Till death do you paaaaaaaaaart!"

The hiss echoed around the tiled room so that it felt closer than Noreen knew it could be. She whimpered and allowed her body to careen off stoves and counters as she made her way to the door on the other side of the room. The knives she was holding found it first, slashing against the cold metal. Before she could push the door open, a wave of aquatic decay washed over her. It was perfectly complemented by the feel of something spongy and wet grabbing her ankle. She screamed and kicked out.

"Till…death…do…you…paaaaaaaaaaaaart!"

Her foot made contact with what she assumed was Terry's face. She swung out with both knives and felt them cut through something tender. So she knew Presa was only a foot or two in front of her. One knife got caught in God only knew what part of him, but she was unwilling to let go of it. She pulled hard, grappled with his lone arm in the dark, felt herself losing balance, and slammed backward into—and out—the kitchen door.

The floor beneath her shook, and she realized Presa's body had dropped beside her. Feeling his big hand groping at her without being able to see it was more violating than anything she'd ever experienced… especially since it happened to find her breasts.

"What are you?" Noreen shrieked, smacking away a slimy hand as

she rolled over and clawed at the floor in an effort to get away from him. Now that she was in the main room of wedding gowns there were actually streaks of light ahead, coming in from the window at the front of the store; it was illumination from the lamppost across the street from the wedding shop. But both knives she'd been grasping were gone. She couldn't see them anywhere, didn't know if maybe they were embedded in Presa's rotund body.

Weaponless once more, she found the strength to get to her feet to head for the light. She hurried down the aisle between the ghostly mannequins in white.

A track of filthy water was glistening on the runner in the middle of the shop. The sea stench was already in here.

Behind Noreen, Presa was already getting off the floor. Her legs and mind battled it out. She was terrified to be following that trail of water. She began to run, but not at full speed.

From underneath a beautiful ruffled train that was encircling the rear side of a mannequin, Terry's corroded upper body lunged out and latched onto her legs.

"Till death do you part!"

Noreen crashed into one of her mannequins and went down in a blinding cloud of sequins and veils.

Now it felt like hands were all over her, pulling her back, dragging her down. The more she struggled the more snagged she became. Mannequins were knocked over and showered down on top of her. And it hurt. Her cries and panting drowned out the two degenerate demons taunting the sanctity of marriage with their unison words.

She grappled with dress material and thrust at hard female forms with her arms and legs but soon began clinging to them, holding on to them, using them to pull herself away from the two monster men coming for her. Female body parts came loose in her hands, and she used them to fend off the degenerate demons that were now stinking up the entire place with their emissions and trying to destroy her very existence. She beat them mercilessly as they came for her soul.

And still they croaked, "Till death do you part!"

On her back now and dragging herself along the floor with her elbows, her body sliding over a wedding veil, Noreen looked back and could see she was moving closer and closer to the light. She could practically read the "Yes, we're open" sign on the front door.

She was about to flip over when she sensed the presence towering above her.

Because he still had use of his legs, Presa had the advantage over his partner's dragging body and was about to overtake Noreen. A beam of light cutting down the center aisle lit him up completely. His bald head and puffy face had taken on a gelatinous appearance and were a sickly sea green. His beard looked like moss, and things seemed to be moving in it. Huge chunks of his head were gone and…stuff…was oozing from them.

A splattering sound as repulsive as a person losing control of their bowels was the only warning Noreen got before a grotesque substance hit the floor with a splash that sent it shooting between Presa's legs. She was drenched in it, and the odor was unbearable, like a combination of rotten meat, rotten fish, and rotten feces.

And there was Terry, dragging himself over the puddle of slime to peer at her from between Presa's legs. And just to add a finishing touch to the horrific display, another underwater critter crawled from his eye socket.

Noreen lashed out with her leg and hit Presa in the calf. Expecting the leg to be as solid as he had looked in life, she was shocked when the flesh around the calf gave in without a fight and the bone beneath snapped.

Presa's huge body tipped forward. He was coming right at her. She screamed and did the only thing she could think of to do; she held a mannequin hand up like a spear.

Fake fingers pierced facial flesh, and Noreen was again covered in wet stink. She pushed the mannequin arm with all her might and was able to toss Presa's dense form to the side as she slid somewhat away from him.

Terry grabbed her foot, his purple lips smiling maniacally. He began to crawl up her calf then her thigh, almost as if teasing his way to her most sacred of regions. She had a quite literal knee-jerk reaction at the thought of being violated by such a monster. She crammed the toe of her shoe into his mouth, causing him to choke rancid liquid around the tip.

"God will not let you have me!" Noreen screamed.

Terry was knocked off his elbows, and his chin hit the floor with a meaty plop.

Both degenerate demons were (barely) out of commission for the moment, so Noreen dug her heels in, found her faith once more, and used that power to get to her feet. She raced for the front door of the wedding shop.

##

Just like the sudden vision he'd been the first time he came to her, Noreen's guardian angel appeared. He was right outside, framed in the door to the wedding shop, his head peeking through the glass, seeming to float just above the "Yes, we're open" side of the store status sign that hung there. Despite being formed in the image of an incredibly unremarkable looking man—he had the most average, forgettable features she'd ever seen—there was something so penetrating and alluring about his presence. It was like he'd reached inside her soul, given it a hug, and promised to love, cherish, and care for her.

When he'd made his existence known to her it had been like love at first sight. She had known instantly that this was the man she would follow until the end of time. That her life with her husband had been nothing more than an earthly, pedestrian coupling. That this was the higher calling beyond mortal life that she had so deeply believed in.

Despite the horror she had left on the floor not too far away, Noreen actually felt a smile spreading across her face as she grabbed the handle of the door. She was safe now. With her angel.

He wasn't smiling back. He just peered at her through the glass, his eyes empty and uninterested as they had been during their first meeting. He showed no human emotion with his facial muscles, which was something Noreen had assumed was beyond heavenly existence, where one was always complacent because things couldn't get any better.

The door wouldn't open, which didn't make sense. It was designed to lock only from the outside when she closed up for the night. She frantically fought with the handle. She glanced over her shoulder. In the light streaming in from outside she could see the two hideous monsters crawling across the floor toward her, both of their gory, gouged faces lit with sinister smiles, one with a mannequin arm still protruding from it.

"Help me!" Noreen gasped quietly against the glass, feeling semi-confident that she was safe. He was, after all, her guardian angel. But he continued staring at her blankly, the panel of impenetrable transparency between them the only thing keeping their lips from connecting in a kiss. "I did everything you commanded. I don't know what happened! They got the better of me. Look! They're monsters! It's like they're revealing the true degenerate demons inside their homosexual souls."

The monsters stopped only feet away from her as if stunned at the derogatory words and unaware that they deserved to be labeled as such.

"We always knew they were monsters," her guardian angel said. "You just wanted so badly to see it for yourself. That's why you were the perfect choice to do the dirty work."

Noreen shook her head. "No. Not dirty work. The Lord's work."

"Come now," the guardian angel said, his poker face not shattering even slightly. "You killed the big ugly one's parents."

"Because…they supported him! Encouraged him! You said it yourself! They hurt society!"

"Oh. Definitely. But they didn't support him. They loathed his disgusting lifestyle."

"What?" Noreen looked back at rotting, fishy smelling Presa, whose jelly-like eyeballs appeared sad, the mannequin arm serving as a new nose between them. "But…then why? If they knew what he was doing was wrong and detested it, why did you make me kill them?"

"You have free will. I didn't make you do anything you didn't want to do in the first place. Besides, they deserved it. They didn't put a stop to it," the guardian angel said. "They let him out into the world to continue doing what he was doing with other men."

"What choice did they have? How could they stop him?" Noreen asked. When the guardian angel stared at her coldly, she knew what he believed they could have done to stop him. "No. Not their own son…."

"Why? You were going to do it."

Noreen shook her head. "I didn't. I couldn't. Look! Those monsters are already dead!"

"Indeed," the guardian angel said.

The glow cascading around him, which was previously white and inviting, now seemed an apropos shade of putrid, murky green that drenched the monsters behind her. The two bodies, the big one barely standing because of its broken leg, the other still on the shop's floor, were shaking and quivering, limbs flapping, giving the illusion of the pair being some hideous water creatures.

"That's pretty much how I found them," the guardian angel said. "Flushed out to sea from that God forsaken city of sodomites. Devoured by a beast of nature. Just what they deserved."

"But then why?" Noreen's knees gave out. She slumped down the length of the door, clinging to the handle for strength. "Why bring them back?"

"Because it was just too easy for them. They even died at the hands of a creature that was trying to practice the same perversions as them. I needed them to suffer more for what they chose to be in life. It just irks me that they died of causes not inflicted by one of my own creations. So I captured their souls to make sure they would suffer in my purgatory before going to hell."

Noreen screamed as a spongy, bony hand swiped at her ankle. She pounded on the door with one palm while keeping the other glued to the handle.

"Till death do you paaaaaart," Terry moaned.

"No! No!" Noreen cried to her guardian angel. "Save me! You promised."

The guardian angel crouched so that his face was level with hers. He simply shrugged.

"You…tricked me!" Noreen sobbed. "You're not a guardian angel. You're evil! You're a liar!"

"I prefer the term 'deceiver'," the guardian angel said. "And I do it for the better of society. And really, it's you who was trying to deceive me and rally against the Lord."

Noreen squealed as Presa's huge smelly body came crashing to the floor next to Terry's. To avoid contact with him, she curled up into a ball as best as her old legs would allow. She glared through the glass at the deceiver. "*You're* the monster! *I* am an angel! *I* am a servant of the Lord!"

"I'll give you that. You did do the Lord's work by ridding the world of those degenerate-spawners rotting away in your basement. But you're not righteous. You're self-righteous. Convincing yourself you live sin-free. You never gave anything to this world. Barren and you knew it, yet instead of refraining from lustful temptation, you spent your life reveling in it."

Noreen couldn't believe what she was hearing. "But...I wasn't able to procreate! It was beyond my control. It's just how God made me! Physical relations are a natural and important part of expressing love!" Noreen squealed and lashed out with her foot as Terry's and Presta's hands tried to grab her feet. "Get off me! Don't touch me!"

"But you like being touched," the deceiver said. "And it's been so long since you've had your husband around to desecrate your body. Your sinful existence is what let me know I could get you to do the awful things you did. Perhaps you'll be forgiven for your sins considering you've helped make the world a little better. Sometimes it takes evil to fight evil."

Noreen shook her head frantically. "No...not me...not evil...."

"And don't worry about your mortal reputation. Evidence left behind will convince your neighbors that these two did the unthinkable to you because of your adamant refusal to help them plan their farcical wedding."

"No! NO! NOOOOOOO!" Noreen banged on the glass door with both hands.

The two monsters clawed at her legs until they had firm grasps and then began to yank them in either direction.

"Now," the deceiver said, "death *may* do you part."

"Fuck you!" Noreen shrieked, not even realizing she was cursing as pain shot into her pelvis where her legs were being pulled wider and wider apart. "You will never have me!"

She yanked the mannequin arm from Presa's menacing face and used it to beat both degenerate demons. Their spongy faces caved in with little resistance, yet they still grappled with her legs. But now their grasps were weaker, and she was able to pull free.

She truly found her faith and knew *this* had been the test—the deceiver had tried to bring her over to his darkness. She would not let him. She was up on her feet in an instant and running for the back exit, leaping over fallen mannequin brides with ease. She ignored the ominous feeling that the still standing mannequins were somehow moving closer and closer to the center aisle, sealing the route of her escape. It was all a test. As she ran through their valley of death, she would fear no evil.

It worked. She was almost there. The escape route through the storage room was only yards away.

But as darkness consumed Noreen the farther away she got from the front windows, shadows played tricks on her. She was almost convinced a bride and groom were standing under the arch of the doorframe, blocking her way.

Then she saw the eyes. They glowed green and inhuman in the darkness. She slammed on her foot brakes as fast as she could. But she was so close now that she could make out the familiar bodies of Presa's parents—previously hunched and feeble, then dead and unmoving, now the revitalized victims of an unholy resurrection. Their faces were hideously deformed, demonic, with gruesome, leaking craters and deep, bloody gashes. Their cracked and split lips, despite being abnormally swollen, could not hide the mangled rows of jagged, slimy teeth that glistened between them. The green eyes intensified and the mouths yawned open, allowing a bowel-like stench to spew in Noreen's direction.

"I told you, you son of a bitch!" Noreen bellowed in the direction of the deceiver. "You will never have me!"

As she turned to look back, her heart practically blocked her throat. The corpulent corpse known as Presa was quickly hopping up the aisle on one leg, the legless body of Terry tossed over one shoulder almost lovingly, as if he was being carried over the threshold. The thumping noise of foot hitting floor was accompanied by the squishing plops of flesh dropping from their jiggling, bouncing bodies.

As if transported into place as a barrier, the deceiver suddenly stepped out from between two bride mannequins and stood right in front of Noreen, obliterating her view of the hopping monsters. He brought his face right to hers and said, "I don't want you. You have blood on your hands. So impure."

With a simple knock of his hands against her chest, the deceiver thrust Noreen into the open arms of the hellish married monsters behind her.

"Till death do you paaaaaaaaaart!" the approaching degenerate demons groaned as the deceiver stepped aside to let them join the wedding party.

Noreen shrieked until death had her in many parts.

Blood Will Tell

by David D. Warner

Alexander sat in his favorite high back chair in front of the bay window reading the morning edition of *The Washington Post*. "1905 Exposition to Open in Portland" proclaimed the headline. He scanned the article. The Exposition, it said, would include among its many wonders "extensive exhibits featuring amazing new technologies." As Alexander read down the list of planned attractions he was struck by the spectacle of the modern world.

It was the dawn of a new century and the things that learned men of science and engineering created these days were, literally, transforming the world overnight. It was as if the pace of new technology accelerated exponentially. He wondered how anyone was able to keep up with it all. The world was evolving rapidly, sometimes too rapidly, and not always for the good.

Sometimes he yearned for the simpler, less complicated days of his youth.

Alexander put the newspaper down on the small tea table in front of him and gazed out the window. It was a beautiful, sunny morning in the District of Columbia. People were already strolling through the park across the street. Springtime, in his mind, was the best time to be in the Nation's Capital, once winter had run its course and the dog days of summer were still three months hence.

Alexander's house—more a mansion really—was a grand Victorian brownstone located on the east side of Iowa Circle. It had been built just after the Civil War ended. Though it had fallen into considerable disrepair after years of neglect, Alexander fell in love with it the moment he laid eyes on it and he procured it without hesitation. After he took possession he immediately began its rehabilitation. While he was at it he added those few modern conveniences that would not detract from the structure's Old World charm, such things as plumbing inside the walls, electric lights, and even one of those new-fangled in-home telephones that, he believed, would one day put Western Union out of business. In homage to the past, however, he restored the gas lights out front. The house was stunning once again, and it was his pride and joy.

As he stared out the window at the traffic circle and the small park it enclosed, Alexander heard the *clop clop clop* of horses' hooves on cobblestone well before he actually saw the hansom cab that pulled up in front of his house. A well-dressed and fine-looking young man emerged from the carriage and paid the driver. The hansom pulled away and the young man walked up the front steps and entered the house through the front door.

"Alex," he called out as he crossed the threshold, "I'm home!"

Alexander hurried to the foyer to meet him.

"Stephen, Darling! I didn't think you'd be back so soon! Take off your coat. Then come here and kiss me … like you mean it."

The two men embraced. Their kiss was long and deep.

"I've missed you, my Love! I hate it when you travel."

"I've missed you as well, Pet, and I hate it when we're apart, but a man has to make a living. Let's go upstairs and I'll make it up to you."

"I would love to, Darling, but it might prove to be somewhat … *awkward?*" Alexander grinned sheepishly from ear to ear.

"And just why is that?"

"We are about to have company—I've already prepared a pot of tea for the occasion."

"So who is this mystery guest?"

"Well, it so happens that a Western Union man stopped by yesterday afternoon with a telegram from my dear, old friend Nance O'Neil. It informed me that she was taking the overnight train from New York and she would be here this morning at about half past nine. By now, she and her companion should be at the Pennsylvania Railroad station … and they will likely be here any moment."

"Nance O'Neil? *The* Nance O'Neil? The actress?"

Alexander nodded his head in assent.

Stephen frowned and put his hands on his hips.

"Alexander Sheridan!" he said sternly. "We have been together for nearly a year and a half and you have never told me that you are acquainted with the darling of the stage. 'America's Sarah Bernhardt' they call her. I am one of her most ardent admirers … and all this time …"

"Sorry, Darling. I didn't think it was important. I sometimes forget her celebrity. But, yes, Nance and I go way back. I knew her when she was still plain, old Gertrude Lamson, from Oakland, California. She was a tiny little thing, you know. You would swear her bones were hollow just like a little songbird. And she got ever so cross with me when I called her Birdie Gertie."

"I probably would have been cross with you too were you to say such a thing to me."

"Don't worry, Darling. Your parts are definitely not birdlike."

Stephen leaned in and kissed Alexander on the mouth.

"Look who's talking!"

"Sweetheart, where are your bags?"

"They wouldn't fit in the hansom so I'm having them sent around later."

"Darling, you must be exhausted. Come inside and sit with me while we wait for Nance and her friend to arrive."

The two men went into the parlor and sat side-by-side on the settee.

"So, Alex, to what do we owe the pleasure of this sudden visit from the infamous Nance O'Neil?"

"Well, I'm not exactly certain. Her telegram was a bit cryptic. She said that her companion was in need of a consultation."

"What kind of consultation?"

"The usual, I suspect. Someone close to her is dead and she wants to make contact."

"But, Sweetheart, I thought you weren't doing that anymore."

"Believe me when I say that I don't plan to make a habit of it again. But Nance is an old friend. I can't very well say no."

"Of course not." He paused. "So who is this companion anyway?"

"I'm not certain of that either. Nance referred to her only as Lizbeth. I suspect she's Nance's new sweetheart. I really can't keep up with her. Nance has always been a bit fickle when it comes to romance. She goes through women like ... well ... a man! Whoever she is, I can guarantee you that she will be someone of intrigue. Nance likes to surround herself with interesting people … especially interesting people with money."

"But I thought Nance O'Neil was married to her manager … what's his name … McGee or McKee something or other."

"Right! McKee Rankin. Darling, that's just a rumor those two cooked up together. They do work quite well together and they decided it was best for both of their reputations if people thought they were *together* together. Rankin himself is dedicated to the mentoring of aspiring young actors, if you get my meaning."

"Loud and clear!"

The sound of horses' hooves drawing nearer caught their attention.

"I do believe your guests have arrived. Shall we see them inside?"

"Yes, Darling, let's."

Alexander and Stephen rose in unison and walked into the foyer, and then exited the house to greet the two women who were being helped down from their hansom by the driver. Alexander met them at the curb and paid the driver his fare.

"Alex, my Dear," said the younger of the two women, "it is so delightful to see you again. You are looking well."

"As are you my little Birdie Gertie. It's been too long." He hugged her and kissed her cheek.

Nance looked up at Stephen and smiled broadly.

"Nance, Dear, this is Stephen Teasdale. I am sure you will come to love him as much as I do."

"How do you do, Mr. Teasdale? It is a pleasure to meet you. Any friend of Alex is a friend to me."

"Then do call me Stephen, please … the pleasure is all mine."

All three turned in the direction of the other woman. She was much older than Alexander had expected—mid-forties, he guessed—and a little plump. She looked rather more like a school teacher than a friend of Nance O'Neil. Alexander assumed she must be rich.

163

Nance took the other woman's hand.

"And this, gentlemen, is my new companion, Lizbeth."

Alexander said, "It is a pleasure to make your acquaintance Miss … Lizbeth. I am Alexander Sheridan."

Stephen followed suit and introduced himself.

Lizbeth nodded her head and replied, "Gentlemen!"

Alexander invited them into his home.

Once inside the parlor, he offered them a seat.

"You ladies must be exhausted. Would you care for some tea? I made a fresh pot shortly before you arrived. Have you had breakfast?"

"Tea would be nice, thank you," Nance said, "but we dined this morning on the train. The food was quite good."

Stephen excused himself to get the tea.

"So," Alexander asked, "what can I do for you lovely ladies this fine morning?"

"Lizbeth is in need of a consultation … the kind of consultation that you used to do so very well … she needs to make contact with her father."

"But surely there are Spiritualist mediums in Boston, or even New York City. Why come all the way to Washington, D.C.?"

Well," Nance continued, "it is a most delicate matter … and one that requires the utmost discretion. No one must ever hear of this."

"Nance, you of all people know that I am a man of honor."

"Of course, Dear, that's why we came to you."

Lizbeth spoke again for the first time since their all-too-brief introduction. "Nance tells me that when you go into one of your trances, you remember nothing that transpires while you are channeling the spirit."

"That is correct," Alexander lied. The primary reason that he quit doing consultations was that, as he got older, his own awareness during trance grew ever clearer. He found that he was remembering bits and pieces of the session afterward, often from the vantage point of the spirit that he was channeling, as if for that brief time they were sharing a common mind. And he found it increasingly disturbing having someone else inside of his head, being privy to their thoughts, their feelings, and even their memories. The more it happened, the more he grew to dislike the intrusion. But he would do this thing one last time … for Nance.

Stephen returned with a tea tray.

The foursome made polite small talk as they sipped tea with milk and honey from delicate porcelain teacups. They talked about the theater, the upcoming Exposition, the situation between Russia and Japan, and the recent Inauguration of President Theodore Roosevelt.

When the tea was gone, Alexander rose from his chair.

"Shall we get started, Lizbeth?"

"Yes, Mr. Sheridan, I think we should. Nance, Dear, it is best if Mr. Sheridan and I do this alone. Father might not tell me what I need to know with others in the room."

"I understand perfectly, Dearest. Stephen and I will keep each other entertained."

* * *

Alexander and Lizbeth retired to the room at the back of the house that Alexander once used for consultations. He invited Lizbeth to sit down at the small wooden table in the center of the room. He drew the heavy curtains to darken the room, lit the long, white taper candle in the center of the table, and turned off the electric light that hung overhead.

Alexander sat across the table from Lizbeth.

"How long has it been since your father passed? I ask so that I know how far back I will have to go to find him."

"It will be thirteen years August next."

"Join hands with me now, Lizbeth, and while I prepare myself for trance, it is imperative that we have absolute silence."

Lizbeth nodded her head and the two joined hands across the table.

It had been a long time since he'd done this and he was a little nervous. He took a couple of deep breaths to relax himself.

He stared into the candle flame, projecting his consciousness deep into the light ... deeper ... deeper ... deeper ...

* * *

Lizbeth watched Alexander closely as he sank deeper and deeper into trance state. His breathing slowed, his expression grew blank, and slowly his eyes closed.

After about a minute, Alexander's eyes opened wide.

"Why have you summoned me, Daughter? Our business is through." It was Alexander's voice, of course, but most definitely her Father's cadence and inflection.

"What's the matter, Father? Are you not pleased to see me?"

"State your business quickly ... and allow me to get back to mine." Clearly it was also her Father's temperament.

"I need for you to tell me where you put the deed to the Alden Street mill."

"Why do you need to know this?"

"I mean to sell it, Father."

"Foolish woman, why should you sell it? It is a valuable asset that provides you considerable annuity and its worth grows with each passing year."

"The mill belongs to me now—to me and to Emma. Emma has no head for commerce and cares nothing about financial matters.

Indeed, she cares nothing for money at all. But I have other uses for the currency that mill could bring."

"What other uses?"

"That is no business of yours. Just tell me, where is the deed?"

"You always were an impetuous child, reckless and impulsive. I see that nothing has changed now that you are a woman of independent means."

For a few moments no one spoke. It was Lizbeth who broke the silence.

"Father! Answer my question!" Her impatience was forefront.

"You answer my question first, Daughter, and perhaps I will answer yours. Just remember, I could always tell when you were lying."

"Oh very well! My friend, Miss O'Neil, wishes to appear in a new stage play. She will, of course, have the starring role. It is a brilliant piece of theater, sophisticated and erudite. It is to open next spring in Boston ... and I intend to finance it."

"That harlot you dare parade around for all the world to see?" he roared. "You want to spend my hard-earned fortune on that ... *woman*? A wanton thing that nature abhors? This is blasphemy, Daughter! This is ..."

"Enough, Father! Enough! I do not seek your approval."

Silence followed.

Then, in a softer tone he continued, "She preys on you, Daughter. She preys on your loneliness ... your shame ... your guilt. Your sins are many and she uses that to her gain. This vile creature cares nothing for you. It is your ample purse she covets. She will divest you of your fortunes and leave you alone as she goes forth in search of another benefactor."

Lizbeth did not respond.

"What does your sister say about such foolishness?"

"You know Emma, Father. She has always been the weak one,

timid, set in her ways, afraid to take risks. She would not know a good investment from a handbag. She cowers at everything, such are her fears. She is even afraid of me sometimes, did you know that?"

"For good reason, her fear, do you not think? She knows all too well the kind of things you will do to get your way."

Lizbeth said nothing.

"And what does Emma think of your disgraceful alliance with this … *actress*? She must be sickened."

"Emma would also be sickened to know of your disgrace, Father. You remember, don't you? Those vile acts you committed against your own daughter … against me … late at night … under the cover of darkness. Or tell me, Father … does Emma already know? Did you, perhaps, visit your depravity upon her too? Is that why she's afraid of her own shadows?"

"Enough of this, Daughter! Those old scores between you and I have long been settled. My debts to you are paid."

"So they are, Father."

She paused.

"Emma and I have battles of our own now. When she musters any courage at all, she makes ultimatums. Now she threatens to move to New Bedford."

"Then I suggest that you heed her or you will have no one left."

"I will have Nance."

"*Pah!* Until the money runs out. I have seen the way she spends it. She fritters it away on foolishness. Fix things with Emma, Daughter, and set this succubus aside. Emma is your family. She is your blood."

He chuckled. "Though we both know how important family is to *you*."

His chuckle became a cackle.

"I tire of this, Father. You make sport of me. Just tell me. Where is the deed?"

"Very well, Daughter. The deed is in my strongbox."

"Emma and I found no strongbox among your belongings."

"That's because I hid it. Your Uncle John was always trying to get his hands on that property. As I said, it is worth a tidy sum."

"Where did you hide it?"

He cackles again, even louder this time.

"You have really undone yourself this time, Daughter."

"What is so funny now, Father?"

"My strongbox is still in the house on Second Street, hidden in the basement, under the stairs, behind a pair of loose bricks."

His laughter thunders now throughout the room.

Lizbeth's shoulders drooped.

"But you know the very spot already, don't you, Daughter? Because you once hid something there yourself, didn't you? Something very … *implicating.* In those days, Daughter, my reach was much longer than yours. All you had to do was reach in just a little bit farther and it would have been yours for the taking. Now it is too late. The bricks are sealed over by your own hand, and the house no longer belongs to you."

His laughter rolled on. When it died off it was replaced by anger.

"That was your home, Child. I gave you a home … you and Emma … I built an empire for you … and you threw it back in my face. You sold that house even before the worms had reduced me to bones."

"What you gave us, Father, were nightmares. How were we to continue living there after … ?" She paused, lowering her head and sighing heavily, "Maplecroft is our home now."

Lizbeth lifted her chin and looked her Father in the eyes, or rather, into Alexander's eyes.

"So it is lost to me then. You were toying with me this whole time. And I shall never be able to give my Nance what she wants."

"I'm afraid not, Daughter."

Another outburst of laughter.

"You always were a monster."

Silence.

"Are we through here? Can I go?"

"Yes Father, you can go now, back to wherever it is you go. Surely, it cannot be Heaven."

"Make amends with your sister, Child. Or trust me; you will die a lonely, old woman."

"Good-bye, Father. May you rest in peace."

* * *

Slowly, Alexander returned to himself.

His mouth was dry, his head was spinning, and the entire right side of his face throbbed with a dull pain. He rubbed his eyes.

"Are you ill, Mr. Sheridan?"

"No ... Lizbeth ... coming out of trance ... it just makes me ... a bit confused," he lied.

He lied because, for the first time ever, he had been *fully* conscious during the trance state. And he remembered everything.

* * *

On wobbly legs, Alexander escorted Lizbeth back to the parlor to join the others. As they entered the room they found Nance and Stephen laughing it up like two old friends.

"Lizbeth, my Dearest, did you get what you needed?"

"I got my answer, Nance, but I was not happy with what I learned."

"Does that mean ... ?"

"Yes, I am sorry to say it is true."

The two women were quiet for a moment.

Stephen leaned in close to Alexander and said softly, "Are you okay, Darling? You look a little pale."

"I'm fine, Pet." Then, faking a smile, he addressed the ladies again, "Would you care for more tea? And will you stay on for lunch?"

Nance said, "I'm afraid we cannot, Alexander. We must be on the midday train back to New York … Dear, you *do* look a little ashen. Perhaps it is *you* that should eat something."

"No … no … it's just my usual re-entry into the world of the living. It's nothing serious. It will pass."

Alexander was quite relieved to learn of their imminent departure.

"Well then, Lizbeth," Nance said., "… shall we take our leave and allow these fine, young gentlemen to get on with their day?"

"We shall."

The foursome walked into the foyer, through the door and down the stairs. The hansom was still parked out front.

"As ever, it was wonderful to see you again Birdie Gertie. And take care of yourself." At the last he glanced in Lizbeth's direction.

Nance gave Alexander a kiss on the cheek. Then she did the same to Stephen before he helped her up into the hansom. Alexander walked around to the other side of the carriage to assist Lizbeth while Nance and Stephen resumed their spirited banter.

Once situated comfortably inside the hansom Lizbeth said to Alexander, "Thank you, Mr. Sheridan. Though I am disappointed by what I have learned today, you have been most kind."

"It was a pleasure to meet you too, Miss Borden. Perhaps we'll meet again one day." As soon as the words left his mouth, he knew he'd betrayed himself.

For a moment, Lizbeth said nothing. Then she raised her chin and looked him straight in the eye. Her stare was ice cold.

"Perhaps we will, Mr. Sheridan. Perhaps we will."

As the carriage departed for the train station, Alexander said, "Stephen, Darling, come inside quickly. You're never going to believe this!"

Going Home
by Peter Saenz

Jarod is pretty nervous about returning home. He understands he shouldn't be. It's a place where he has fond memories and lots of childhood friends. Still, his youth back in Louisiana seems like a remote memory. It's almost as if it could've been lived by someone else completely. So much has happened to him in the years since he left home to first attend college in a faraway state, then on to become what he is now on the other side of the world.

Passing by the overgrown wildflowers outside the car window, Jarod's thoughts go back to his growing up years. Despite being very poor then, he was almost always happy. Not having money never really bothered him much. That was something only the other kids seemed to have had an issue with. For some reason his more affluent peers felt the need to constantly point out his hand me down clothes or failure to come up with the money for the latest toy everyone else seemed to possess. This is possibly where his ability to decipher people's intentions and levels of honesty began. Now being driven back home in a town car complete with hired driver seemed a little too ironic. He'd much rather have driven himself, but with his current circumstances, he knows better than to be behind the wheel of a car anymore. Driving himself contained the very real possibility of having another episode occur mid-transport. Waking up in a ditch somewhere bloodied and bruised is not something he relishes in reliving ever again. No, a driver is needed, plain and simple. To hell with what his detractors may think.

When the car finally pulls up to the motel Jarod notices his grandmother waiting for him beside one of the bungalow doorways. She has a huge smile on her face, which infects Jarod with one of his own. Seeing his grandmother always made Jarod the happiest. She smelt of baking cookies, one of her favorite pastimes. Closing his eyes Jarod could swear he smelt them still. When Jarod steps out of the car though, his grandmother is nowhere to be found. He continues smiling though, knowing she'll return later.

Jarod tells the driver he needs to check in and will be back in a moment. As he walks to the motel business office, Jarod feels a bit guilty that he isn't staying at his old home. Part of him wants to go back to the car to tell the driver to turn around and take him there now. The loss of his father is too great though. Being back in his old home knowing his father isn't there to greet him is too much for him right now. Besides, he never got along with his father's new wife. Better to keep things separate for now, lest his prediction of ugly family squabbling over material possessions come to him all the sooner.

A tired looking woman well beyond the onset of her twilight years comes into view. She is in the next room watching *Wheel of Fortune* on an old box television. The sound of the bell ringing once Jarod opens the front door grabs her attention. Like Pavlov's dog, she slowly gets up off of her plush loveseat and over to her walker. Shuffling the aluminum contraption towards him, Jarod has a faint image of the old woman eventually falling from it and breaking a hip. He keeps this forethought to himself.

Smacking her lips a few times, "Can I help you?" finally escapes her wrinkled mouth.

"I need two rooms please. Preferably beside one another." Jarod states.

As the woman slowly reaches for the keys, she eyes Jarod closely. "Funny accent you got there. You look familiar." she says. "You're not from around here, are ya?"

"I used to be." Jarod says shyly. "I'm Jarod Price. I'm Constance Price's grandson."

Throwing the keys on the table, the old woman says, "Oh. You're him. I heard about your father. Guess you're here for the funeral, eh?"

"Yes ma'am." Jarod answers with a tone of respect.

"Humph." The lady replies. "Heard you shacked up with a bunch of heathens in England somewhere doing witchcraft and God knows what else."

Jarod then notices the figure of an old man standing next to the senior woman. He is slightly older than her and slightly more crotchety. He stares at Jarod with bitter eyes. The ghoulish phantom emanates a feeling of unwelcome.

Looking back to the old woman, Jarod says, "No ma'am. I work for a group of people overseas who try to help solve cases normal police can't figure out."

"Satan stuff if you ask me.," the woman says. "I hope you're not staying here long. I'm a Christian woman and can't have people like you spending a lot of time here. And I don't accept no credit neither. Cash only."

Jarod looks back at the old man who has now crossed his arms, eyeing Jarod in disgust. Jarod takes out his wallet and removes several bills. Placing them on the counter, he says, "We'll only be here three days, four days max Mrs. Arnot. This should cover it with a little left over for your inconvenience."

The old woman eyes Jarod again, taking the money and placing it into her bra. Jarod takes the keys and returns to his driver, giving him the one tagged 8. The driver nods and begins taking out the luggage from the trunk of the car.

Jarod uses the key tagged 7 to open the door to his suite. Once inside he sees the figure of the old man from before. Mr. Arnot stares at him coldly, whispering the words *get out*. The apparition startles Jarod at first, confused as to why there would be someone already in his room. Before he can respond, Jarod's grandmother appears next to him. She takes in Mr. Arnot's full measure with a distain of her own. Her posture is a clear signal to anyone around that she is not to be trifled with. The two spirits have a duel of wits for a moment before Mr. Arnot finally submits, disappearing into the shadows.

"Thank you grandma." Jarod says. The smell of baking cookies overtakes him as his grandmother disappears from view too. Only in town a full ten minutes and Jarod can tell it's not going to be an easy trip.

After settling in, Jarod knocks on the door to bungalow 8 to tell his driver that he plans to take a walk and to call him if he needed anything. Jarod zips up the front of his light pullover hoodie as he takes the first few steps away from the motel. Jarod knows from experience that this time of year the warm fall day will quickly shift to a chilly evening at the turn of a dime.

More memories flood his mind as he walks the familiar streets, passing homes he previously had overnight sleepovers in. Another house brings back the memory of Halloween trick-or-treating, relishing in the discovery that the then owners gave out silver dollars instead of the usual sugary candy sweets. Still another home passed brought back the memory of a mean mixed breed dog that would bark at him viciously every time he'd pass on his way to and from school.

The feelings Jarod experiences on his walk surprise him in their potency. Things he hadn't thought on in decades now vividly return. Up the way he can see his childhood home. It's changed a little since the last time he was there. The once open carport is now closed off and there is a large boat stall standing where the backyard dog house used to sit. He knows his stepmother is inside, expecting him to knock on the door any minute. Jarod thinks on it a moment but he changes his mind against it. The drive was too long and his warm reminisces are much too nice to be spoiled by one of Pam's overly soap opera tinged scenes.

Instead, Jarod turns down another street allowing the smell of jasmine to guide his newly routed journey. The fragrant floral scent was everywhere in the town. On some especially humid summer days its intoxicating aroma can be more than one could bear. It was while picking jasmine blossoms on the roadside when it all started for Jarod. He was too preoccupied to notice the swerving car coming his way. Otis, the town drunk, had been drowning his sorrows at the local tavern like always. No one at the bar objected when they saw Otis stumble out the door and into his ramshackle Chevy pickup truck. One minute young Jarod is busy picking flowers to give to his grandmother and the next he is staring down at himself in a hospital bed.

Below him Jarod saw his lifeless, color void body being attended to by several doctors and nurses. The sight of so many tubes coming out of him was something he didn't care for. The bright floating doorway behind him beckoned for him to enter, and Jarod was tempted. He

177

could hear voices on the other side. Sweet voices he hadn't heard in years. Their calling was infectious. He was about to walk through to greet them when he noticed his grandmother and father arrive. They threw themselves on his body below with anguished pleas for him to wake up. Seeing them cry took Jarod out of his trance-like fog. He couldn't leave them. Not now. They needed him. A moment later Jarod opened his mortal eyes again. It would be several weeks before he would realize that he also awakened his new gift in the process.

Something snaps Jarod's attention. He notices it's that same tingling sensation he occasionally feels at the back of his neck when a potent spirit is near. The feeling crawls from his nape to the bottom of his spine. This alarms Jarod. His now years long experience in using his gift has trained him to know that a full body reaction only triggers when an especially dangerous spirit is approaching. Now free from his mental wanderings, Jarod looks around to see where his walk has led him. Panic hits when he realizes he's now standing in the middle of the town cemetery.

The sun is setting off in the distance and except for the sound of the buzzing cicadas, the cemetery is completely quiet. Even when he was little, the hometown cemetery gave him the creeps. Local stories were told about the many strange sightings the property held. He made sure when his grandmother took him there to place flowers on the family gravestones that they didn't linger. Little Jarod would tug on her arm to return to the car but his grandmother would tell him to stop his nonsense and that he was being silly. Now that he's older and gifted, Jarod knows all too well the hidden horrors cemeteries can bring.

Since awakening from his coma all those years ago, Jarod has become a beacon of sorts. Spirits are pulled to him. They can sense his gift. They draw themselves close, asking him to aid them in some way. In his investigations with the London Company Jarod has seen a lot of things. He now knows that there is more to the spirit world than just his sweet grandmother or lost loved ones trying to reconnect with their families. Some spirits evolve. Bitterness or anger in the mortal world, if allowed to grow and fester, can become dark if carried over to the other side. These restless spirts can become malevolent. Then there are the spirits who were never human to begin with. They covet the human soul and are often dangerous.

It's this dangerous type spirit that Jarod feels lurking nearby. Looking around, Jarod can see several ghost phantoms wandering listlessly. It's actually a pretty common sight for Jarod when he enters a graveyard actually. These spectral figures are usually harmless, unaware that they're even dead. Jarod has seen hundreds like them before. Their lives are a constant loop, drifting among the areas familiar to them with no awareness of anyone or anything around them. No, these figures aren't what's heightening Jarod's apprehension. It's something else. Something sinister.

That's when Jarod spots it. He doesn't know how he could've missed it before. Unlike the wispy transparent figures drifting to and fro, the spirit in question is something altogether different. It has a red aura about it that gives its hazy features a mixture of crimson and scarlet hues. It has the shape of a middle aged man with sharp angular facial lines. It wears old fashioned clothing and is smoking from a long cob pipe. Its bowler hat is tipped low on its brow, giving its face a dramatic spray of shadows. Its eyes, however, are stark white. It leans back on a tall ivy covered tombstone with one foot propped up for added relaxation. It takes in a long slow inhale from the smoking apparatus, savoring the effect it brings. It holds in the smoke for a full minute before letting the misty cloud drift out of it's nose and mouth. Slowly the spirit turns its head toward Jarod, allowing a Cheshire smile to creep upon its sadistic looking face.

More chills streak down Jarod's spine as the spirit silently pushes off from the grave marker. It stands fully on its two feet and positions its body toward Jarod while holding its maniacal grin. It is tall, somewhere just over 6 feet in height. Its pose, intimidating.

"I see you too," the spirit tells Jarod. Its voice is a twisted combination of sweet and ominous. It cackles softly. "Time to play."

The wind whips around Jarod as the spirit begins to walk slowly towards him. In previous occurrences when dark spirits challenged him, Jarod had a full team of peers on hand. Never go on an assignment alone. That was one of the central rules at the London Company. This wasn't one of his many assignments though. Jarod was on personal leave and now utterly alone. Though he desperately wishes otherwise, Jarod knows he doesn't have the luxury of a co-worker to aid him now. The thorough training he received at the Company for such instances though comes racing to his mind. He takes in a long deep breath and thinks on a circle of white light surrounding him. In the light he imagines safety, protection and love. He imagines nothing dark able to penetrate its barrier. The spirit stops in its tracks. Its grin stops with it.

"Witch trained you are," it spits out at Jarod.

"Why are you here?" Jarod barks at the spirit.

The spirit sneers at its opponent. It doesn't like being questioned. The pipe in its hand becomes a long switch. The spirit uses it to rap several tombstones nearby. Each thwack against the worn stone graves sends more chills down Jarod's body.

"I've always been here," the spirit hisses. "I've been here long before you were born."

"You're not welcome here." Jarod stares straight into the spirit's white eye sockets. "This is a sacred place. Leave. Now."

The spirit stops its slow advancement. "I've seen you here before boy," it says. "Small, scared, afraid." Cackling for a moment, the spirit pauses to look Jarod over. "I think you're still afraid now. Yes, you are." The spirit's grin becomes a serious stare. "You should be."

The spirit's aura triples in strength. This alarms Jarod but he knows he can't show the spirit any sign of weakness. Allowing the spirit to see fear will only strengthen it.

"I said you don't belong here," Jarod says plainly. "Leave. Go back to the darkness from where you came."

Jarod can sense his grandmother materialize beside him. Her presence boosts his confidence. He looks on at the spirit with a determined gaze. The spirit isn't impressed.

Laughing, the spirit boasts angrily, "Do you think I'm some common ghoul? Your protective phantoms can't hurt me boy. I go where I wish. I do what I will!"

The spirit howls, sending the local apparitions into a state of panic. They look around themselves with sudden concern, not knowing what to do. Some vanish from view while the remaining haunts cower in fear of the unknown. The crimson figure thwacks it's switch several more times against the grave markers. The remaining cemetery ghosts whine as if in pain. It laughs sinisterly at the effect it brings.

"Stop it!" Jarod barks. "You have no authority here. Go, now!"

The spirit eyes Jarod coldly. It sneers at him, taking in his full measure. By its expression Jarod can see that the spirit is enraged. It looks as if it is about to lunge at Jarod but stops at the appearance of several other figures. Materializing on either side of him and his grandmother, Jarod sees more relatives that have long since passed. Some spirits he doesn't recognize. They are dressed in clothing from eras of days long ago. Every spirit around him though carries the same feeling of family protection. Each new figure also eyes the vengeful spirit before them with disgust.

The spirit growls at the beings beside Jarod. The wind whips even harder, signaling its anger has risen. The familial phantoms stand their ground. Their determination is unwavering.

"Go back to the other side and don't come back. You're not welcome here."

The strict tone of Jarod's command is unmistakable. A few more Price Family spirits appear, reinforcing the strength of Jarod's words. The white imagined circle around Jarod visually manifests, bringing a light to the entire cemetery. The glare brings an obvious hurt to the spirit as it uses its arm to block the intensity.

Behind the malevolent being, a dark portal opens. Icy air escapes, chilling Jarod to the bone. Low moans can be heard within. Goosebumps flash across Jarod's skin as the cold dusk air changes its direction toward the open doorway.

The crimson spirit sees the doorway and screams out into the night. "No! You won't send me away! I am too strong!"

The Price Family ghosts walk forward in unison, challenging the spirit to get past them. The spirit howls, knowing it has nowhere to go. Now trapped, it uses its switch to rap the nearby tomb stones again. A few of Jarod's ghostly guardians flinch somewhat, but continue in their steady yet purposeful direction.

Curses fill the night air as the wind gets ever stronger. The force of the wind blows several tree branches and bushels of jasmine into the pitch black opening. It begins to pull the spirit towards the blackness as well. The spirit screams out desperately, clutching on to the tombstones nearby. In doing so it drops the switch it is holding. Jarod looks on as the switch is blown into the unearthly doorway. Seeing it disappear also, the spirit now strikes a look of fear. Its red hues turn to a bright fire engine red. When the Price Family spirits finally reach the red glowing demon, they push the evil off of its earthly anchor. It wails in a guttural cry as it stumbles backwards and onto the ground, just in front of the entrance to its purgatory.

The spirit claws at the ground in a vain attempt to stop its descent into the void. It tumbles backward even more. Soon its feet are in the doorway. It sinks its now claw looking appendages into the dirt, screaming at an intense pitch. An even stronger gust of wind appears, almost knocking Jarod off his feet. It billows past him at an incredible speed, hitting the spirit squarely. The deafening screams fall silent once it is knocked completely through the portal. Jarod uses his extrasensory gifts to sense any trace of the dark spirit. Nothing.

As the doorway closes, locking the tormenting spirit within it, Jarod feels a new presence appear beside him. Looking to his left he sees the spirit of his father. The figure emanates a feeling of protection and love. Somehow Jarod knows that it was his father's spirit that was responsible for the last bit of strength needed to banish the evil energy.

Jarod turns to embrace his lost father but his hands fall through his father's form. It's a rookie mistake. Jarod remembers that his father is now only a phantom of his old physical self. He'll never again be able to hold him like he once did before.

"Dad."

Jarod's father smiles at his son. Slowly the various Price Family spirits begin to vanish. Soon, the only figures left are that of Jarod's grandmother and father. The two of them hold hands and vanish as well. Jarod is then overtaken as the strong smell of jasmine in the air is replaced with the scent of freshly baked cookies. In his ear he hears his father's voice say '*I love you*'.

Jarod smiles and says out into the darkening sky, "I love you too dad."

Under the Dock
by M. Van London

T'was a cold and windy Wednesday night in Malibu, California, December 2007. I could feel the cooling breeze on my face through the open sliding glass doors that were ajar. My lover and I foolishly danced around the living room sipping on whiskey and snorting lines of cocaine off of his expensive glass coffee table. Things were always easy and careless at this time in my life and these bohemian affairs, that some might die to experience, were often thrown into my lap. I remember being obsessed with Carol King's album, *Tapestry*, and I played it on a loop because it seemed fitting, and it put me at ease when I had gone too heavy on the fantasy that I was living.

After what seemed like days of heavy partying and running through the streets of Los Angeles in search of whatever pleasures we could find, my lover finally passed out on the couch and I found myself alone. Wandering to the balcony I sat on a sun chair to watch the waning moon. I waved my cigarette back and forth in front of me making faces with the smoke and giggling at whatever this life was, or what it was supposed to be to everyone else. I suppose there were questions I had at the time about myself, what I wanted or what I wanted to live for if anything. The darkness always surrounded me. Darkness I myself had conjured for the sake of writing songs and spinning the tales of misfortune on myself to live through extreme examples. Someone once said to me, "You know if you keep socializing with weirdoes you're going to end up being a weirdo." I guess they were right but little did I know however, how weird this night would get for me.

To be honest, I cannot remember what spurred me to leave my moon bathing in the stars but something was calling me to the beach. I threw on some loose fitting blue jeans and canvas shoes and walked out the front door into the cold night. To my immediate right was a set of stairs which led from the front deck of the house to the ocean side. The house sat on stilts because it was on the waterfront, a sort of dock to keep it above water level. I began my decent down the wooden staircase; I remember having an overwhelming feeling of numbness roll through my entire body, the hairs on my neck standing to attention as I gulped back my swallow. I finally reached the last step, and then my right foot hit the sand. I looked over my shoulder. Under the dock, however, was pure blackness, and I knew the moment that I looked over at it that something was looking back.

The moon was lighting up the entire beach except the lonely void of darkness the dock created. My eyes fixed on that void; I walked clockwise around its shadows. The ocean was loud and waves were smashing behind me like a beautiful orchestra. It was at that moment that I saw the ominous shadows shift under the dock and the light from the moon made them undulate in my perception. My mind began to race as I murmured to myself, "What have I just seen?" I knew in my heart whatever it was, it mostly certainly was not human. It however did have an upright body, limbs, torso and a head.

I backed up, one tentative foot after another slowly until my feet were met by the water and the waves splashed on the back of my pants and soaked my shoes. Even in this horrifying moment I sensed the elements were with me, on my side and in some strange metaphysical way- working for me. I felt empowered by these rushing waters as I took a few steps forward I pointed directly into the blackness, "I see you... you ... will NOT frighten me." The shadow, the being that lingered in the dark seemed to taunt me as I walked closer. Something in my mind shifted and to my left I noticed a small pride of cats gathered by the edge of the water, watching me, watching them. I walked towards the cats and they scattered back down the beach leaving me alone again with this thing, face to face with this harbinger.

The air seemed to stand still as I had a faceoff with this spirit; whatever it was. It was brave, yet showed fear, it was human but not. The truth is, I was terrified but felt this immeasurable surge of courage rush through me. The ocean roared behind me and the comforting earth beneath me held me close. I stepped forward toward the blackness and I saw that it fell back further beneath the dock. As I gained momentum this spirit of darkness lost its power to terrify me.

Finally I stood on the edge of where the light and the darkness met and there was only a few feet from where the dark figure was and where I stood. I placed my hand in the darkness, waving my fingers, my eyes glaring while walking sideways to the stairs. Breaching the gap of light and dark, entering its world only by a little, maybe to show that I was brave, maybe it was my last stand approach, I'm still not sure.

It seemed to quietly hiss and coil up in the furthest corner of the dock as I ascended the creaking steps.

When I reached the very top of the stairs all the courage I had mustered dissipated and I ran into the house screaming, waking up my lover and telling him what I had experienced. He told me I was crazy and that I needed some rest, dismissing the entire experience to that of fatigue or an over active imagination. But I knew. I knew what had happened. I knew that whatever had visited me that night was real and what scared me the most was the idea that I would see it again.

Four days later I nearly died in a car accident. The driver took a wrong turn whilst I was in the passenger seat and by a stroke of luck I was not crushed by the sideswipe. I believe somehow that what visited me that night was the Harbinger of Death. Somehow I was lucky enough to sway him from taking me that evening or from that near fatal car wreck...I'm still not sure. One thing I can be sure of is this; there are things under the docks. There are things that linger in the darkness. They will try to lure you out of the light, for their own naughty thoughts.

The Returning
by David Berger

Normally, Sagerville, Oklahoma had an unhurried pace about it, but when people went missing, Detective Ross Reynolds came in early and worked late. So far, eight people had disappeared in a matter of weeks. Investigations had come up cold, so he wanted to talk to the families once more. He'd barely had a sip of his precinct coffee at 8 a.m. when an officer brought Gretta and sixteen-year-old Jackson Jenkins to his desk. Gretta's husband and Jackson's father, Andy, had disappeared, and they had been brought in for routine re-questioning.

"Sorry to bring you in so early, Gretta. We're trying to rule out suspects and get more background. What if anything can you tell me that might help our investigation?" He noticed her pull her sleeve over

189

her wrist. Jackson was slumped forward in his chair as if he had better places to be.

"Don't know what you want her to tell you." Jackson chimed in. "She didn't do nothing wrong."

"I didn't say she did, Jackson. Why don't you tell me about your father? Personality traits. Habits. Anything that might shed some light."

"What do you want to know?" Jackson barked. "He was a loser. I'm sure *you* probably know stuff."

"Jackson!"

"It's all right, Gretta. Okay, Jackson, if that's how you want to play it. You're right. I have domestic abuse reports from Social Services and arrest reports on your father. I also know that you've been to the hospital a few times for cracked ribs and a fractured arm. Can you tell me about that?"

Jackson pushed himself upright and wrapped his arms tightly around his chest. "My dad and I just had a few... disagreements. That's all."

Ross noticed the barrier to discovery. He needed to prod further.

"And how often were these disagreements?"

Tapping his foot, Jackson wouldn't make eye contact with Ross. A few moments passed, and Gretta nudged her son with her shoulder.

"Look, my dad's an overweight, unemployed day laborer. A trick knee keeps him outta work. He's frustrated. Sometimes, he... he lets off steam."

"Detective Reynolds, my husband isn't a bad man. Like my son said, he's had some trouble getting work, so he gets ornery. He's really not a bad man." She looked at the floor.

Jackson's eyes fell on his mother's wrist, and when she noticed, she tugged her sleeve.

"Everything okay, Gretta?"

Her slight smile and quick nod was more obvious than she thought. She tugged on the other sleeve.

"Gretta, something wrong with your wrist?"

Her empty eyes fell after a minute.

"It's nothing, Detective. Sometimes, if I come home from volunteering at the library, and sometimes dinner's a little late, well, sometimes Andy is a bit... disappointed. It's my fault."

Raising the cuff of her blouse sleeve, she revealed bruises. Some even looked fresh. Ross noticed a few lacerations that had started to heal, too. Jackson reached over and pulled her sleeve down. She hung her head.

Jackson looked at his mother, and his voice was barely above a choked whisper. "He tells her that 'no respectable woman is gonna wear T-shirts and shorts, showing off her body to every man she sees.' That library ain't got no air conditioning, so she brings shorts and T-shirts with her. Dad makes her wear long sleeves and pants, even in summer. If she forgets to change before she leaves, well... you see what happens."

"Gretta, how does he act afterwards?"

"He yells. He'll notice the bruises and say, 'you wouldn't be hit so much if you'd stay home and...'" She pressed her eyes shut and tears trickled down her face.

"And what?"

Gretta pulled a tissue from her purse and dabbed her eyes. "And... *entertain* him."

Ross saw that Jackson used his arms to hide his own tears. He could guess what *entertain* meant. He was going to change his line of questioning, but Gretta started muttering, looking away.

"Every time he touched me... it felt like acid had been poured on me. If I pulled away, he would... he would tie me to the bed. He had certain rights as a husband, he'd say. Once, Jackson came home early from school. What was it, a test day? Well, he came home and saw his father and me…"

Jackson leaned forward, his face flushed.

"He had her tied to the bed with his belt. I could hear him slapping her from the living room. I… I yelled at him to stop."

"What happened?" Ross fidgeted in his chair. These types of admissions always hit him hard.

"He took a pipe to my shin. That's what happened! 'That'll teach you to sneak up on your mother and me when we're making love,' he said."

Ross took the information down in shorthand. He'd elaborate later.

"Every time I had to walk past him," Jackson continued. "Every time I had to walk past him snoring away in his recliner so I could leave for school, my eyes… I wished I could set him on fire by looking at him."

He hated to ask, but Ross needed to know if there was anything else. Gretta sat without speaking, but then she looked over at Jackson and cradled his cheek in her hand.

"He always read from the Bible."

Gretta sounded as if she was about to recount something positive to diffuse the situation. The woman probably needed to hold onto something, a good memory to diminish the pain.

"Right before dinner, he'd read from the Bible. I remember the day, about six months ago, was it? Jackson asked him why we had to hear Bible verses right before dinner. That night, Andy had read from Proverbs 13:24…"

Ross knew the verse from his own upbringing. *Whoever spares the rod hates his son, but he who loves him is diligent to discipline him.*

"Jackson lost a tooth just for asking that question."

Gretta dabbed her eyes again. Ross wasn't sure how much more he needed to hear. He suggested they take a few minutes while he grabbed more coffee. He returned while they were arguing about the time Andy had burned a book of poetry she'd brought home from the library. Andy apparently wanted her to volunteer there so she'd be smarter, but he saw the book on the coffee table and, when he couldn't understand it—he had a fourth grade education, Gretta interjected— he tossed the book into the fireplace. She had to excuse herself to use the ladies' room.

"Jackson, I have a report here of a domestic disturbance last year. Neighbors say your father was yelling at you around midnight out on the lawn. Do you remember what that was about?"

"It was my birthday."

The detective said nothing. Jackson's face reddened, and he crossed his leg over his knee.

"My dad… he took me to Bridge Street to…"

Bridge Street was the seedier side of town where prostitutes plied their trade.

"He said, 'No kid of mine is having a lame ass party with pizza and pop.' He wanted to 'make me a man'."

"What happened, if I may ask?"

"He stayed in the room so he could 'bear witness,' he said. I couldn't do 'it.' I couldn't, you know, with him right there. When we left, he shouted the whole way home about what a faggot I was since I couldn't even screw a girl."

Other similar reports sat on Ross' desk. Each time was due to a domestic violence call from the neighbors who swore they could hear the belt strikes and broken glass from across the street with their windows closed. One of the last times Det. Reynolds had to pay a visit was when Dispatch interrupted dinner with his boyfriend so he could find Andy, drunk and half-clothed, waving a lawn rake and shouting what a waste his son Jackson was. He'd called his son "Jack Off Jenkins."

"Jackson, when was the last time you saw your father?"

Gretta returned. She seemed more put together, a little more at ease.

"Like I told the other officer, it was about two weeks ago. Dad had finished one of his rants about politics and the news when he announced he was going to Quik-Mart for some beer and smokes."

Det. Reynolds remembered questioning the owner and sole employee, a 23-year-old woman named Patty. All Patty could tell the officer was that Andy came in the store around 11 p.m., bought his beer and cigarettes, and left. During the interview, Det. Reynolds couldn't help but notice that Patty seemed a bit nervous, but when he asked her about it, she simply said that Andy Jenkins was not a nice man. In fact, he was one of the evils of the world. Sagerville wasn't a large town, Det. Reynolds had told her. Andy Jenkins would have to turn up somewhere. If she remembered anything, she should call him at the precinct.

"All right. Thank you both for coming in. I'll let you know if I have any more questions."

Gretta put her arm around Jackson as they left. Ross watched as the door closed after them, and in his gut, he didn't think they had anything to do with Andy's disappearance. He'd have to add his notes to the case file before the next interviews began.

Patty Simms said she couldn't go into the precinct for an interview since she had no one to work for her, so Det. Reynolds had always talked with her at the store. Interviews with witnesses or suspects were always conducted at his desk or in an interrogation room. She'd been the only one who knew Marcia Poore, rumored to have set stray cats and dogs on fire and then toast marshmallows over their fiery body and David Walsh, a teenage boy who had allegedly stolen money from his elderly neighbors. All Patty could tell Ross was that she'd seen them come into the store occasionally. Patty had grown up in

Sagerville, and she tended to know most people since Quik-Mart was the most central place to shop. Once a gas station and a convenience store, Quik-Mart went to being a small food store after other gas stations moved in nearby.

At noon, Bob Tillson, a janitor at St. Catherine's Elementary, found his way to Det. Reynolds' desk. Ross was finishing up some paperwork when he heard the man clear his throat.

"Oh, hey, Bob. Thanks for coming in. Have a seat."

Bob, a balding 55-year-old man with an arboreal stature, pale and thin, sat holding his wool cap.

"So, you knew Sam Parkins?"

Bob nodded. "Yep. We both started working at St. Cat's the same time. About three years ago."

"What do you know about him?"

"Well, not much. He lived alone. Liked to play cards. I think he was from Missouri." Bob lowered his voice. "Do you know what happened to him?"

Shaking his head, Ross told him that that what was they were trying to determine. He asked Bob to talk about what he knew as to why Sam was let go from St. Catherine's.

"Complaints from parents, I think. Some said that Sam was talking to their kids. About where they liked to play. Whether they liked to go fishing. Stuff like that. Enough parents complained that the school had to fire him. After that, all he ever wanted to do was sit in the park and feed the pigeons."

"The park across from the school?"

Bob nodded. "Yeah. He'd get his bag of Wonder bread from Quik-Mart and sit and feed pigeons. Kinda sad, actually."

Ross finished writing a sentence. "Bob, what can you tell me about seven-year-old Danny Wallace?"

195

Bob smiled. "He was a cute kid. He used to fly paper airplanes at recess."

"Witnesses said they saw Sam feeding the pigeons in the park the day that Danny disappeared. Teachers said they saw Danny waiting for his mother, but then Sam walked over and offered to walk him home. A few days later, Sam also went missing."

"Did... did you ever find Danny?" Bob's eyes watered.

Ross hesitated, and then he nodded. "He was found in the woods. An autopsy revealed... foul play." That was all Ross could reveal, but he hoped that Bob knew what he meant. Danny had been sexually assaulted and died of blunt force trauma to his head, probably while trying to flee. "Bob, did Sam ever talk about the students at St. Catherine's at all?

"Well... he did mention a few times how adorable the little ones were. I didn't think he meant anything by it. I mean, aren't little kids supposed to be called cute or adorable?"

"Did he ever say anything else?"

"He said they were so young." Then, Bob perked up a little, and his face went pallid. "He also said once they were soft. Young and soft. Oh, my God..." He put his head in his hands. "That sick bastard... I didn't even see it."

Ross handed Bob a tissue. "Do you know if Danny's parents ever suspected anything with Sam? Before Danny disappeared?"

Bob shook his head. "All I know is that Sam bought his bread at Quik-Mart before he'd sit in the park."

It was obvious that Bob had had no clue about Sam's proclivities. What Ross needed to understand was who would have known enough about Sam to do something to him. Danny's body was found pretty easily. Sam's DNA confirmed he was the one who had abducted the boy.

"Okay. Thanks, Bob." He shook his hand. "I'll let you know if I have any more questions."

Once Bob left, Ross leaned back in his chair, brushed his hair back with both hands, and exhaled sharply. Then, he called Alex. He knew talking to his boyfriend would make him feel more at ease, especially after the past few days.

Ross and Alex were watching TV later that evening when Alex asked if there were any leads on the disappearances. Ross said he hadn't found any, and that no one had found a trace of Andy Jenkins or the others. It was as if they had vanished. Alex commented that these people sounded like they were the darker parts of society, taken over by the evils of the world. Ross laughed, saying that was the second time someone had referred to them as evil. The first time was from Patty Simms. Alex couldn't disagree. Sagerville was a small town, and word traveled fast about who was doing what to whom or with whom. Ross knew that all too well, especially since he and Alex had had their share of trouble when Alex moved in. All because they were gay. After they lived in town for a while, people saw them as another couple and stopped getting in their business. The evening ended with a news report that the Green family was asking for any information about their daughter, Frannie, who had also disappeared recently. That was going to be his next interview the following day. It never got easier having those conversations.

"Mr. and Mrs. Green, thanks for coming in. Thank you, Allison, too."

Allison was Frannie's five-year-old foster sister.

"Mrs. Green, you said you were the first one to know Frannie was missing. What can you tell me?"

Mr. Green took his wife's hand, and his eyes bore all of his pain and anguish. Hers mirrored his.

"We had heard some rumors from neighbors that Frannie had

been, well, touching Allison. In places a sister shouldn't touch. The other kids had told this to their parents, and I just told them they were being horrible to say such things. Frannie loves her sister." She looked over at Allison who was playing with a doll.

"Mrs. Green, when did you know Frannie was missing?" He hated having to repeat himself, but he needed to get the information. With a minor present, this conversation could easily go south.

"Well, two Thursdays ago, I came back from the hairdresser and saw Allison playing with her doll. She looked like she'd been crying. When I asked what was wrong, she said Frannie hadn't come home yet from the store. She'd gone to Quik-Mart to get some candy, I think. By the time 8 p.m. came, I went by the store, but Patty said Frannie had come and gone. Before I walked in the house, I heard some of the neighbors' kids on the sidewalk talking that they heard that Frannie had… been inappropriate with Allison, and that she'd run away after what she'd done."

Det. Reynolds remembered the news interview right after the disappearance. Mr. Green said on camera that he and his family wanted their daughter back safely, and they believed her to be the victim of a cruel prank. Ross had a hunch Frannie had done exactly what she was accused of and had gone missing like the others. His gut instinct was rarely ever wrong.

In talking with Frannie's parents, Det. Reynolds noticed that the younger sister sat in the corner, playing with a Barbie doll, and said nothing. She didn't even look up. At one point, when he asked the parents if they had any reason at all to believe what the students had said, he noticed the girl raise her head and look away. That told him all he needed to know. Sagerville had become a town he didn't really know anymore, especially since the disappearances had shed light on behavior he had never considered in the town where he grew up. In a way, and he would never say this aloud, he was somewhat grateful that these individuals were no longer hurting innocent people. As a police officer, though, he had to remain impartial.

"Well, I have all I need for now. I'll be in touch if I have any news or if I have any more questions."

He knew his next call would have to be to Social Services. Maybe they could work with Allison and learn something. He wasn't that great talking with kids.

A few days later, the Millers came in to talk about their son Robby's disappearance. Since this case involved the Smiths, too, Det. Reynolds had them sit in the interrogation room, but on opposite ends of the table.

"Detective, what are you doing about what their son did to my daughter?"

"Mrs. Smith, let me assess the situation. Hear about what happened. Then, we can talk more about that. Katy, since you're the last person to see Robby, would you please tell us what happened? The whole truth."

Katy Smith pushed strands of her long blonde hair behind her ear, not quite making eye contact with Det. Reynolds, or anyone else for that matter. She pulled herself closer to the table, again pushing strands behind her ear.

"As you know, it was Sagerville High School's senior prom." Her voice had a softness that barely breached the tension. "Robby Miller and I were going together, and it was held in the town square. Near the gazebo. I'd wanted to go to my senior prom ever since freshman year. The school called it 'An Evening Under the Stars.' We danced while the school band played, and then... then Robby wanted to go for a walk by the lake."

"Katy, it's okay. Take your time." Mrs. Smith put her hand on Katy's arm.

She nodded at her mother. "We sat by the lake for a bit, and then Robby wanted to kiss me. His hand moved toward my chest, and I pushed it away. I thought that was it, but then he tried again. I moved his hand, but then things changed. The band had started to play a bit louder since the fireworks had started. Then, it happened."

"What happened, Katy?" Ross' heart sank.

She inhaled and exhaled deeply. "He forced himself on me. At first, I didn't know what he was doing, but before I could move, he had pinned me down on the grass and was pushing my dress up. The whole thing didn't last long. When he was done… when he was done, he fixed himself and ran off. I just sat there for a while, crying, but eventually I got the strength to walk home. I didn't say anything to anyone." She looked at her mother. "Not even my parents."

"What did you do the next day?"

"I went to school. On the way, I passed Patty Simms who was opening the Quik-Mart. I tried not to let her see I was crying, but she could tell something was wrong. She asked how the prom was, and I must have touched my wrist because she saw my bruise. I couldn't talk with her, so I went to school. I think that's when she called you, Detective."

"Mrs. Miller, you said you hadn't seen your son since when exactly?"

Agnes Miller had been sitting in her husband's embrace the entire time Katy told what happened. When she heard Ross address her, she snapped out of her reverie.

"I'm sorry, Detective. The last time I saw him was the morning after the prom. I saw him off to school, as usual, but he didn't come home afterward. I thought he'd been playing with his friends, but they hadn't seen him either."

"Katy, do you have any idea where Robby might have gone? A special place? Somewhere you two might have gone, maybe with friends?"

She shook her head. "No, Detective. We'd only recently started dating."

Hope seemed to have left Sagerville. The police had been following every lead, examining every place they could, but they could find no trace of the missing. Word now was that people feared to leave their homes, and paranoia blanketed the town. Neighbors were watching neighbors through barely parted blinds or curtains. Few if any people left their house at night. Det. Reynolds knew he and his department would have to find a clue soon. This town was far too small for such an occurrence to have gone unnoticed. This was why he wanted to question those connected a bit more. The stillness that permeated the town wasn't a natural one born of serenity and security. Fear had worked its magic, and it would take some careful sleuthing to break this spell.

Det. Reynolds' last interview a day later was with a street hustler named Angel. She'd known the last victim, Johnny Rand, pretty well, along with his pimp, Eagle.

Angel walked in wearing a leather miniskirt, red thigh boots, and a leather jacket over a T-shirt. Her hair had been teased up a bit, and her makeup had more coats than most houses. She was 17, but tried to pass off as if she were older. Cracking her gum didn't help her performance.

"Okay, Angel. Is that your real name?"

"Yeah, a real ironic twist, eh?" She checked her nails.

"So, you work on the south side of Sagerville, in the warehouse district. How long have you been doing that?"

"Just about a year." Her lack of interest made Ross edgy. He'd been dealing with so much loss lately, and this young woman had more attitude than he was comfortable with.

"What can you tell me about Johnny Rand and Eagle?"

"Johnny's a real sweet kid. He does his business, guys or gals, and he doesn't step on anyone's toes, you know? He's got class."

"And the night he vanished?"

"He'd met his usual customer, a salesman from Omaha. Eagle

thought he had potential, you know? He promised Johnny protection in exchange for being good in the business. With a face like Johnny's, he wouldn't have had a problem with getting customers." She popped her gum. "Eagle liked him for his body and his jawline. 'Chiseled,' Eagle called it."

"Did Eagle ever give Johnny any trouble?"

"Nah. He called him his 'streetwise Adonis.' We all kept wondering why Johnny'd want a street life when he could have been a real model. Anyways, word had been that Johnny was keeping more than his share and keeping some from Eagle."

"What did Johnny usually do when he met his customers?"

"He'd have the guy drive him to the Quik-Mart to pick up some condoms. Good old Patty would smile. You know, that nervous smile. She didn't like what we did, but she once told me that at least we used protection. She'd tried to convince Johnny and me to give up the street trade, but I told her the money was too good."

"You *know* we found Johnny and his customer, their throats cut, behind St. Catherine's. We tried to find Eagle to question him, but he's not been seen since Johnny was killed. You sure you didn't see anything that might help us out?"

"Detective, you're one of the few cops in town who gives a crap about us entrepreneurs. If I hear of something or see something, I'll let you know."

With so many disappearances, Det. Reynolds needed a new lead, but he didn't know where to look. An absence of evidence made any investigation almost impossible. On his way home, he stopped by the Quik-Mart for a gallon of milk and some Kit Kats, his one guilty pleasure. Alex had him eating pretty healthy stuff. He asked Patty if, by any chance, she had seen or heard anything about Johnny, and she grew silent. With a raised eyebrow, he leaned forward. Her cheeks turned pink when she told him that she had sold Johnny some condoms the night before, and she knew he was going off to do his business. Ross told her he knew about that. Her embarrassment about saying this aloud revealed an innocence that Ross found re-assuring. In a town where so much had gone wrong in the past few months, he was happy to know someone still seemed a bit more normal. He asked if she minded what Johnny did, and her reply was simply,

"He was doing what he needed to do to survive, I guess. I wish he hadn't, but he was at least trying to be responsible about it."

That struck Ross. Of all the people in town whose behavior wasn't being judged as harshly, unlike Andy Jenkins or Sam Parkins, Johnny was trying to keep himself fed and clothed, albeit through the auspices of a thug like Eagle. The detective was almost home when he radioed in a request for more information about Patty Simms. He needed to be sure he had covered everyone in town. The records officer said he would have the information in the morning. When he got home, Alex was reading in the living room. After he took off his holster and hat, Ross sidled up against Alex, leaning his head on his boyfriend's shoulder. No words needed to be spoken, and Alex went from reading silently to reading aloud. It didn't matter what the book was: Alex knew the sign that Ross needed some attention, and this way, they both got what they wanted.

When Det. Reynolds returned to his desk the next day, a printout awaited him that showed a pristine history of Patricia Simms. She'd been born and raised in Sagerville, had attended the local community college, and had an Associate's degree in literature. She became manager of the Quik-Mart not long after graduation, and she lived alone. Her parents, both deceased, died of natural causes, and she had no siblings. Her father had been a food distributor for Quik-Mart that might explain how Patty got her job, and her mother had been a seamstress in town. In fact, Det. Reynolds seemed to remember that his mother would take her dresses to a Sadie Simms. That possible lead turned out to be a dead end, and he was no closer to learning more about the disappearances.

The next day, Det. Reynolds was eating lunch at his desk when an officer at the next desk commented that her sub from the Sandwich King wasn't as good as the ones she used to get at Quik-Mart. Ross searched the Internet and found out that after Quik-Mart's owner died and a local supermarket chain bought out the company, some of the smaller distributors went out of business. New ownership, new distributors, and the Quik-Mart sandwich franchise fell apart. He also learned that some of the old food processing plants were on the outskirts of Sagerville.

The next evening, after he finished looking into some other cases, a radio call came in that he needed to go to the Dillard residence. Apparently, another man had vanished. Lynn Dillard was sitting with Det. Long when Ross arrived. According to the wife, her husband Harvey had gone out for a drive the night before, but he never returned. Ross asked where he might have gone, and she only said he might have gone to buy cigarettes or to visit his sister across town. Lynn had called Harvey's sister who told her she hadn't seen him in a week. Both detectives said they would see what they could find and let her know as soon as something turned up. Back at the precinct, Ross checked Harvey's cell phone records and credit card transactions, and he noticed one discrepancy, the Jackpot Casino on the Comanche reservation. The casino refused to answer his questions and denied him access to surveillance footage. Ross called a judge and said he had probable cause for foul play with regard to a missing person. The judge, after an affidavit had been filed, granted a warrant for the casino to relinquish the surveillance footage with the express instructions that it only be used to obtain information about Harvey Dillard. Sure enough, Mr. Dillard had been there, but he had been thrown out due to misappropriation of funds. Working with a man inside, he had defrauded the casino out of thousands of dollars. Apparently, Mrs. Dillard had no idea.

On the way home, Ross stopped by the Quik-Mart for a few things, and Patty asked if there was anything new about the disappearances. He told her he couldn't reveal anything about an ongoing investigation. She said she wished there something she could do to help, to which Ross replied that she should report anything abnormal, no matter what. She agreed she would.

The weekend passed, and Ross did some more digging into Mr. Dillard. While he didn't see anything about the gambling, he did notice that Mr. Dillard once worked for Quik-Mart as a meat distribution manager. Something triggered Ross' intuition, and he wanted to satisfy the hunch. He went back to talk to Patty, but all she could remember was that he used to work for the company. She said her father had been tight-lipped about corporate business. The reason she continued to work for the company was for the health benefits, otherwise she would leave town for better opportunities. With the recent upswing in disappearances, she didn't think Sagerville was the best place for her. *Too much evil going on*, she said.

There was that reference again, Ross thought. He needed to follow up on a few ideas.

Det. Reynolds found the dirt road two miles outside of town blocked by a weathered wooden sign that bore the words 'No Entry' in faded red paint. His headlights brought out the jarring color even more, and he walked around the barrier to find tire treads. He called Alex to let him know he'd be late, but the call went right to voicemail. *He's probably gone up to Quik-Mart*, he thought. He'd try to call him again later. He needed to check on this first. In the distance, he could see the silhouette of a massive building blackened against a starless sky with only the waning moon to show the contrast. With latex gloves, he slid the barricade out of the way and drove up the dirt road toward the abandoned packaging plant. A faint gray-yellow hue illuminated the interior of the building, coupled with a faint mechanical sound. Parking about fifty feet away, he drew his gun and moved toward the side of the building where a blue Mustang sat. A hand on the hood told him that whoever was inside had arrived not too long ago, and a cool wind brushed past him, making the hair on his arms bristle. The door to the warehouse hadn't closed entirely—whoever was inside probably hadn't expected anyone to find this place let alone go inside. A musty heat pushed its way out as he pulled open the door, and the smell of something acidic hit him hard. He had to fight back the urge to vomit.

Conveyer belts coated with dust and cobwebs lay dormant at one end of the plant, and the hum of fluorescent lights above gave the impression of a mechanical graveyard. The stench of a slaughterhouse pushed into his nostrils, the pungent smell of blood and engine oil clinging to the air. Det. Reynolds moved his head in all directions, unsure what he would find: a group of men hell-bent on ridding Sagerville of its darker element or a mad butcher hoping to bring divine justice to those who would defile the innocence of a small town. The farther he walked, the more erratic his heartbeat was, and it collided with the sound of machinery elsewhere in the building. The sound of scurrying feet made him spin around and aim his weapon, but all he could see were rats scampering for the dark corners. It was at this point he realized he should probably have called for backup, but he realized he'd left his radio in the car.

Rounding a corner, he heard a faint buzzing and realized that flies seemed drawn by the stench. Everything he saw and heard made his imagination run rampant with images of death, perhaps his own, but he had sworn an oath to serve and protect, and he would not betray that. Shadows emerged from beyond a metal door at the end of the walkway, and he could see the flies crawling all over the walls. His sleeve over his mouth wouldn't suppress his urge to vomit much longer. Breathing through his mouth was small comfort, especially when he thought of inhaling whatever contributed to the smell of decay. Each footstep closer made his skin tingle, and the flies buzzed in his ears, distracting him. He had to focus, though, since whoever was here could be lurking anywhere, and he didn't want to be taken off guard. By the time he reached the door, the noise he had heard earlier became louder, and he could hear the sound of a voice. A singular voice. Using his foot to open the door, he held his breath, hoping that the door's hinges wouldn't squeak, or if they did, the machine's rumbling would cover the sound. Along the left wall, half hidden in shadow was neatly folded clothing. On the wall above, written in blood was,

"The earth is full of evils, and the sea is full; diseases come by day to people, and by night, spontaneous, rushing, bringing mortals evil things in silence."

He didn't understand what that meant, but the words made his heart pound. The first pile of clothes was a pair of worn slacks and a plaid shirt. Sitting on top was a gold watch, its face cracked. With his free hand, he checked out the watch. On the back was engraved, "To Andy, Love Gretta." Ross felt a lump in this throat. The next pile, also neatly folded, was a woman's blouse and a pair of jeans. A piece of masking tape on the blouse had the initials "M. P."—Marcia Poore. *Dear Lord*, Det. Reynolds thought. The rest of the clothes were otherwise labeled with the initials of the others who'd vanished, but before he could check out all of them, a grinding noise made him turn his head, and he heard that voice again, a little louder. A woman's voice. Another sound came through as well, muffled—another person's voice. Now he wished he truly had called for backup. Past the end of the table was another room, the one where the machine sounds emanated, and he took a deep breath, ignoring the fetid smell. This door was wide open, and the sound of crunching was louder. He slid

207

across the floor, one foot at a time, gun ready, shaking his head as the flies buzzed around him. His foot stopped right before the opening, and he saw splatters of red liquid on the floor. Det. Reynolds' heart thumped harder, and he knew once he turned the corner, whatever was there he could never unsee.

Poking his head around the door, gun held up, he gasped. Thankfully, the machine noise covered it. To the left, a pile of limbs and body parts sat in a pool of blood. An industrial meat grinder was suspended above a large ceramic container. The outside of the container had what looked like ancient symbols, painted in blood. Metal stairs led up to a platform next to the grinder, and a woman could be seen dropping body parts into it. Ross couldn't hear all the words, but he was able to make out the name 'Harvey Dillard'. That was the last man to go missing.

Ross knew that if he tried to climb the stairs, he'd put himself in a precarious position, and he didn't know if she had any accomplices, so he waited until she descended the stairs before he stepped forward. First, he saw her bare feet, spotted with blood, and then he saw a green Greek-style tunic. Her hands hanging at her sides were so blood covered it looked as if she were wearing red gloves. She stepped off the stairs, and her face came into view. Her hair was tied back into a bun, and she had bloody splotches on her face, but he knew her.

"Gretta Jenkins," he muttered. "Holy shit."

She moved toward her right, at which point he heard the muffled voice even louder. He moved closer, ready to apprehend her and glanced to the left. Another pile of clothes. His eyes widened as he recognized the T-shirt and jeans. He lurched forward to where she had gone and saw her, blade in hand, about to cut down the naked man hanging by his wrists, duct tape over his mouth.

"Step away, Gretta! Drop the knife. Now!" He aimed the gun right at her.

She turned.

"Detective, you don't understand. This man is evil. Like the others. Like Andy. He must be returned."

"Drop the knife now. Last warning." His eyes met his boyfriend, Alex's.

Moving behind Alex, she cut the rope keeping his arms elevated, but then placed the blade at his throat.

"He must be returned. You don't understand the evil."

"Gretta. Does Jackson know that you've done this?"

Without realizing it, she had looked over at the table next to Ross. A quick scan revealed to him another set of clothes, neatly folded: a pair of worn jeans, a plaid shirt, and a book.

"But… why? What could he have possibly done to—"

"*For whatever the Father does, that the son does likewise.*" Her eyes didn't leave the pile of clothes.

Ross realized the book was Bible.

"John 5:19. You're taking that out of context, Gretta… What could Jackson have done?"

Gretta used Alex's body as a shield as she backed up toward the metal stairs leading to the grinder. Ross kept his gun on them, looking for an opening to shoot her, preferably to wound, but she was small enough to hide behind Alex. Weak and shaken, with a bloody knife at his throat, he moved with her backwards up the stairs. By the top of the stairs, she leaned against the lever to turn on the grinder, the sound vibrating the air. Stale flesh, blood, and bone from within mixed with the air, and Ross gagged, but his eyes never left Gretta and Alex.

"Before you do this, tell me why. I need to know why." By keeping her talking, Ross hoped to catch her off guard. "Why Alex?"

"You're a good man, Detective. You help people. You listened to us without judgment. This *man*, though," she pulled Alex's hair to expose his throat, "is evil. You defile yourself with him."

"What did he do?"

Gretta didn't answer right away. The grinder roared beneath them.

"He... he was unfaithful to you."

Ross crossed his brow.

"Gretta, who do you think he was he unfaithful with?"

"Last Friday morning. I was walking to the store, and I saw him in another man's embrace. Another man vied for his heart and won. You were nothing to him. Infidelity is an evil that must be ended." She paused. "I thought I had love once, but then he... well, you know what Andy became."

"How did you know about the others?"

"Small town gossip, Detective. Everyone's in everyone else's business."

"Why kill them? Why, Gretta?"

Again, she said nothing. She wouldn't look at him. He was getting to her, and if he could get the right shot, he would take it.

"I am not Gretta. Gretta was weak. Gretta enabled. Gretta was insecure."

Ross started to grasp what was happening. This woman was no mere sociopath, but, instead, had completely lost her grip on reality.

"Who are you then?"

Her eyes glazed a bit and looked off for a second. "Pandora." There was an odd lilt to her voice, almost melodic, when she said the name. "I made the mistake of freeing the evils of the world by opening the jar. Now, I have to put the evils back and seal the jar. Those people were evil. I have to atone for what I did. I have to right my wrong."

Ross shivered. *I'll do what I have to do to save him*, he thought. He lowered the gun toward Alex's body, slightly below his rib cage.

"What—What are you doing?"

"What does it look like, Gretta? You said it yourself. Alex is evil. He must pay. Don't worry. I'll take care of this."

210

Gretta gasped. "What? No, then you will be evil, too. It has to be me who does this!"

Ross saw Gretta's hand move away from Alex's neck a little, and before he could do or say anything, Alex backed his body against hers, and her hand opened. The knife clanged against the side of the machine, and Alex jumped away from her. Gretta lunged for the knife, but she fell forward into the grinder. Ross turned his head away as heard the blades tear her apart, her screams eventually silenced. Alex made his way to Ross who removed the duct tape and the rope from his hands. They descended the stairs, watching the bloody remnants of Patty fall into the earthenware jar.

Shaken, Alex needed help putting his clothes on, and Ross helped him to his car where he then called for more assistance at the scene. When the crime scene investigators arrived, Ross took Alex to the hospital to be checked out. Gretta's accusation stuck in Ross' mind, though, as they drove, and Alex looked over when they parked in the hospital parking lot.

"She was wrong, by the way. I haven't been unfaithful."

"Eh?" Ross came out of his confusion.

"Last Friday, while you were at work, my brother Scott came over to drop off a book he'd borrowed. If she saw anything, she would have seen me hug him before he left."

Ross caressed Alex's cheek.

"Come on, let's get you checked out."

While Alex was with the doctor, Ross reflected on the past few weeks. Gretta had not only been the victim of abuse, but she also had heard about more malevolence in the human spirit than she could probably handle, and it pushed her over the edge. Gretta had become a victim of her own mind.

The Gift

by Peter Saenz

Aaron is at his lowest. Lying in bed, he stares up at the ceiling and wishes death will come swiftly. Everything in his body aches. He tries to lift his hand to better position the blanket against him but his strength leaves him halfway through the process. He groans into the darkness as his hand lands back down at his side. 'Is this going to be the night?', he thinks. 'Is this going to be the night I'm finally through with the pain?' He's wondered this many times over, but by some horrid circumstance his body pushes through, forcing him to see another sunrise instead of the blissful feeling of nothingness he so desires.

Cancer is a bitch. Especially the type Aaron has. Not only are his vital organs shutting down, but he is beginning to hallucinate. Tired of the freezing cold hospital room with the icy medical drips and repetitive noised machines, Aaron called his lawyer and had him take the necessary actions to have him receive home hospice care. Better to die with the comforts of your own home than in a sterile room where you're only seen as a bed number. A hospice worker had initially been tasked to come every day to check in on him and to make sure the pain wasn't too unbearable. At this late stage though, they've moved up their visitations to once every few hours. Hearing the front door click shut, Aaron knows he will have a few more hours of peace and quiet before anyone else comes in to puff up his pillows, give him a bath, or provide him with another infuse of morphine.

Looking out the window, Aaron stares at the moon as a gray night cloud slowly drifts over it. Off in the distance he can hear a car horn and the sound of a group of friends laughing. The thought of people young, healthy, alive, and enjoying the world makes Aaron angry. He knows he will never have that again. At his prime, he was a gorgeous specimen. Beautiful, rich, popular... He was the envy of everyone who knew him. Now, at this end stage of his illness, his beauty has faded, his once vast wealth has depleted due to greedy relatives and mounting hospital costs, and he hasn't seen even the most faithful of his former friends in many months. In his mind Aaron knows that death would be a welcome escape from the remote horror that is now his life.

"But what if you could live again?"

The voice startles Aaron.

"Kent, is that you?"

Aaron shifts a bit, trying to look around the bedroom doorway for the burly blonde male nurse. He hears no answer and can sense no sign of anyone nearby. Aaron could have sworn he heard the hospice worker leave the house and drive away a few minutes ago, but if it wasn't Kent then who spoke just now?

"Hello?"

Aaron's voice falters as the effort to speak above a whisper stings his throat and sends waves of nausea into his head and stomach. 'Damn it.', he thinks. 'Not another hallucination.' The thought of dementia overtaking him in his last days frightens him as he remembers his grandmother's final days passionately talking to people who obviously weren't there.

"I'm no hallucination. You can have life again, if that's what you really desire. You just have to know how to make it happen."

Aaron can now tell the voice doesn't belong to Kent. It's too deep, too commanding. He looks around the room again.

"Where are you? Who are you?" Aaron's anger rises.

From the corner of the room a silhouette subtly moves into view. Aaron's eyes widen in shock. The stranger is tall, somewhere around seven feet in height. He has broad shoulders which dramatically frames the thin black cloak he is wearing. Aaron tries to see if he recognizes the face, but the room is too dark to properly make out his facial features. Even the stranger's eyes seem shrouded in shadow. Whoever it is, by his proportions alone the feelings Aaron has in the presence of the stranger are that of ominous and foreboding.

"I don't have any money," Aaron tells the shadow. "My thieving relatives came and took everything I had when I was still in hospital care. The only thing you'll find here is a penniless, dying, bitter queen filled with angst and regret."

The figure remains motionless, peering at Aaron from an aloof distance away.

"I'm not after money." The stranger's voice is matter of fact, but kind. "I merely would like to strike a deal."

Aaron stares at the dark figure.

"I'm almost dead!," Aaron screeches at the shape. "I have nothing!"

Pain stings like mini lightning bolts through Aaron's head at his exertion. He would retch if only there were anything in his stomach to release. The many tubes tied to his appendages are the only sustenance his body will currently allow to enter it. The pain makes his eyes water over. He mentally screams out for death to take him, lest he passes out from the pain.

"I don't offer you death." Aaron can barely make out the stranger's words over the pounding in his skull. "I offer you a return to what you once had. I offer you a body filled with strength and vitality. A body that will allow you to get revenge on the ones who've spurned you. That's what you've been dreaming of these past few months, isn't it? The chance to get back at your enemies? To make them feel the pain you feel now?"

The words resonate in Aaron's mind. Yes, that's exactly what he wanted. Screw the pain. Screw the sickness murdering him from within. He wants revenge against every fake asshole who's ever entered his life and told him that they loved him only to run away first chance they heard the word 'cancer'. That would show them. That would be a pleasure to experience instead of the torturous pain he constantly feels. 'Oh, if only it were true.', Aaron thinks. 'If only this weren't one of my morphine derived delusions.'

In a more stern tone the stranger says, "I told you, I'm no hallucination!"

Aaron looks sharply toward the dark figure. It's patience is being tried, and Aaron can sense it. Whoever he is, he's deadly serious. Aaron wonders just how far he's willing to take the proposal.

"So dark angel, you want to help me get my revenge?"

The shape laughs. "Yes, I do. It's my forte actually. It's what I do."

Aaron closes his eyes. He takes several deep breaths inward, trying to will the sharpest of his body pains to ease. 'Could it be? Does this midnight visitor really want to help me fulfill my dreams?'

"I told you I would."

Aaron opens his eyes.

"So you can read thoughts too?"

The dark shape laughs again.

"Let's just say, I deal in things where words aren't needed. I've heard your longing for some time now. I could feel your pain, your yearning to be free. That's why I'm here. Your spirit called, I answered. So here I am."

Aaron slowly lifts his hand above him. It is skeletal thin. He can almost see the bone beneath the now paper thin skin. Several purple veins and arteries slowly pulse between them.

"You can turn this back into what it once was?," Aaron asks.

"Why would you settle for a reversion?," the stranger asks. "Even at your peak you carried this sickness within you. Dormant, yes, but ever present waiting to come to the surface. Wouldn't you want something better? Stronger? Disease free? Something with power enough to make sure your enemies suffer at their last breath as you do now?"

The stranger's words entice Aaron. At present the only thing Aaron has to look forward to is a painful death. Death while knowing that the people he once loved had used him and are living off of what he once had. Anger fills him. What he wouldn't give to see them all get what's coming toward them. If only he could be there to see karma come and bite them all. 'Oh, that would be so wonderful…'

"But you can see that happen Aaron. Tell me you want this and we're halfway there."

Looking back at the shape, Aaron asks, "Halfway?"

"Yes," the stranger says in a lower tone. "There is still the matter of payment. In life, you can't get something for nothing you know." The stranger displays his palm to Aaron, silencing him before he can respond. It is pale white with long black fingers. "In this deal money serves no purpose, as I told you. There are…other forms of payment. Other things much more precious."

Confused, Aaron asks, "Money is all everyone ever wants from me. If you don't want my now missing money, what kind of payment are you looking for?"

The shadow gathers itself up and in a benevolent tone says, "Your soul!"

Flashbacks of campfire stories in his youth immediately flood Aaron's mind of dark folktales were the devil came upon dangerous criminals and killers in the dead of night, making unholy pacts to steal their souls.

The stranger cackles. "I steal nothing. All is given to me of free will."

A cold fear overtakes Aaron's body. All control of movement and voice leave him as he stares at the figure that is now slowly approaching the bed. Sweat breaks out on Aaron's forehead and a dull numbness fills his chest and appendages. The stranger openly laughs in response. Within moments the man's once shrouded face comes into the moonlight cascading through the window, allowing Aaron to view the face once hidden from him. Aaron gasps as his internal mantra of not wishing to see evil take shape manifests against his frantic wishes.

Standing before him is a misshapen visage, one too ghastly for timid constitutions. The man's eyes are bulbous and glow as if lighted behind a thin gauze. His nose is nonexistent. In its place is a gaping hole. Below it is an oversized mouth filled with jagged, stained teeth. A thin, long tongue falls from it. It's tip jerking left and right like a serpent with a mind of its own. The man's ears point upward and are flanked by two large horns. His skin is sickly white except around the eyes. There, the blackest of pits frame the large glowing orbs now staring down at Aaron.

Aaron clenches his eyes closed, afraid to look back upon the demon. More cackling can be heard. As before, Aaron's mind races back to his childhood. Instead of scary fireside stories though, this time his mind goes back to being a young child in Sunday school. He can distinctly remember Mrs. Von Tassel in her black high collared dress leering over her half-moon spectacles with a ruler in hand. The Devil laughs as he sees the image too.

"Sunday school lessons won't save you now boy! *DECIDE!*"

The memory continues in Aaron's mind, particularly of one lesson taught by the no nonsense schoolmarm. He can almost hear her high pitched voice say, "Once the Devil was a beautiful angel. The most beautiful of God's creations in fact, until he lost his way."

'Why-oh-why isn't that true?', Aaron thinks to himself. 'Why isn't he beautiful anymore? God, why can't he be beautiful now and not the nightmare that's looking back at me?'

Aaron can hear his heartbeat pounding loudly in his ears. He knows he can't keep his eyes closed forever. Gingerly Aaron opens them and looks back at the demented creature still standing over him. This time, though, when Aaron looks into its eyes he sees a slight change in the face's previous menace. In some indecipherable way, Aaron notices a softness come across the Devil's features.

"You were beautiful once." Aaron forces the words out as best he can as fearful tears begin to form in his eyes. His statement barely escapes his lips as a whisper.

The Devil takes a step back and regains his composure.

Several moments of silence fill the room before the creature responds. "Yes."

Gesturing towards his face, Aaron says, "Then this…?"

Slowly the Devil's facial features begin to shift and reform. Instead of the monstrous look from before, the Devil's face begins to resemble that of a human man. A very beautiful human man. He looks at Aaron, angered over his temporary moment of weakness.

"I take on the expectation of what others believe me to look like. To most people I'm a monster with scales, horns and a tail. To others I'm a simple black figure with an overpowering aura of terror. Sometimes I'm compelled to take the shape of a gangly old man with a pointed beard and cane."

Feeling some of his previous apprehension leave him, Aaron wipes his eyes. He forces saliva to form in his mouth to overtake the desert dryness that's recently settled there. He looks again at the fallen angel, surprised at the dramatic transformation. Gathering up his strength, he says in as close to a normal voice as he can manage, "Is this your true appearance then?"

The beautiful face says to Aaron, "No, not really. Even now I take on the appearance of what you yourself believe 'beauty' to be. If I were to show my true form to you, you would be incinerated within a second."

"So the story of man being made in God's image…"

"Ha!," the Devil laughs. "That is an entirely different tale I don't have the patience to go into."

"Then why…," Aaron begins to say.

"Power, my dear boy. I feed off of the subjection of humans. I feed on their sorrow, their anger, their fear. It's in their pure emotion directed towards me that I channel and gain strength!"

Searching the face of the now more approachable demon before him, Aaron asks, "Then if you can get that, what do you need with souls? With MY soul?"

Grinning seductively at Aaron, the Devil says, "Ah, but you've asked the right question then." The tall figure glides over to Aaron's bedside and sits. "Emotion sustains me but the ownership of souls is an exquisite delicacy! Imagine, if you will, the feeling of eating a leaf of lettuce. It is sufficient. Mildly satisfactory. Enough to squelch the hunger you feel for a short time. Now, dear Aaron, imagine the difference you feel when you eat a slice of the most succulent steak ever made. Imagine the scrumptious flavors cascading over your tongue, and warming your body with its heat. That is the difference that exists for me too. Sure I can live off one, but I CRAVE the other!"

"I understand.," Aaron states. He looks again at his frail body and knows that death can come at any time. He wonders if his soul is even worth anything in the state his condition is in. He looks up at the Devil and sees his new brilliant green eyes staring back at him.

In a soft, kind voice, the Devil says, "Your soul is beautiful. Even now. Believe me."

Aaron breathes deeply several times pondering what was just told to him. "If my soul isn't as tainted as my body is, that works in your favor, but what happens to me once my soul is removed? Do I cease to exist? Will I become a mindless spirit set to roam the land? Am I destined to burn in hellfire for all eternity?"

A slight grin appears on the Devil's face. "You watch too much television Aaron Davis. You had a Sunday school upbringing, yes?"

Aaron nods in agreement.

"Tell me then," the Devil continues, "what were you taught about what happens when you die?"

Pondering the question a moment, Aaron says, "Well, the good people go to heaven and the bad people go to hell."

The Devil rolls his eyes slightly and sighs. "Go on."

Perplexed by his reaction, Aaron says, "Supposedly the good people become angels and the bad people are tortured for eternity. I guess… that's it."

Looking on at Aaron, the Devil says, "Please forgive my sarcasm. I mean no disrespect to you specifically, but humans in general are grossly ignorant to what actually happens in the afterlife."

"I'm sorry." Aaron struggles to say. "I don't understand."

Sighing again, the Devil says, "While the Creator does have some morbid sense of love for all humans, he doesn't quite see them as anything other than what they are. I'm afraid to break it to you, but He would never allow a human to elevate themselves to the status of an angel. We're celestial beings, each carrying a specific purpose in the grand scheme of things. Humans, well, are not. Despite what you were taught, when people die, good or bad, their souls are reborn into new vessels. Those He deems worthy are reborn into lives of pleasure and esteem. Those who create strife or worse for others are placed into lives that fit their crimes."

"You're talking about reincarnation."

"Yes," the Devil answers. "Reincarnation, exactly."

Still confused, Aaron asks, "And for those persons who've promised you their souls? What of them?"

Wringing his hands, the Devil says, "Ah, that's where the fun twist comes into play." Pointing upward, the Devil continues, "He has control of unclaimed souls or those given to him. The souls that are willing given to me though are taken completely out of that equation."

"So I won't be reincarnated like everyone else?" The look of confusion on Aaron's face grows greater as the conversation continues.

"If that's what you really want," the Devil says, "I'm willing to eventually put you back into that cycle. It's a rather boring choice if you ask me, but even kings must eventually bow to the will of their people. Before you make that request though, I have other tasks for you to carry out. Tasks I think you might enjoy."

The Devil stands and walks over to the window. He motions towards it and it begins to shimmer. In the windowpane several moving objects begin to form. In it Aaron can see his former friends and relatives. A gnawing hatred begins to form in the pit of his stomach. Behind some of the figures he can see his former possessions. In others he sees some of the familiar faces are driving new cars and boats, some even playing videogames on overly large screened TVs. He knows these nouveau riche purchases were all bought with his stolen fortune. The fact that they are laughing and enjoying their newly augmented lives while he lays in his bed dying alone infuriates Aaron beyond measure.

"I can sense the hate you feel, Aaron." The voice is low and sympathetic. "You resent every one of these people, don't you?"

"You have no idea," Aaron responds.

Walking back to the bed, the Devil sits beside Aaron again. He gently takes Aaron's face in hand, locking eyes with him.

"What if," the Devil tells him, "I could give you the ability to take revenge against these people? What if you had a chance to give them exactly what's coming to them? Would you take that opportunity? Would you be willing to bring them swift justice as you've only imagined?"

Stunned, Aaron stutters, "You, you, want muh-muh me to…"

The Devil lets go of Aaron's face. He leans in and seductively whispers into Aaron's ear, "I want you to do what comes naturally. Do you think you can do that?"

Pulling back, the Devil looks down kindly at Aaron. "I told you that humans were meant to live within a constant reincarnated cycle." Gesturing back to the still animated windowpane, the Devil says, "HE has deemed these souls to live lives of tragedy. In their previous lives they've done terrible things. Things that you wouldn't believe. You are right to think that they are vile people. Do you think allowing them to live happily with what you see here is just? Especially considering what they've done, in not only this life, but in others?"

Looking back at the window, Aaron sees his enemies laughing and sipping on cocktails in posh night clubs. Coldly he says, "No."

The Devil takes Aaron's gaunt hand in his. "I also told you that we celestial beings all carry a specific purpose. Contrary to what you were taught, mine is not to incite blind chaos and evil. HE would never allow such disorder to happen on our level of being. I too have a purpose as well. One He bestowed to me long, long ago. Believe it or not, my assigned purpose is to ensure that the humans on Earth who are to be reborn into degraded lives meet their intended end justly. It is my duty to make sure none slip through His righteous cracks. With or without you, the people you see across the room there will all die horrible deaths. I or one of my other minions will see to that. In exchange for your soul, I give you the opportunity to mete out how that happens. To act as my own right hand, if you will."

The offer plays out in Aaron's head. His endorphin levels begin to rise at the thought of terrorizing his enemies, watching them die horrible deaths each.

Turning back to the Devil, Aaron says, "Say I take your offer. Say I murder these low lives. What then? After my mission is complete, what happens to me?"

The Devil leans in to Aaron's face until both of their noses touch.

"You become mine," the Devil says.

In Aaron's mind a series of mental flashes appear. In some he sees himself killing other people who are meant to die cruel deaths as the Devil watches. In others he sees himself traveling the world, exploring distant lands he's only seen in photographs and movies. In these places he sees himself enjoying free time there, waiting for his next assignment. And in other flashes he sees himself dressed scantily, being seduced by the Devil. He sees himself having passionate sex with him. The look of ecstasy on the alternate Aaron's face is euphoric. The emanating feelings he experiences cause his real life self's extremities to swell in response. The sound of the Devil's voice snaps him back to reality.

"So," the Devil asks, "what do you say?"

Aaron takes one last look at the IV drip connected to his arm.

He hears the sound of the machines humming softly around him. He looks at what's left of his body, feeling sickened at what it's become. Then he looks at the windowpane again, eyeing the bastards who ruined him living lives they don't deserve.

"I'll do it."

Still at his bedside, the Devil asks, "Are you sure?"

Looking back at the fallen angel, Aaron says, "Yes, I'm sure."

The Devil gently takes Aaron's hand and holds it palm side up. The pointer finger on the demon's other hand morphs and becomes a long, sharp claw. Quickly the Devil makes one quick slash at Aaron's hand. Instantly a cut appears. Leaving Aaron's now wounded hand in place the Devil slashes at his own hand until a bloodied wound appears there as well.

"So be it," the Devil says.

The Devil then places his wounded hand on top of Aaron's. Once their blood mingles together both of their bodies pulse. Both of their eyes roll back as their union in blood takes place. Waves of pleasure ripple across both of their beings. Aaron can feel his body growing stronger. The constant pain he's felt over the past months slowly ebbs away. Where once Aaron felt weak he now feels great amounts of strength. As his body doubles, then triples in size, the IV tubes fall from their insertions and onto the floor. Soon Aaron is surging with energy where once he had none. Now robust, he is consumed with the urge to stand on his own two legs again. Something he hasn't done on his own in quite some time. Sensing his need, the Devil releases his hold on Aaron and takes several steps away from the bed.

Aaron swings his legs over the edge, and before he knows what is happening, he is standing again. Still struggling with slight entropy, Aaron tries to balance himself in his new body. Once he does, he turns toward a mirror placed on the far wall. What he sees causes Aaron to gasp.

Looking back at him, Aaron sees a pale but very robust man looking back at him. The man is teaming with muscles. The size and amount make him feel a great sense of foreboding. The skin is very pale, almost white. Aaron sees that his once brown hair has now turned black. The medical gown worn by the man in the mirror is tight fitting. Aaron can then sense just how snug the garment is on him and rips it off with ease. Looking down at his body, Aaron can't believe what his body has become.

To the Devil he says, "This…this isn't me."

Smiling, the Devil says, "No, it's an improvement. This is your new base form. Can you see how much more powerful you've become?"

"Base form?," Aaron asks.

"Yes.," the Devil answers. "Your old body is much too recognizable to people. I require you to have a new one. One that can't be traced. Like me, you have the ability to change at will. As my servant, I will require you to gain access to many places and people. You will need to become a chameleon, blending in where needed. You will take the form of others, if need be, to accomplish my goals. Do you understand?"

Aaron looks at his new muscular arm. "So I can change? How?"

"Concentration." The tone of the Devil's voice is calm and patient. "Simply focus on what you wish to become and see it happen in your mind. Your body will react and make it happen. Try it."

In Aaron's mind he imagines what he used to look like, long before the cancer ravaged his body. He concentrates hard. He can feel his body changing. In an instant the change stops. Looking back into the wall mirror, Aaron sees his old self again.

"So I can change back into my old body after all?" Aaron sounds surprised.

The look on the Devil's face turns cold.

"Yes," he says, "but as I just told you, it is way too recognizable. If you insist on changing back to that form too often, I will be forced to block you access to it."

Aaron can see the darkness beginning to form on the Devil's face. A slight chill passes before him. Seeing that the Devil's patience is being tested, Aaron says, "You don't have to worry about that. If I really am going to kill those bastards for you, I just want to know that the last face they see before they die will be my face. My true face. I want them to see that it was me who got the last laugh in the end."

Aaron walks over to the Devil and caresses his face. He continues saying, "Once the last of them is dead, I'll say farewell to this body forever. After all, there's so many more I'd like to try out."

Aaron's body changes again, this time to a seductive redheaded woman, then to a powerful looking black man, then back to his new base form. The Devil smiles.

"You take to the shifting with ease."

Aaron smiles back. He takes one backwards step then lifts his hands before him. They individually become long savage looking claws. His smile turns more sinister.

"So boss," Aaron asks, "how do I do this?"

With seductiveness in his voice, the Devil says, "Oh, I really think I'm going to like working with you Aaron." He chuckles slightly. "Go then. Think on your first victim and your new body will do the rest."

Closing his eyes, Aaron thinks hard on his once best friend. The one who hurt him the most. Large black leathery wings suddenly erupt from his back and engulf his body completely. The now black cocooned form then begins to dissolve from view until it is no longer visible at all. All that is left is the now still room that housed the once decaying body of Aaron Davis. The Devil smiles, content on the success of his latest acquisition.

Looking out the window, the Devil grabs onto the thick frame and breathes in the night air deeply.

"Ah, but how many more of you are out there? How many more will I claim for my own?"

The Devil turns, looking at the reader of this story.

"You, perhaps?"

The demon laughs sinisterly as large black leathery wings erupt from his back and engulf his body, disappearing into the dark night air. The laughing continues and the world weeps.

Moving On
by David D. Warner

After an arduous, two-hour climb I arrived at my destination, high above the clouds at the craggy summit of the mountain. The ancient Inca had called this place Huayna Picchu—*the young mountain*—though it was ancient long before the Inca ever walked this Earth.

From this vantage, I gazed out over the vast Urubamba Valley. My legs—my whole body, in fact—shook uncontrollably from the exertion of the steep climb … and, truth told, some amount of anticipation at what I had returned to this place to do.

I sat down on the rocky ledge to slow my racing heart. My feet dangled over the edge.

Through the low-hung mists I could barely make out the

229

serpentine route of the Urubamba River as it sparkled in the late afternoon sunlight and wound through the rainforest, nearly 9,000 feet below me. The colors refracting off the distant peaks shimmered and changed subtly from one instant to the next as the sun sank lower in Western sky.

Every soul I had ever encountered who had hiked this mountain to its zenith described this panorama in flowery, poetic terms. More often than not they used emotion-draped adjectives the likes of *breathtaking*, *awe-inspiring*, or *majestic*. Words such as I, myself, had used the last time that I sat on this very precipice … with John at my side.

But this time … this time I felt nothing.

Of course, John was with me now too. The only difference this time was that I carried John in my backpack—in a 6" x 6" x 9" polyurethane container.

All that was left of him, anyway.

I took a deep breath and rubbed the sweat off my brow with the back of my hand. It wouldn't be long now before the sun sank behind those distant peaks and inky Darkness bubbled up and over the mountains and coursed, thick like molasses, to fill the valley below.

By now, however, I was quite at home in the Darkness.

I sat there, on my lofty perch, taking silent measure of time's gentle passing, as the first stars appeared above the Eastern rim … and I shivered slightly as I felt the Darkness draw nearer.

John had told me several times after our third and final trip to Peru that if Death chose to take him from this life before it chose me, he wanted his ashes spread at the summit of Huayna Picchu. Though initially, this wish was born out of humor—and his admiration that after two failed attempts I'd finally beaten my phobia of high places—it became something more symbolic once we'd returned home. Symbolic of new beginnings and new frontiers. He was quite serious about this. He wanted his earthly journey to end here, on this spot.

So I made this trip for John—mostly—but also, I made it for me—on what would have been our 25th anniversary.

I needed to have closure. I needed, at last, to let go of everything that had kept me trussed up for so long now.

After all, hadn't people been telling me for the better part of the last year that it was time for me to move on.

"John died," they'd say, "not you. He'd want you to live your life fully … he'd want you to move on …"

Move on.

I hadn't been able to move on. I needed more time alone with my grief.

Sometimes, I regretted the lie that I told to John that day on the mountain. I hadn't really conquered my fear at all. I had only sublimated it because I hadn't wanted to see the disappointment in John's eyes again if I failed to reach the top of this summit and stand beside him.

He'd been so proud of me that day, and I loved him for it all the more.

Truth told. I wasn't supposed to be up here at all. Before I set out this morning my hired Andean guide had warned me not to go off on my own. He also said that the trail back down to the lodge at Machu Picchu—the very same trail that had brought me up here today—was too dangerous to traverse after dark, especially this time of year when the rains came so regularly and the mossy rocks were slippery, even for seasoned hikers like me outfitted in sturdy hiking boots. Indeed, I had lost my footing more than once during my ascent. But I wanted—no I *needed*—to perform this task alone, and under cover of Darkness.

Yes, coming up here at this late hour was forbidden, but anyone who had ever visited this place before, as I had, knew that all it took was a couple of twenty dollar bills slipped discreetly into the palm of the gatehouse guard to gain admittance to the citadel after the site had closed its doors to the public. And after the masses had boarded their tourist buses and gone back down the mountain by way of the switchback road to their comfortable tourist hotels in the sleepy village below, I paid my tithe and entered the ruins.

The gate clicked loudly behind me as the guard keyed the lock.

Of course, I assured him in my less-than-fluent Spanish, that I would return promptly by 7:00 p.m. to be escorted out of the Lost City and back to my luxury room at the lodge.

I looked at my watch. It was nearly 7:00 p.m. now. Part of me was sorry for this lie too, and I hoped the guard would not get into too much trouble over this … but we do what we must.

This certainly wasn't the first rule I'd broken, or the first lie I'd had to tell to return here … with John. Smuggling human remains across international boundaries is frowned upon just about anywhere you go.

I'd been lucky that I hadn't been found out by some overzealous Customs inspector in Lima. Perhaps it was my unassuming smile that won her over. I'd certainly practiced that smile enough over the last few months to have confidence in its efficacy.

The biggest lie, of course, was the one I told practically every day now. The one where I told my mother and my sisters, John's family and our friends, my coworkers, the guy at the coffee shop, and the dry cleaner's daughter … the lie where I told these people that I was okay.

Okay?

Perhaps it wasn't a lie after all. I don't think I really know what that word means anymore.

No.

It was a lie. And I'd come up here to tell the truth … at least to myself. I knew very well the meaning of the word. And I wasn't okay.

I would never be okay again.

Okay?

232

John died a little over a year ago.

It was an unremarkable winter evening. John was riding his bicycle home from work, as he always did, when a distracted driver snuffed out his light. It was a young woman behind the wheel, with a cellphone stuck, like glue, to her head. At the height of rush hour, she veered over the solid white line into the bicycle lane—and into John.

At that very moment—10 blocks away—like a limb ripped cleanly from its socket, I felt John torn from this world and from my life. The pain was physical, and it pierced me body and soul. I fell to my knees where I stood and wailed inconsolably until the telephone began to ring with the terrible news.

That was the moment that the Darkness found its way in.

They told me that John had died instantly, that he hadn't suffered. But isn't that always what they tell those of us left behind? They think their lie a kindness. They think it gives us peace of mind.

It doesn't.

How could he *not* have suffered, being torn from me so abruptly, his other half? I had suffered surely and I was certain that he had too.

At first, I couldn't believe it was real. John could not be dead.

This was the kind of thing that happened to other people, not to us. Any minute he would walk through the front door, kick off his shoes, and tell me all about his day.

John couldn't be dead.

Only he was.

We had built a great life together, John and I. We were both 30 years old when we met and it was, believe it or not, love at first sight. Some clichés exist for a reason. After our first night together, we were inseparable. Several years later we celebrated our bond in a private ceremony on a moonlit beach—purely symbolic it was but it meant the world to us. And when it was finally legal, we went down to City

Hall and got married by a magistrate on the 18ᵗʰ anniversary of that fateful day that we met.

Even after two decades together, we were happy. And we had plans for our future. We would retire early, move to Southern California, and build our dream house in the desert. And we would travel the world together.

None of those things would happen now.

The first few weeks were the hardest. I couldn't eat. I couldn't sleep for more than a couple of hours at a stretch. I cried myself to sleep every night and cried again each morning when I woke up and realized that John's side of our bed was empty and cold. I went through life as if in a fog, not unlike the mists that filled the valley below me.

Eventually, even some of our closet friends—and John's family—stopped calling me to check in.

I wasn't the only one who'd lost John and yet, there I was, a living, breathing reminder of their loss … of their pain.

I spent most of my time quietly … alone.

Sometimes, in that quiet, I blamed myself for John's death. No, I wasn't the one driving that car. But wasn't it my job as his wedded spouse … his longtime companion, his lover … to keep him safe?

I had failed him miserably in that regard. I hadn't held up my end of that sacred bargain.

Mostly, I just sat alone in the dark, sipping my Scotch … or vodka … or gin … until I was too numb to feel much of anything at all.

It was then that I first began to notice the Darkness.

At first, I saw only the shadows. Darkened corners, spaces obscured from ambient light, the dark, dusty margins beneath furniture. These shadows seemed, somehow, darker than they had before … more fulsome somehow, as if there were substance and texture to their makeup.

I attributed it to the shorter days and low winter sun and put it out of my mind.

When spring came, however, with its longer days and more open windows, the shadows did not recede. In fact, they seemed longer, more pronounced and more nuanced. Often, when I walked into a room, I imagined I saw motion amidst the gloom. Fleeting movements out of the corner of my eye. And I sometimes imagined I heard faint scratching or skittering noises in the dead of night.

By mid-summer, I knew I was not imagining these things.

As the Darkness grew stronger, it also grew bolder. No longer were the shadows relegated to corners and liminal spaces. Rather, they came out into the open. They came out into the light, and they did not dissipate. Sometimes, they passed boldly in front of me. Sometimes, in addition to their scratchings and scrapings, I heard whispers.

I had never given much thought before to such things as hauntings or ghosts, but I knew right away that this was not John. If John had come back to me, he would never have come so surreptitiously. It was, plain and simple, not John's nature to be timid.

This was something else—something decidedly *not John*.

Yet I wasn't made the least bit afraid by these sights and sounds. In fact, I didn't really feel much of anything at all, and hadn't in months. Of course, I told no one about any of this lest they think I had lost my mind completely. But I began to read about such dark hauntings in books I checked out of the neighborhood branch of the public library and on some of the more ... *speculative* ... pages of the Internet.

It seemed it was not uncommon, according to these sources, for people in the throes of grief to be visited by such dark presences. Some went so far as to theorize that these dark *entities* might be, in fact, grief itself. Grief so deep that it was made manifest by the sheer force of its gravity. Consciousness, it is said, is the underlying force of all matter, in the quantum soup from which all things emerged. Perhaps these

Dark things existed because I had willed them into being. Would then, they not be in some sense, my children? Children born from my love for John?

How, then, could I ever fear them?

As the months went by, I spent less and less time out in the world and more of my time at home. And as the months passed, the Darkness became less of a mystery and more of a balm. Sometimes, in the dead of night, I would talk to the Darkness, tell it the stories of my life with John. And now, when I cried myself to sleep, the Darkness wrapped itself around me like a blanket, much the same way that John had once done. It would whisper soothing words in my ear and assure me that it was never going to leave my side and it would be my succor until that day I was reunited with John once more.

During the daytime hours, I played my part well. I went through all of the socially accepted motions—I went back to work, I said the right words, I did the right things. I nodded at the appropriate times in conversation. And I endured without protest the worried looks of family and friends and coworkers, as well as their never-ending encouragements to put the past behind me and move on with my life. I convinced everyone that I was, indeed, nearly ready to do just that. I'd become the master of this, my greatest lie.

But at the end of the day, I'd return to my empty house and give myself up, wholly and completely, to the Darkness that had become my sole companion.

The one-year anniversary of John's death came and went quietly. I spent the day making arrangements to return to this mountaintop and to honor John's final wishes.

And now, here I sat, my reverie at an end.

I looked up at the darkened sky. The sun had completely set now and I looked at my watch again—the watch that John had given me for my 50th birthday.

It was time.

I stood up and brushed the dust from my clothing. I reached for my backpack, unzipped it, and took out the 6" x 6" x 9" polyurethane container that contained the ashes of my dead husband and lover. I placed the empty pack on the ground beside me.

Pop! I broke the seal that held the lid in place.

I just stood there, stock still for a moment, steadying myself. Then I spoke silently to John.

"It's time now, my Love. It's time to do what we came here to do."

I held the container in front of me and slowly tipped John's ashes over the side of the precipice.

The Darkness was so thick now that I couldn't see much past my nose, but I imagined the winds carrying John's ashes outward and over the valley. I imagined John smiling up at me from the dark abyss beneath me as tears flowed unheeded down my cheeks.

When the container was empty, I dropped it on the ground next to my backpack.

I turned once again toward the precipice and spread my arms wide, breathing in the cool night air and feeling the cool breeze caress my wet face.

Once more I spoke to John.

"Good-bye, my Love. You are free now. Free from anything that can hurt you. And now it's time for me to move on too."

I smile, then, for real this time.

I bent my knees and jumped …

… and as I plummeted to the earth, the Darkness below opened its arms to welcome me home.

Worst Day Ever
by Patrick Raith

"Um, this isn't right."

God fucking damn it. Rebecca closed her eyes and quietly took a deep breath. *Of course it's not right, you mean, nasty bitch*, she thought, *it's never right.* Opening her eyes and forcing her frown into her most convincing smile, when all the muscles wanted to grimace in defiance instead, she turned back around to the handoff where she had placed the steaming mug down for the unruly, dissatisfied customer.

Jesus Christ, she thought, *it's not even noon yet.* If she could just make it for a couple more hours, she would be out of there.

"I'm sorry Phoebe," she lied, a little bubblier than she had wanted to. "What's the matter?"

Two things floated into her mind before she blinked the glaze away from her eyes as she subconsciously began to look beyond the awful woman standing before her. The first thing was the thought of, *I wonder what's more pretentious: this meticulously ordered chai latte or this annoying, stuck up, entitled fucking bitch?* The second thing was her imaging the moment her patience finally exhausted and the result being the latte tossed right out of the mug and into Phoebe's face, followed shortly after with the mug being smashed down on her head.

Phoebe, at five foot five, still managed to somehow loom over the counter top where her mug sat, untouched, as though she were a furious titan rather than the annoying, irrelevant little pest was. From her short, asymmetrically cut, chestnut hair, down her navy blue pants suit, to her Italian leather shoes, everything about her screamed *I'm better than you.*

Everyone in the shop thought she was utterly revolting, and, for whatever reason, Rebecca always, **always**, seemed to be the one to have to deal with her.

Leaning across the counter, with one hand on her hip and the other tapping perfectly manicured, French tipped nails over the wooden surface, she stood, eyes widely questioning and in silent demand of a response. "Uh, you didn't make this right," she snarled.

Rebecca continued to smile as opposed to the alternative, which would be to punch the woman in her loud, obnoxious mouth. "But you haven't touched it yet," she replied cheerfully. Phoebe's eyes narrowed at her response. *God I hate you so much.*

"There's not enough chai in it," Phoebe argued before she snatched the mug up, narrowly avoiding the dribble of liquid and foam sailing off of the surface of the drink and onto her suit jacket as she made an obnoxious scene out of taking an equally obnoxious, loud sip of the liquid. "See?" she spat, her moist, spicy breath spraying Rebecca's face. "I can barely taste it. There's supposed to be *six* pumps of the concentrate in it, not *four*." She loudly put the mug back down on the counter, spilling about a half inch of the contents in front of her. "I *know* what four pumps tastes like."

"I actually put seven pumps into it this morning," Rebecca smiled, her eyes slightly narrowing in spite of the very fake look she was fronting. "I know how you like to order it stronger than everyone else does, but here," she reached over and picked up the now partially wet mug, "I'll just go and add a bit more." She turned back to Phoebe and spared a glance at her coworker Terry, grinning from ear to ear at her from where he stood at the register waiting for a pair of twenty-something girls to make up their minds about what they wanted to order. Rebecca briefly curled her front lip back mouth and widened her eyes in a goofy face at him before she pumped several blasts of concentrate into mug.

Phoebe reached her hand into her pocket shortly before pulling out her cell phone. "Put more milk back into it too," she ordered before glancing down at her touch scream.

"Oh, yessa massa," Rebecca muttered under her breath before grabbing a wooden stir stick on her way back to the handoff.

After setting the mug down in front of the she bitch, she placed the stick into the liquid before Phoebe could reply, "Make sure you stir it," and began to stir the newly added concentrate into the drink as Phoebe continued to order her about like a servant, all the while praying that the foam had not dissipated during the entirety of the woman's chastising her.

"Here you go," Rebecca replied while Phoebe completely ignored her and began talking erratically into her phone at some other poor soul.

"Hey Becks," Terry called to her from register. Glancing over to her coworker, Rebecca nodded back before turning to back Phoebe.

"You have a awesome day, Phoebe," she said, her words entirely fake and dripping with contempt, knowing full well the woman would no longer be acknowledging her existence any longer that day. Not even looking up from while talking on her cell phone, Phoebe picked up the mug before turning to walk away. "Bitch," Rebecca muttered after she rolled her eyes at the departing woman.

Turning away from the now empty counter, still feeling a bit frazzled despite Phoebe's absence, she walked over to the registers at the front. "Hey," she began, "what's up?"

Terry smiled before he reached into his apron. "Your tips, m'lady," he replied, pulling out an envelope. Terry was very cute, there was no question about that. Though not nearly as short as her best friend David's hair, it was the exact same shade of dark brown, and his eyes were the lightest blue of anyone else she had ever seen.

Rebecca recalled last year, during the first two weeks of starting work, their boss had assigned Terry to teach her what their job consisted of. Catching on fast, she had only needed a week before she had absorbed the basic knowledge of what, as a barista, she needed to know. Terry, however, was always close by and had continued to remain in said proximity in spite of that.

Soon after, nearly a month to the day, Terry had asked her out and everything "got awkward" for all of five minutes. Though she really liked him, Rebecca was not interested in anything beyond friendship. It had been nearly two years since her messy departure from a four year relationship, and that, coupled with a crush she still harbored for her best friend, had dulled her senses in terms of being on the lookout for guys to date. Thankfully, Terry had been completely mature and understanding regarding her decision, and she felt grateful that he was more than happy to accept the alternative of friendship.

Smiling, Rebecca reached for and took the envelope from him. "Thanks," she replied as she folded the money filled paper in half before placing it inside her apron pocket. "That's my cell bill and lunch after this hellshift." Terry nodded.

"I hear ya. What's for lunch," he asked, "because Indian sounds good to me." Rebecca nodded in agreement, and was about to ask if he wanted to head to the other side of the park for lunch with her after they were finished with work, since she knew he would stick around for an hour after clocking out for her to finish, when an arm slid around her neck to dangle from her shoulder.

"*I'm* always up for sushi," came the voice of their coworker Cariba from behind Rebecca.

Terry frowned. "I bet you are," he jeered. Cariba stuck her tongue out before tossing a pen at him, frowning when he managed to catch it and place it into his pocket after. Rebecca smiled, always amused at the sibling-like banter between her two coworkers.

Whereas Terry's brief, innocent advances had been slightly awkward, Cariba's had been borderline obscene and on the verge of sexual harassment. A complete extrovert, and notoriously open about her sexuality, there were not many lines she was afraid of crossing. When she had noticed that flirting was not working, Cariba had flat out had asked her if she was into girls like she was, guys, or both.

Rebecca had nearly spit out the coffee she had been drinking at the time, coughing and sputtering instead of answering, her reaction much to the delight of Cariba who loved getting a rise out of others. After telling yet another coworker that she was not interested, and thank you, Rebecca had been relieved after Cariba had only shrugged and said it was no problem. The flirting from her, however, had not ended.

"So, how 'bout it kids?" Cariba asked, lifting her arm and detaching from Rebecca's shoulder. "You know, my shift ends the same time yours does Rebecca."

"We had sushi last time," Rebecca reminded her. "And Terry and I feel like Indian."

243

Cariba grimaced. "Oh gross," she pouted. "I hate Indian food."

Terry crossed his arms as Rebecca chuckled. "Well too damn bad, that's what we're having, so there." Cariba swung her head back overdramatic, with a tortured expression on her face before planting her forehead on Rebecca's shoulder.

"But it suuuuucks!" she whined. Running her hand through Cariba's fire engine red, shoulder length, pixie cut hair, Rebecca smiled when she whimpered in response.

"But you like spicy food," Rebecca reminded her. Cariba turned her face towards Terry, the side of it now on Rebecca's shoulder. "Come on," Rebecca gently patted her head, "come with us. There's bound to be something you'll like."

"Oh fiiiiine," Cariba lifted her head from Rebecca's shoulder and crossed her arms. "Only because you're so cu—" The sound of something slamming into the front glass door startled the three of them, Cariba shrieking in surprise during the interruption. Rebecca looked past Terry, who spun around in the direction of the lobby and front entrance. Two people, a man and woman, appeared to be locked in each other's arms, struggling against one another.

"What the hell?" Terry whirled back around and rushed past his two coworkers. Rebecca stared along with the rest of the people in the coffee shop at the struggle happening outside the door. The woman's back again slammed up against the door, a gasp came in reply from the two previous customers Terry had just helped who were sitting near the door. Now on the other side of and nearly halfway past the bar, he made his way toward the front of the lobby.

"Terry!" Rebecca cried out. Terry stopped and turned to look back at his coworker who shook her head.

"Yeah, they're fighting or something," Rebecca turned noticing Cariba had found the cordless store phone and was talking into it now, presumably to the police. "No, I don't know who they are, some guy and some chick. *No,* I said they're fighting," she told the person on the other line. "Yeah, well the guy looks freakin' nuts." She looked over at Terry who had started to turn towards the door. "Yeah," she began as she snapped her finger before pointing at him, "Terry, don't even think about it—oh hey, there's a cop."

Rebecca and Terry each shot glances back to the chaotic scene happening on their work's doorstep. From several feet away, a police officer hurriedly made his way towards the pair, yelling protests and ordering them to stop. Rebecca walked to the edge of the counter, Cariba following while Terry resumed his approach toward the lobby.

Rebecca felt her blood run cold as she watched the man's head snap backward, his eyes wide with the crazed expression plastered across his face. As his head reeled back, she gasped as he opened his mouth almost impossibly wide before lunging for the space between the woman's lower neck and shoulder. In reply was the shrill, pained scream of the now injured woman, joined by several cries from the patrons in the lobby.

"He's fucking biting her!" Cariba screamed into the phone, startling Rebecca out of her fear-induced paralysis. "Oh, fuck this!" Cariba tossed the phone aside to the registers. "Terry!" she called to their coworker before she vaulted over the counter. Go!" she ordered while running past him and toward the doors.

"Everybody stay where you are!" Terry ordered as he hurried after her. Rebecca tried to move, but stood frozen, so afraid even her mind was blank. All she could do was stare as the man savaged the woman's neck, blood spraying from the grizzly wound and onto the glass of the door as the cop, who had reached the pair and joined in the struggle, managed to yank the man's gnawing mouth away from her. *Oh my god,* she was finally able to think to herself, *what the hell is happening?*

Cariba reached the door just as the man snarled and decided to let go of the woman and turned his attention to the officer instead. The woman fell forward and to her knees, thankfully, and Cariba gave a brief prayer of thanks in the moment as she turned the doorknob and swung open the door. "Terry!" she screamed over her shoulder. "Help me!"

Terry closed the gap between the both of them and followed Cariba beyond the open doorway, each taking a hold of one of the woman's arms and yanking her into the store while she tried to help by back peddling her wobbly, uncoordinated feet. Cariba held the injured woman in her arms as Terry stood up. Several people in the lobby began to push and shove past each other as they fled from the open doorway, carefully avoiding struggling pair in front of the shop.

"What are you doing?" Cariba demanded as he rushed back to the open door. Outside, the officer gripped the crazed man's arms and was able to toss him to the side. Terry held the door open and waved the cop towards him.

"Hey! Get inside!" he screamed to the officer who noticed and immediately made a run for the opening, grabbing the radio at his shoulder and screaming into it along the way. From behind, the man immediately leapt to his feet and screamed before he began sprinting after the officer. Terry, holding the door, swung to the side as the officer rushed in past him in, the howling man nearly on his heels.

"Terry!" Rebecca screamed as the man closed in on the open portal. Gripping the door with one hand, Terry pivoted back into the doorway and reached for the doorframe with his other. Cariba and Rebecca both screamed as the man snarled and reached for their coworker and was met with a devastating kick square to his chest from Terry's foot instead. The blow sent the crazed man sailing backward, head over feet to the ground.

"Get the fuck inside!" the officer roared as he reached for the door and pushed it closed.

The man sat up, not appearing remotely phased by the attack, and snarled before launching himself from the ground to the door. Terry braced up against the officer and the door as the blow from outside knocked him back. "Help me!" the officer screamed. Terry pressed his hands against the door along with the officer before he remembered the store keys inside his apron pocket. Reaching inside with one hand while bracing the shuddering door with his other, he fumbled through the contents of his pocket before pulling out and dropping the keys. "Shit!" he cried as they fell to the floor at his feet. Another loud slam echoed throughout the lobby as the door slammed open several inches before the officer managed to push it closed again. "Shit!" Terry screamed again as he returned his other hand to the door. Looking over his shoulder down at Cariba who had torn off her apron and was pressing it in a bundle against the injured woman's neck in an effort to halt the bleeding, he turned back towards the register counter. "Rebecca!" he screamed. "Help! Get the keys!"

Rebecca felt the jolt of adrenaline to her body, now screaming to life, and climbed over the counter top between the two registers. The door shuddered again as she hurried toward the door.

"Jesus Christ," the officer cried. "What is he on!"

Rushing past Cariba and the woman, Rebecca dropped down to a crouch and scooped up the keys, before rising up to the door and the two men braced against it. Pressing a hand up against the door in a feeble attempt to aid them, she brought her other hand in possession of the keys towards the lock. Her hand shaking, Rebecca was about to press the small bit of metal into the key hole when she shrieked and missed, stabbing the key into the door instead when the man outside had snarled and pressed his face up against the glass in front of her, his mouth spraying several droplets of bloody spittle against the glass as he shrieked at her.

"Fucking lock it!" Terry screamed. Rebecca closed her eyes and pressed the key into the keyhole before turning the lock into place. The man shrieked at her again and punched the glass in frustration.

The door trembled from the impact of the crazed man's assault yet remained closed. Rebecca retreated backward from Terry and the officer as the two men eased away from the store entrance, Terry sighing as the officer panted. The crazed man refused to give up and continued to pound on the door, growling and screeching unintelligibly as he fought to get inside. Rebecca looked into his wild, angry blue eyes for a split second before he closed them and bashed his head against the glass, his skin and dirty blonde hair leaving behind a smeared, sweat filled impression of his forehead.

"Rebecca!" Rebecca whirled around, her eyes falling to the floor and Cariba. "Go and get the first aid kit and some towels," she ordered from the floor where she held her apron, now an ever darkening mess, against the woman's wounded neck, "I need to stop the bleeding."

"The first aid kit has some clotting sponges inside," Terry replied. "I'll go. Rebecca," Rebecca glanced over her shoulder, trying her best to not look at the door. "Make sure everyone inside is okay. I think Phoebe might be in the restroom."

Annoyed, Rebecca clenched her teeth. "Oh you suck," she muttered as Terry made his way past them.

The officer took a step back to the door and the man outside shrieked and pounded on the door erratically. Rebecca turned and glanced over at the small table where the pair of frightened twenty-something women, the only other two people in the room with them, stood terrified. The woman on the floor, despite how much blood she may or may not have lost, was hysterical and struggling against Cariba.

"Let me get my phone!" she shouted over Cariba's protests for her to remain still and calm. "I have to call my husband! I need to tell him what happened! I need to go to the hospital!"

"What you *need* is to stay still!" Cariba argued. "You're bleeding really bad! Terry," she shouted over her shoulder, "hurry up with that kit!"

Rebecca looked to the officer again, who appeared to be fumbling with his utility belt, searching for something. Though a little huskier than he probably should have been, his arms suggested either a current or a past practice of weight lifting, and she wondered for a moment if he was married. Probably once spiked or product styled hair was a mess and drenched in sweat, several beads of it oozing down his pale face. "Shit," he muttered.

"What is it?" Rebecca asked, taking a few steps past Cariba. "What's the matter?" The officer turned and looked at her, the weight of his powerful gaze freezing her in place. *Whow*, she thought as she stared into his green, almost jade, unnatural-looking eyes, *you've got beautiful eyes*.

"My radio," he replied. "I don't know if it was him or one of the others who tore some of the utility clips off of my belt, but it's not working. One of them must have damaged it." One of the two girls' eyes widened, bulging behind the lens of her glasses as she clung to the arm of the other one.

"Them?" she squeaked from behind the dark curtain of ebony hair that circled her face. "You mean there's more?" The other girl, frightened, though not on the verge of hysterics, had clearly had enough as she yanked her arm away.

"Emily," she hissed, "for fucksake!" she had to pry the girl's tightly clamped, white knuckled hand from her arm, as she gave a whimper of protest. "Get it together!" she ordered as she took a few steps from her friend and ran her hands through her own shoulder length, dishwater-blonde hair.

"I'm Officer Sprague," the officer began, "what are your names?" he asked.

"Jana," the calmer of the two girls replied as she walked towards one of the tables in front of one the large windows she and Emily had been seated at before all hell had broken loose, "and she's Emily," she said while jabbing her thumb past her shoulder to where her friend still stood, nodding in reply to the acknowledgment.

Rebecca initially thought to go to Emily and get her seated and calm before becoming apprehensive towards the idea. Given the current state of things, she really couldn't afford the possibility of a clingy, weeping, hysterical mess of a girl clinging to her. It was actually pretty surprising to her how well Cariba was keeping it together considering how she normally reacted to even the slightest bit of blood.

"My name is Rebecca," she nodded to the woman and her coworker on the floor, "that's Cariba. What's yours?" she found herself asking and immediately felt foolish and wished she had not.

The officer, Sprague, gave a cold, uninterested look as he answered, "Officer Sprague," before checking his pants pockets. "Shit," he muttered.

"Hey," Jana called as she leaned across the table, "I think I see your phone or—" she shrieked and jumped backward, tripping over her feet and falling flat on her butt as the man outside unexpectedly slammed his hands against the window, screaming and pounding in a fury.

"Hey!" Sprague shouted, walking over to the fallen girl. "Stay the hell away from the windows," he ordered before helping Jana to her feet.

"Sorry," she said dejectedly and visibly embarrassed as she got to her feet. Rebecca heard a snort from the floor before she turned and looked down at her coworker.

"Idiot," Cariba muttered annoyed before lifting the apron and checking the woman's bite wound, blood immediately pooling at the site of injury in reply to the absence of pressure from the nearly entirely saturated garment. "Shit!" she hissed as her face paled. Clamping the apron back over the wound she looked up at Rebecca, the woman moaning in reply to the returned pressure. "She's bleeding out! Get Terry!"

Rebecca hurried several steps away, nodding in reply at her coworker before turning and shrieking in surprise as she found her arms suddenly gripped by two strong, fingerless gloved hands.

"Whoa!" the owner of the hands, nearly a foot taller, and a woman, cried out in surprise. Rebecca gasped as she felt her heart descend from her throat and back into its home in her chest. Looking at the woman, as she released Rebecca's arms from her grip, from her ruined jeans, black workman boots, and her white, tight-fit, graphic t-shirt, emblazoned with a dark, tribal design of what appeared to be a bird emerging from flames, Rebecca thought she looked more at home in a biker bar than there in a coffeehouse.

"Where did you come from?" Rebecca gasped rather than said, her heart still furiously pounding against her chest from the passing shock of the surprise. The woman reached up and flung the dark blonde braid that hung at her chest back over her shoulder, narrowly missing Rebecca's face, before jabbing the thumb from same hand towards the direction she had come from.

"Men's room," she replied. "Some jackass was taking forever in the lady's." Rebecca rolled her eyes. *Ugh, Phoebe,* she thought. From behind them, Cariba slapped her hand against the floor, the sound of it echoing briefly.

"Woman! Dying! MOVE IT!" she roared at the two of them.

The woman looked past Rebecca, her eyes widening in surprise. "Oh shit," she said before putting her right backhand against Rebecca's shoulder and pushing her to the side. Compliant, Rebecca stepped away as the woman shoved past her before turning to run towards the backroom. Terry turned, eyes wide, as she burst through the swinging doors. "Rebecca," he started to say before she cut him off.

"Where is first aid kit?" she demanded. Frustrated, Terry shoved everything off of the top shelf of the metro rack in front of him, and grabbed the red bag that had been behind the discarded items now on the floor. Rebecca nodded, even as she noticed that the bag did not appear to be as full as it usually was. "Go," she said pointing towards the lobby, "hurry!" before she made her way to her manager's desk. Reaching for the telephone, she immediately dialed 911.

Worried she would not know the first thing to say when the operator picked up from the other end of the line, Rebecca was both surprised and relieved when an automated voice recording answered. "You have reached Guerin 911. Please do not hang up. We are experiencing heavy call volume. Your call will be answered by the next available emergency operator."

Should have expected that, she thought as she hung up the phone and sighed before she remembered her friend Aidan stopping in earlier that morning during her shift. David, their mutual best friend, had been hung over and was absent from the duo who had made it their routine to visit her every Friday morning. Rebecca had sent their loud, flamboyant friend on his way with coffee and bagels, along with several extra goodies for their sick friend, and now she herself felt sick inside while she wondered whether or not her friend had made it to their friend's apartment without incident.

To the left of her manager's desk, a locker tower loomed over Rebecca, several of its doors unlocked or ajar. Reaching for the door with a piece of tape with her name written across it, Rebecca opened the locker and pulled out her flip phone, forgetting how much she detested cell phones and actually grateful to have it for a change. As she shakily scrolled through her list of contacts, she made her way through the doors and back out into the lobby and the commotion that had begun to build. Several shrieks rang out, and Rebecca's thoughts immediately went Jana and her hysterical friend.

Aidan, on account of his name, was the first she immediately dialed. Shockingly, it did not even ring a single time before it went immediately to voicemail. Officially worried, as her friend's cell was always on and attached to his hand, she immediately dialed David. After several rings it went to his voicemail, which was really not out of the ordinary for him.

"David, it's Becky," she said, surprised at how shaky her voice sounded even to her. "Listen, I'm not really sure what's going on. I've tried calling you and Aidan. There's a police officer in the store and he had us lock the door. There's some really messed up guy outside."

"I know it hurts!" Cariba's voice echoed from beyond the counter. "You need to hold still for us or we can't help you!" Rebecca sighed as she made her way around the counter, wondering how the hell today had ended up like this.

"Something is going on across the street at the park, I don't know what," she continued. "The officer has a woman with him who is hurt— was...bitten, by that guy outside, but Cariba's taking care of her and Terry just found the first aid kit and is going to help patch her up." She reached down into her front pocket, unfolding the fabric of the garment's internal pouch in preparation of her phone. "Anyway, call me or text me, or something. Please." Rebecca snapped shut her phone just as she nearly collided with Phoebe, shrieking in surprise.

"Jesus," she hissed. "Pay attention to where you're going! What's going on?" she demanded. Rebecca felt the remaining drops of her reserves of patience finally evaporate into nothing. Shoving into her pocket the phone she had nearly dropped when Phoebe had almost walked into her, Rebecca spun on her heel, ignoring the unruly woman, and made her way back towards the lobby. "Hey!" Phoebe called after her, her tone a mixture of annoyance and surprise. "I am talking to—"

Rebecca whirled around, her face a mask of rage. "Shut your goddamn mouth!" she roared, the woman in front of her briefly flinching in surprise at a tone she was not at all expecting from her. "Someone is hurt!" she exclaimed before turning and hastily making her way back to her coworkers and the injured woman.

"Hurt?" Phoebe called out while jogging after her, the clicking of her ridiculously pretentious shoes echoing after her. "What the hell are you—!" her annoying questioning ended in a shriek.

Just as Rebecca was about to join Cariba and Terry, she spun back around to see Phoebe, as pale as her spray on tan allowed her to be. The lawyer stood wide-eyed, covering her mouth with her hands as she stared past Rebecca. Lifting one of her manicured hands from her face, Phoebe pointed past her and toward the lobby. "What the hell is wrong with those people?" she screeched.

"Rebecca!" Terry called from the floor. "Grab those towels from over on the counter!" Turning back to the front of the room, and Terry's voice, she froze when she saw them. Emily sat underneath the table she and Jana had been sitting at, her knees brought up to her face as she shook her head, rocking back and forth with her hands clamped on her ears. The man from earlier continued to pound on the window above, only now he had been joined by two more men. Rebecca gasped as she looked at the grotesque versions of what had once been the people standing outside the shop.

The older and stockier of the two arrivals stood the closest to the first man. His dark, graying hair was soaked and fell in several unkempt locks across the forehead of his sickly pale, yellowed face. The fabric of his already dark, navy blue tracksuit pants had several suspiciously spots and blotches that were darker still and quite obviously blood.

Pounding nearly in unison with the first man, Rebecca swallowed and put a hand to her mouth when she noticed that the older man was pounding only with a single hand while the strands of the shredded sleeve of his track suit jacket flapped about in the absence of his left arm. The older man's eyes bulged out of their sockets, his expression twisted into a vicious face of madness as he snarled and howled at everyone inside of the shop.

Officer Sprague stood shouting into the shop's cordless phone as Jana tried to shake her friend from her hysterical fit. Frustrated at Emily, showing no signs of coming out of her delirium, Jana grabbed a hold of her friend's shoulder with one hand as she wound up her other before slapping Emily across the face with it. Rebecca gasped, as Emily's head recoiled from the blow, snapping to the left and in the direction of the length of window glass underneath the window.

It was only a moment Emily froze before her eyes widened and she began screaming her head off at the third person outside who held himself up from the ground by leaning against the lowest portion of the glass window that shown beneath the table. Once a blonde, teenage boy, now an almost lipless revenant crowned with a mass of soiled, gore covered hair, growled and scratched at the glass blocking him from the two girls. An explosion of crimson stained the pallid skin beginning at the bottom of his ruined mouth that fell past his chin and ended in a shrinking trail of several bloody stains over his once now only mostly white hooded sweatshirt.

The woman who had brushed her aside earlier stood crouched near Cariba, searching inside the first aid kit. "You said there were clotting sponges in here?" she asked before she looked up at Rebecca. "You," she said pointing at her, "whatever your name is, bring those goddamn towels over here!" Rebecca shot forward from the spot she had been frozen to in shock of what was happening outside in front of them. Listening to the sound of the moaning woman on the floor and the sounds of the frantic people all about the room, she forgot her fear for a moment as she dashed up to the counter and seized the pile of towels someone had thankfully forgotten to put away.

"I need to get out of here!" Phoebe screeched. Rebecca turned from the counter, gazing at the lawyer before continuing on.

"You need to sit down," she said before hurrying over to the woman and Cariba. Her normally stoic demeanor had completely dissolved and Rebecca wondered how long it would be before Cariba completely lost it. The girl's hand was now completely drenched in blood, her soiled apron becoming more and more saturated by the second, her eyes glistening with now falling tears.

"Why the fuck isn't it getting it?" she sobbed. "I can't get it Becky!" Rebecca crouched down and put her hand on her coworker's shoulder before the woman who ordered her to grab the towels seized them from her hand and moved in close to the woman and Cariba. Dropping a few, she folded several together into would be a tight compress.

"Hon', I need you to look at me," she said to the injured woman whose mouth hung open as she took slow, controlled breaths. "My name is Susan, can you tell me yours?" The woman closed her mouth and swallowed.

"Kirstie," she rasped before she swallowed and began to cough. The woman Susan, nodded. Cariba glanced down at her blood-soaked hand and gulped, visibly nauseated.

"Oh god," she grimaced, "I think I'm gonna be sick," she choked out. Noticing her hand begin to loosen its grip over the waded up apron, Susan slapped her hand over Cariba's, forcing it back down, re-pressurizing the apron against the wound. Kirstie winced in reply though she remained silent. Cariba's eyes snapped shut as her lips moved gently apart before she took a deep, long breath.

"Okay Kirstie, I need you to keep your eyes open and I don't want you try to move because this is gonna hurt a bit," she replied before looking at Rebecca. "Okay, the second I move Red's hand here, I'm gonna clamp these towels down on Kirstie's neck." Rebecca nodded, not sure exactly why she was telling her this.

"I can't get through!" Phoebe shrieked from the front counter, holding her cell to her ear. "They're not picking up!" Jana, who sat holding her uncommunicative friend, glanced up from and over at the hysterical woman.

"Who?" she asked, annoyed at the second person now to have lost their shit.

Phoebe, hysterical as she was, still managed to roll her eyes at the girl. "Who do think, moron? 9-1-1," she fired back. "All I'm getting is a message that I'm on hold, waiting for the next person to pick up!" Officer Sprague, finished talking into the cordless phone, set it down on the table above the two girls seated below it. The two standing, crazed men outside beat furiously and more agitated against the glass in reply to the officer's sudden closeness. Emily shrieked in reply to men's snarls and increased pounding.

"Ma'am," he said as he pointed to Phoebe, "I need you sit down and remain calm. Help will be here soon."

Phoebe laughed as she shoved her phone into one of the front pockets on her pants. "Keep calm. Right, because those windows are going to hold forever," she taunted. "What the **fuck** is going on?" she demanded, walking towards a table slightly closer to the group on the floor before sitting down to it.

"I don't **know** what is going on exactly," Sprague replied, "but you need to calm down, right now." He glanced down at Kirstie. "How is she doing?" he asked. Susan nodded at Rebecca.

"Okay so, uh," she stopped as she shrugged her shoulders, waiting for her to reply. Rebecca swallowed, nervously anticipating what would be coming next.

"Rebecca," she answered, Susan nodded her head in reply.

"Rebecca. Okay, so here's what we're going to do," she began. "I need you to get ready to switch places with Red—"

"It's **Cariba**," Cariba snarled, cutting her off, "Don't fucking call me that!"

The corner of Susan's lip rose slightly for a brief second before she continued. "With *Cariba*." She glanced behind her at Terry who had stood silently watching the entire time. "You," she replied, her eyes burning holes into his. "Get ready to help Cariba." Terry shrugged.

"With…what?" he asked confused. Susan frowned.

"Away from Kirstie and up from the floor," she answered annoyed. "Then you go find those damn sponges that **aren't** here." Eyes still locked on the younger man, who stood in bewilderment, Susan nodded toward the three people on the floor with her. "Move!" she ordered. Terry's body jerking to life in reply, hurried past the older woman and crouched down behind Cariba. "Okay," Susan replied looking at Rebecca. "Ready?" she asked, glancing at Cariba next.

"Yeah," Rebecca replied, rising to a standing crouch in preparation. Cariba closed her eyes and rapidly shook her head in protest.

"No!" she screeched as Terry moved in closer to her left side, his left hand closing around her forearm while his right hand snaked behind her, clamping against her waist.

"Awesome," Susan facetiously answered as she nodded, "Okay Cariba, I'm counting to three, and on three you're gonna ease up your right hand from Kirstie's neck."

"Be careful," Sprague replied as a sneer came from the table behind them.

"Do you even have any idea what the hell you're doing?" Phoebe demanded. Susan, hands still raised and poised for what she was about to attempt, glanced up and in the direction of the woman.

"As a matter of fact," she replied, "I do." Phoebe chuckled and rolled her eyes.

"Yeah," she laughed, "of course you do." Annoyed, Rebecca closed her eyes and sighed before shaking her head.

"Please Phoebe," she pleaded. "You are so not helping right now."

From where she sat, Phoebe shrugged. "Whatever. Not my fault if that woman dies and you're all responsible for it." Susan turned her attention back to the injured woman in front of her.

"Ignore her," she replied. "Okay," she began raising her hand holding the folded up towels, the fingers of her other hand tightening around Cariba's hand. "One," Cariba began to cry.

"Oh god, I can't do this!" she wailed. Rebecca leaned over and took her face in her hands.

"Yes you can," she replied. "Just let go when she says and go with Terry. It's going to be okay." Terry leaned in closer still to Cariba.

"You've got this," he said quietly in her ear and she nodded.

"Okay," she said before taking a breath and nodding at Susan who nodded back.

"All right," she began. "One…two…three!" Lightning quick, she flung Cariba's hand away from Kirstie's neck and clamped the towels over it, all seemingly in one movement. Kirstie cried out in reply, her eyes widening as she gasped.

"Jesus!" she screamed before taking a deep breath. Grabbing Rebecca's hand and placing it tightly against the towels, Susan looked to Terry.

"Okay," she began, placing her hand against the center of Rebecca's back, between her shoulder blades. "Terry, go!" Pulling Cariba towards him, Terry pushed up from the floor and away from Kirstie. While the two rose to their feet, Susan pushed Rebecca forward who pivoted around and behind the injured woman, Susan's other hand gripping Kirstie's opposite shoulder to keep her steady and in place. Once planted behind her, Rebecca let Kirstie rest against the front of her body. Kirstie sucked in another breath and slowly exhaled, nodding at Susan.

Placing her hand over Rebecca's, already tightly pushing down against the towels, Susan began, "Keep pressure—"

"I've got it Susan," Rebecca replied. Susan smiled back before letting go of Rebecca's hand as well as Kirstie's uninjured shoulder, gently patting it. Sprague walked up to the women and knelt down next to Susan.

"What's her condition?" he asked. Susan closed her eyes and sighed, rubbing each of the temples of her face with her thumb and middle fingers as she gripped her forehead.

"I only got a glimpse of the wound and it looks pretty bad," she answered letting her hand drop down to the floor. "And it seems like she's lost a pretty good amount of blood too, but not enough to put her into hypovolemic shock." She reached down and placed her index and second finger against Kirstie's pale wrist. "Pulse is still even."

"Are you a nurse?" Jana asked. Susan glanced over her shoulder and shook her head.

"No. I used to be a paramedic," she answered, Jana nodding in reply. Susan turned and looked at Kirstie. "How you doing Kirstie?" she asked.

Her face pale and beginning to perspire, Kirstie nodded and swallowed. "It hurts," she replied, "but, I'm okay," she reassured them even as she took a deep breath. "But I need to call my husband. We were supposed to meet at the park for his lunch break."

"What happened to you?" Susan asked. "How'd you get hurt like this?"

"She was bitten," Sprague answered for her. Susan's head whirled around to look at the officer at her side.

"Come again?" she said bewilderedly as Sprague nodded.

"By one of those psychos outside," Jana added. Susan turned back to Kirsten and reached for her chin, gently gripping it with her fingers.

"Turn and slowly look to your left Hon'," she said even as she gently began to turn Kirstie's face. "You feel a little warm," she added.

"I don't feel like I am," Kirstie replied. Rebecca lifted her left arm she had been using to hold onto Kirstie and put her free hand over Kirstie's forehead.

"Yeah," she agreed, "she's warm. She's got a fever." Jana, who had crept up behind Susan, leaned over the woman and pointed down at Kirstie.

"Hey," she said, startling both Sprague and Susan. "What's up with her neck right there?" Susan's eyes scanned the site of the wound and the area surrounding the compress Rebecca held over it. Tiny purplish lines beneath her skin had begun to poke out from beneath the bandaged, bruised area surrounding the bite wound.

"I'm not sure," Susan replied, "but bites, human or animal, are bad news."

Cariba, having collected herself, poked Terry's shoulder. "Let's go and check the backroom again," she suggested. "Show me where you found the bag." Terry nodded and the two of them made their way further into the store, each ignoring Phoebe and her following eyes as they passed the table she began to stand up from. Rebecca continued to hold the compress to Kirstie's shoulder and decided that rather than continue to worry about her two friends, neither of whom she could get on their phones, she would instead ask the woman she was holding about what had happened to her.

"Do you want to tell us about what happened?" she said gently into Kirstie's ear. Uncomfortable and trying to shift her weight even as she failed, Kirstie nodded to the three people in front of her.

"I said before," she began, "I was going to meet Mark, my husband, on his lunch break. We only ever really seem to see each other at home after we're home from work so we rarely get to spend much time during the day together." She sighed. "I told him that I'd meet him at the park entrance and then we'd go in and choose a place for lunch, only he never showed up."

"Well did you say to meet inside or outside of the park to him?" Jana asked. Kirstie frowned at the younger girl.

"I already said that I told him that I'd meet him at the entrance outside of the park," she said annoyed. "But, after waiting around for him, and wondering why he wasn't picking up his phone, I thought that maybe he made it here first and went inside." Having enough of the floor, Sprague stood up.

"But you never saw him?" he asked. Kirstie shook her head. Susan stood up from the floor and faced the officer, crossing her arms over her chest.

"What were you doing when this all happened?" she asked. Sprague sighed and took another look at the men outside of the windows, still pounding mindlessly on the glass of the windows. Rebecca up at the officer and then the direction he was looking. *Phoebe's right*, she thought while looking at the men outside still assaulting the door, *that glass is pretty tough, but it's not going to last forever.*

"I was in the area and calls were going out about rioting in several different locations, one of them being the park. I didn't see any other squad cars so I figured that I was the closest." He nodded toward Kirstie and Rebecca on the floor. "I saw her being chased," he pointed in the direction of the first of the three men outside, "by that guy. We were close to here so that's why I assume she ran towards the shop."

From the floor, Kirstie nodded. "I kept hearing screams, or echoes that sounded like screams, I don't know. I thought that man outside was hurt when I saw him limping around." She closed her eyes, visibly uncomfortable as she told them what had happened earlier. "I thought he might have been hurt so I called over to him and asked him if he was okay or if he needed any help. When he saw me, he…"

"It's okay," Rebecca whispered. "You don't have to say anymore." She felt Kirstie's nod and looked at the officer. "We really need to get out of here. Those people clearly aren't normal and they're not looking like they're going to give up and leave anytime soon." Despite looking annoyed as he was, Sprague nodded. "Are there any other exits out of the shop?" he asked. Rebecca shook her head and he sighed. "You're serious? You're telling me that this place doesn't have a backdoor?" It was Rebecca's turn now to be annoyed.

"No, officer, this place doesn't have a backdoor." She answered flatly

"There's a window in the lady's room," Phoebe chimed in from out of nowhere, Sprague and Susan each turning to face her in reply. "It's pretty high up off of the floor, but we can all fit though it to climb out of here." Susan placed her hands on her hips.

"And how, exactly, are we supposed to get Kirstie through the window?" she asked at which Phoebe rolled her eyes.

"So we'll send help," she scoffed. "What? You have a better idea?" Eyes narrowed, Susan was ready to answer when Jana jumped to her feet from the floor.

"Holy shit! Look! Look over there" she shouted, pointing as she hurried to one of the windows, the view from it not obscured by any of the men outside. From across the street, fleeing from several people in pursuit, was a young girl, screaming her head off the whole way. Susan and Sprague each ran to one of Jana's sides, Sprague immediately drawing his gun from the holster at his side. "We need to help her!" Jana shouted in Sprague's direction, or rather his ear. The officer said nothing.

The girl's disheveled, blonde hair bobbed up and down as she frantically sprinted through the street. The collar of her magenta windbreaker torn almost completely from the jacket, flailed about along with her hair, hanging literally by threads and sinewy flaps of torn fabric. The only thing that did not look ruined were her jeans whose knees were caked in dirt.

Turning in reply to the screams, the two men standing at the door snarled and howled before shooting forth from the entrance and toward the girl who screamed as she desperately tried to maneuver around the both of them in her path toward the shop. Sprague hurried to the door and turned the key in the lock before going back outside. Silently, Emily stood from the floor and walked towards the door.

"Is he nuts!?" Phoebe shrieked from the table just Terry and Cariba returned.

"What the hell's going on?" Terry demanded while Cariba hurried over to Rebecca and Kirstie.

"We found them!" Cariba replied and handed several square, white packages to Susan before crouching down in front of Kirstie who appeared to be panting as her eyes fluttered and began to close. "Hey," she said, placing her hands on the injured woman's cheeks. "Are you okay? Kirstie?"

"About goddamn time," Susan hissed while opening one of the sponge packets. Turning and pointing at Jana and Emily she shouted, "You two! Lock that door if anyone other than that cop tries to get in here!" Turning away from the two and crouching next to Cariba, she took hold of Rebecca's hand holding the towels pressed against Kirstie's ruined neck.

"Oh god, what do we do! I can't see him!" Jana shouted back to the rest of them in the store as Emily reached for the doorknob. "What are you doing?" Jana demanded. Emily's hand froze before she looked over to her friend.

"We can get away," she replied. "We can get away Jana, we can get someplace safe!"

Jana shook her head. "No Emily, it's safe right here. Don't open that door. Don't go out there." Emily turned her gaze back to the door and reached for the knob. "Emily don't!" Despite her friend's protests, Emily turned the doorknob and opened the door. Terry hurried towards the entrance as Emily stepped outside. "Hey!" he shouted.

"What are you doing? Stop!" Just finishing placing the clotting sponge over the Kirstie's neck, Susan turned and glanced over her shoulder, her eyes widening as she watched the savaged, young man who had been holding himself up from the ground and against the window crawl towards Emily, despite his mangled leg dragging behind him.

"Watch out!" she screamed, shooting up from the floor and towards the open door, nearly colliding with Terry. Emily turned back to the pair rushing towards her and Jana before she felt two hands seize her leg. Jana screamed as Emily looked down and saw the mangled boy pull himself up from the ground taking handfuls of her pants as he climbed the garment.

Emily screamed as he gripped the waist of her pants and pulled her to the ground. Screaming, the girl fell to the ground, landing on her back, her feet kicking wildly as he took a handful of her hair and yanked her head towards him. Susan dove to the floor and grabbed Emily's ankles beginning a tug of war over the screaming with her assailant. Rushing past the older woman, Terry reached for the boy's head and missed as he lunged for and bit into Emily's cheek.

"Oh my fucking god," Rebecca felt her heart jump up into her throat as Emily let out a blood curdling screams. Kirstie's body went limp and sagged against Rebecca who now struggled awkwardly to hold the unconscious woman up. "Oh shit, hey! Kirstie!" Before Cariba could turn her head back to the two women on the floor she was crouched in front of, she felt a hand clamp over her forearm. Her head snapping back to from the chaos at the doorway, Cariba watched Kirstie's eyes open as she slowly rose her head, her lips curling back from her teeth.

"Kirstie? Cariba said shakily. Kirstie snarled in reply, tugging Cariba's arm while reaching for her face with her other hand. Rebecca pulled the woman back from her screaming coworker as Jana suddenly appeared, trying to pull the crazed woman's hand off of Cariba's arm, sobbing hysterically as she tried to ignores the screams of her friend being torn into.

"What are you doing Kirstie!?" Rebecca demanded. "Stop it!" Kirstie paused with a moment of realization, letting go of Cariba's hand and grabbing Rebecca's left arm. The resistance gone, Cariba and Jana fell backward to floor. It happened too fast for her to realize what was happening and Rebecca screamed, feeling the worst pain she ever felt in her life as Kirstie sank her teeth into her arm.

"Rebecca!" Cariba screamed and began to scramble to her coworker before stopping and looking past the two women in front of her. Noticing movement out of the corner of her eye, Rebecca instinctively leaned back before looking up just in time to see Phoebe swinging a chair over her shoulder and down onto Kirstie's head. The furniture exploded into wooden fragments and Rebecca screamed again when she felt the impact cause Kirstie to somehow briefly bite down harder still before releasing her grip from Rebecca's arms and falling forward.

Phoebe looked down at the three of them. "Run, you idiots!" she shrieked before she turn and ran further into the store. At once, Jana was on her feet and raced after the woman as Cariba snatched up Rebecca's hand and pulled her to her feet.

"Run!" Cariba screamed as she yanked Rebecca toward her once last time before letting go and hurrying after the two other fleeing women, not bothering to look past Rebecca and at the screams from the people at the entrance.

Just as Rebecca began to run, she screamed as she felt Kirstie grab her ankle from the floor. Now enraged, and turning back and looking down at the woman's bloody, psychotic mask of a face, Rebecca swung her foot with all her might into the Kirstie's face, sending whatever now remained of her septum into her head upon impact. Kirstie went limp, and the moment she felt the now dead woman's grip receded from her ankle, Rebecca yanked her leg back and bolted from the spot towards the direction Cariba and the others had gone.

Her arm screamed as she clutched it against her chest, the sounds of glass breaking behind her, and Rebecca continued forward, refusing to look back. Cariba stood in the open door of the lady's room waving her forward, eyes wild.

"They're behind you! Run!" she screamed hysterically and jumping up and down as she continued to wave her forward. Rebecca felt the breeze of something to the left side of her face as she saw Phoebe appear behind her coworker. Cariba screamed as Rebecca turned and looked over her shoulder and saw the same man who had bitten Kirstie earlier reaching for her as he chased after her. Rebecca shrieked and turned narrowly past the counter, the man unprepared for the maneuver shooting forth and slamming into the now closed door to the restroom.

Hurrying toward the swinging doors leading to the backroom, Rebecca heard the sounds of several pairs of feet stomping after her along with the shrieks and howls of their owners. Turning as she threw her hands on the doors, the last thing Rebecca saw was a crazed woman leap up onto the counter she had rounded before running into the backroom.

Seizing the pipe wrench that had been left on the towering metro rack to her right, Rebecca whirled around and slipped the surprisingly heavy, metal tool in between the door handles just as the woman slammed into the doors from the other side. Ignoring the face of the screaming woman pressed against one of the small, plexiglass windows, immediately joined by several other ruined, screaming faces, Rebecca grabbed a hold of the metro rack and screamed as her adrenaline tempered arms yanked the metal rack forward. The contents of the shelves fell to the floor as the large rack toppled over into the wall in front of it.

Seeing the doors held in place by the wrench, along with the tipped over metro rack braced against them, Rebecca took a few shuddered breaths before turning and running further into the room. *Oh god, what if it doesn't hold?* She thought as she raced towards the only other door in the back room, which lead to a supply closet.

Rushing inside, while pressing the lock in the doorknob into place, Rebecca turned and swung the door closed as she felt her feet spin on the slippery floor. Failing to right herself, Rebecca flailed her arms out for something to grab onto and steady herself and grasped at only air. Her feet suddenly off of the floor and over her head was the last thing that she saw before a flash of white light, not even feeling the blow to the back of her head as she fell backward and hit the side of the sink behind her. Rebecca watched her vision return for a moment as she fell the rest of the way to the floor in the now nearly pitch black room, save for the bit of light from underneath the tiny crack below the door.

What bit of illumination there was faded away along with echoes of howls and screams outside and beyond as Rebecca's eyes closed shut.

End

Contributing Author Biographies

David Berger. David grew up with privilege—the privilege of being immersed in reading from a very early age. A fan of fantasy, comics, and mythology, he eventually would become an English teacher where he could help foster a love of literature with his students. This love would bring about the *Task Force: Gaea* series, a Greek mythology fantasy set in the modern world. His first three books, *Finding Balance*, *Memory's Curse*, and *The Liar's Prophecy* are out now. The fourth book, *The Archer's Paradox*, as well as an anthology tied to *Memory's Curse* are due out in 2016. He is living his dream, as it were, and resides in Land O' Lakes, FL with his partner Gavi and their cat, Shayna.

Simon Graves. Simon Graves is an emerging author of contemporary horror, suspense, science fiction and fantasy from Norfolk, Virginia. He released his first collection of horror short stories in September 2014, and he's currently working on a novella. Simon's short stories include *FIND'M*, *Happy Anniversary*, *Bloody Ben*, *Ace*, *Stud Muffins*, and *******: *Your Secret Admirer*.

Daniel W. Kelly. Daniel W. Kelly is the author of the *Comfort Cove* series that includes the horror novels *Combustion*, *No Place for Little Ones*, and *Rise of the Thing Down Below*, plus the horror collections *Horny Devils* and *Closet Monsters: Zombied Out and Tales of Gothrotica*. He is also creator of Boys, Bears & Scares, a website dedicated to gay male horror.

Michael Manschot. Michael "Mikey" Manschot is a 27-year-old Southern horror writer, painter, actor, and horror fanatic. He's been obsessed with the horror genre since he was a kid and found horror to be a great escape from reality. He lived in California for a short while working on some independent films and trying to gain some experience. He realized that Texas would always be home and that he could really execute his horror craft from anywhere. Now he's back in Texas, writing at least one short a month with his writer's workshop group and enjoying life.

Patrick Raith. Born of the frozen wasteland that *is* northern Wisconsin, Patrick Raith is the author of several short stories. Having grown up in a family that has always celebrated the horror genre, he is currently finishing one of the two works centered around his first two loves of said genre: zombies and vampires. He now lives in the (far warmer) Los Angeles area.

Peter Saenz. Peter Saenz was a contributing author on the previous Digital Fabulists/DoorQ anthologies *Queer Tales: A Fantasy Anthology* and *New Year's to Christmas: 15 Queer Holiday Tales*. He is also known for his solo book series *Coven of Wolves*. Raised in both

270

Southern California and South Texas, Peter now lives in the Los Angeles area with his husband Joseph.

M. Van London. American singer and songwriter Michael Van London has honed his skills "on both sides of the ocean and in between them" but has made his home in Los Angeles where he has fronted his band "The Bombs" (featured on MTV) and the "The Black Beverly Heels" while constantly recording and releasing material under his own name. His music has been featured on the MTV Movie Awards 2011 and 2012 and his band "The Black Beverly Heels" made officially available in Rock Band. His song "Feel Love" has been spotlighted in Spotify's "Artist of the Week." In November 2013 he was also in the running for the Oscars "Best Original Song in a Film" for his work in Chris Colfer's 2012 debut film *Struck By Lightning*. He also received the "Best Alternative Album of the Year" award from the Malibu Music Awards in 2013. He is currently working on a new record for 2015. This is his first published short story.

David D. Warner. In addition to compiling this collection, David D. Warner has written a number of LGBTQ-themed horror and science fiction stories—as well as stories in other genres. Under the pseudonym Warner Davidson, two of David's stories were included in the Digital Fabulists/DoorQ LGBTQ anthology *New Year's to Christmas: 15 Queer Holiday Tales*. David currently lives in Washington, DC with his husband Marc of 23 years (4 of them legal). He is currently working on his first full-length novel—a thriller set in Palm Springs, CA—in addition to a number of other works in progress and myriad story ideas swirling around inside his head waiting for just the right time to be recorded on the page.

David Wolfhaven. David Wolfhaven was born in Richmond, KY. He has also lived in: New York, San Francisco and New Orleans, where he had a fascinating journey, for a few years, with famed novelist, Anne Rice. He credits her and musician, Tori Amos, for his passion and acceptance of himself and for all things. He won the National Humanitarian Award in 1986 for his work on the ethical treatment of animals and also studied at Cornell University. He enjoys being compared to Zachary Quinto and Michael C. Hall and has many adventures and stories to tell. He currently lives in Hollywood with, yes, his two cats, Harrison and Zelda.

www.ingramcontent.com/pod-product-compliance
Lightning Source LLC
Chambersburg PA
CBHW051534260626
47170CB00003B/937